THE EMPTY COFFIN

THE EMPTY COFFIN

A Sam and Vera Sloan Mystery

Robert L. Wise

Publishers Since 1798

THOMAS NELSON PUBLISHERS®
Nashville

Published by Thomas Nelson, Inc., in association with the literary agency Alive Communications, 7680 Goddard Street, Suite 200, Colorado Springs, CO 80920.

Scripture quotations are from the HOLY BIBLE: NEW INTERNATIONAL VERSION®, Copyright © 1973, 1978, 1984 by International Bible Society. Used by permission; and the NEW AMERICAN STANDARD BIBLE®, Copyright © The Lockman Foundation 1960, 1962, 1963, 1968, 1971, 1972, 1973, 1975, 1977. Used by permission.

This is a work of fiction. The characters, incidents, and dialogues are products of the author's imagination and are not to be construed as real. Any resemblance to actual events or persons, living or dead, is entirely coincidental.

Library of Congress Cataloging-in-Publication Data

Wise, Robert L.
    The empty coffin : a Sam and Vera Sloan mystery / Robert L. Wise.
        p. cm.
    ISBN 0-7852-6687-9
    I. Title.

PS3573.I797 E47 2001
813'.54—dc21   2001030015

Printed in the United States of America

1 2 3 4 5 6 QWD 05 04 03 02 01

This book is dedicated with
esteem and affection to my friends
Lou and Barbara Smit and
their daughter, Dawn Miller.

1

WITH THANKSGIVING ONLY DAYS AWAY and the remains of Halloween decorations still hanging in a few windows, autumn had already settled at the foot of the Rocky Mountains. A cold evening fell over Colorado Springs, nipping a few surviving plants with a freezing touch of frost that should finally end all blooming. The daily grind at the downtown detective bureau on Nevada Street had already settled into the evening's leisurely quiet pace. A couple of police officers and one detective were still finishing their daily pencil work. Paperwork was a boring necessity. No escape from the grunt task at the station house.

At 8:30 P.M., a battered 1988 Ford van turned onto Nevada Street, chugging through downtown toward the police station. With most of the windowpanes cracked, the van looked like a junkyard reject. The front fenders had been salvaged from other vehicles and the right side still carried a slight green tint, but the opposite fender had a faded gray, unpainted color, appearing to have been picked up from a second-rate scrap yard. The van's body probably had been maroon, but several repaintings hadn't helped. Numerous scratches and dents told their own stories about cutting it too close, too often on crowded streets. A shiny metal stovepipe stuck straight up from the back door into the black night.

After passing two stoplights, the van pulled up in front of the police station, where the rambling disaster came to an abrupt stop. A rattling muffler exploded with a *pop* that did little to conceal the roar of the engine. The dented door opened and an enormous man crawled out.

Looking like he weighed more than 300 pounds, the driver's straggly hair hung down his shoulders toward the middle of his back. His sprawling black beard covered most of the bottom of his face. The vastly overweight character pushed his tattered T-shirt into his greasy overalls and peered around the corner of his van, gawking at the police station. No one seemed to be paying him the slightest bit of attention. He pulled his worn black leather cap down farther over his eyes and stared at the large two-story brick building.

For a few moments, the hulk leaned against the front of the van and stared at the station house. With a quick grab, he pulled out a bent package of cigarettes and flipped one into his mouth. His first two deep puffs sent a curl of smoke up into the black sky. Still no one came in or went out through the front door of the police station, and that made him feel better.

George Barnes was not a bright man, but he had exceptional strength and the neck of a bull. Beneath the fat on his pudgy arms hung large muscles with the capacity to crush full beer cans in a single crunch. In a way that he never understood, his brain and his brawn never seemed to line up right, and they didn't work well together. Often he felt unsure of what to do next and uncertain about himself. Staring at the police station gave Barnes the familiar insecure feeling that for the thousandth time his problems were slipping through his fingers, leaving him on the short end of the stick once more. He didn't like the nagging fear but couldn't decide on anything else but going inside. After one last drag on his cigarette, Barnes flipped the cigarette into the gutter, rubbed his hairy arms, and started for the front door.

The burly man pushed the station house door open and sniffed the air. Smelled like a cop joint. The usual stale, dusty scent of papers, desks, and disinfected floors filled his flaring nostrils. Barnes swallowed hard and shuffled across the floor.

A policeman sat behind a wooden desk, writing on something or another. Two men and a woman sat quietly, as if waiting for someone. Barnes watched the policeman, but he didn't even look up from his work. The cop didn't seem particularly interested in anything except what he was working on. Behind his desk stood a metal detector visitors had to pass through.

Barnes reached up and took the battered leather cap off. He stood in front of the desk, waiting for a response. Nothing happened. After fifteen seconds, he cleared his throat.

"Yeah?" the cop answered. "Whatcha need?"

"Need to talk to somebody."

"Ain't no psychiatrist's office," the cop grumbled without looking up.

"Need to talk with an officer."

The policeman laid his pencil down and glanced up for the first time. Barnes caught the look of surprise in the man's eye.

He'd seen it many times before when people noticed how big he was. The cop leaned back in his chair, giving him a long, more careful second assessment, the kind of look that always made him start feeling insecure again.

"What can I do for you, big boy? Be a tad more exact."

"I seen somethin', somethin' bad." Barnes cleared his throat nervously. "Need to talk to somebody who handles this stuff."

"You jokin' around with me?" the cop pushed.

"No, sir. No, sir," Barnes repeated himself nervously. "I'm just a-needin' to talk to somebody in charge."

The policeman laughed. "Somebody in charge, huh?" He laughed again. "Well, let's see who I can roust out back there." He turned his head sideways as if measuring again the proportions of Barnes. "We're going to need a good-sized one for you." He started down the roster lying in front of him.

"Yes, sir," Barnes grumbled.

"Like I said earlier, be more specific about the problem."

"Well," Barnes began nervously. "You see, it's a bad deal."

"Spit it out," the cop growled. "We ain't got all night."

"Want to talk about a murder."

The policeman's countenance changed, and the skeptical hostile scowl faded. A serious look settled in his eyes. "A *murder*?"

"Yes, sir."

The cop raised both of his eyebrows and looked back at his list a second time. He stood up and peered outside where the man's van was parked. The policeman blinked and looked again. "Dick Simmons is gone . . . Most of the other detectives are out on assignment," he said to himself. "Sam Sloan looks like the only guy around here right now." He picked up the phone and tapped in an extension number.

Barnes watched, wishing even more that he hadn't come inside the station in the first place.

"Sam?" the cop said. "You still back there? Yeah, yeah. I've got a big one for you. I'll put him up here in the interrogation room."

The policeman laughed. "Naww. I wouldn't kid you at this time of the day. By the way, take a gander out the window before you come over to interrogation." He hung up the phone and stood up.

"Thank you," Barnes mumbled uncertainly.

The cop nodded and shouted over his shoulder. "Hey, Jones! Escort this man down to the interrogation room."

The huge man shuffled along behind the young policeman, walking through the metal detector and down a long hall toward the back of the building. Jones opened a door and pointed toward a marred white chair on the other side of the table. "Sit down and wait. Detective Sloan will be here shortly."

"Yes, sir." Barnes nodded obediently and started across the room. The door closed behind him and he heard the lock click. He wouldn't be coming out until this Sloan guy showed up and finished with him. Barnes shuddered.

He'd seen these rooms before and knew how relentlessly cold they could quickly become. A table. Two chairs. A mirror at the far end, police watching on the other side. Nothing else except that the table was narrow enough that the cop could lean across and get in his face like a tiger eating lunch.

Sam Sloan hung up the desk phone and shook his head. The front-door sergeant always had a unique way of drawing him into problems he didn't need. In five minutes he should be on his way home, and heaven knows that his wife, Vera, had expected him an hour ago. She'd call the problem an old but familiar story . . . and the source of constant tension between them.

Detective Sloan completed his report and shoved the papers into the pile on the corner of his desk. Why did he still have to be here when this nut showed up? He shook his head and stood up.

For a moment Sam stared into the small mirror on the wall beside his desk. Streaks of red crossed his blue eyes like erratic roads on a worn map. His normal thirty-nine years looked more like sixty tonight, but he still had the mild, gentle appearance that always deceived suspects into not taking him as seriously as they should. Sam took a second look at the kindly face the other officers teased him about, the boyish features that made him appear twenty years old after a long restful weekend. He could use a shave, but his thinning brown hair still looked decent, except for the bags under his eyes. Sloan started to pull his tie up tightly but stopped. The hour was far too late to worry what anybody thought of his appearance. He'd go down just as he was, no more, no less.

Wondering what the desk clerk had meant about *something* outside, he stopped at the door and took a look out the window. He quickly did a double take.

"Oh no," he groaned. "What is that *thing*? The putt mobile from hell?" The detective shook his head and clenched his fist. "Not one of *those* guys!" He pounded on the door. "At this hour of the night?"

Thinking that whoever had driven the van must be the winner of the All-Time Bizarre Award, Sloan bit his lip and started down the corridor.

2

SAM SLOAN KNEW THE WORN DIRTY WALLS and old asbestos floors of the Colorado Springs police station as well as he knew how to tie his shoelaces. For more than ten years he had worked murder cases and whatever else came through the front door, and he hadn't yet failed to solve a case. Some murders took longer to break than others, but he had yet to miss one. Remarkable.

The police bureau was known to be tough and indifferent. Often the cops' emotional sensitivity carried more than a slight callousness around the edges. Yet Sloan's personal convictions set him apart; in contrast to most of the detectives on the beat, Sam cared, a unique quality for a murder detective.

But tonight he wasn't ready for any nonsense.

Sam Sloan wanted to go home to his wife. Some jerk showing up late caused considerable problems.

The detective stopped at the end of the hall and looked out the window into the cold night. Growing up in Chicago, he'd seen many a winter night, and this one looked on the slight side, but as he glanced across the sparkling lights of Colorado Springs, Sam recognized similarities between this town and a typical November night in the windy city.

Sloan had grown up in a tenement house on Chicago's South Side, not too far from the downtown area. The block he lived on proved to be a hard, tough place to survive. Like his own family, most of the residents were immigrants. Jack Sloan, his dad, had slipped into the United States from Toronto, looking for work and trying to make a buck. Somewhere along the path of his arduous struggle, he'd met Alice Carpenter and moved into the neighborhood because the beat-up apartment building proved to be a cheap place to live. In 1961, Sam was born into what proved to be an explosive decade of confrontation and dissent.

Sam abruptly remembered how often he'd gotten into fights with the kids who lived two floors below him and with others from across the neighborhood. In fact, he'd been quite a scrapper, usually winning. But he'd been beaten up enough times that he'd developed a nasty temper, which still proved to be a problem. At that moment, Sam remembered the incident that changed his life.

A kid from the building next door turned into one of his archenemies. Because he was older and larger, "Duke" Bennington chased Sam at every opportunity. Sam usually avoided Bennington, but one afternoon Duke caught him in the alley behind the tall apartment building. Sloan could still see that pimple-faced kid standing a head taller, looking down on him like a wolf ready to devour a rabbit. A cold wind had swept down the dirty street, blowing dust into his eyes. He bit his lip and wanted to cry. "Hey, look here!" Duke shouted in Sam's face. "I've found the snot-nosed little twit from upstairs. Time to straighten you out again, creep."

Sam quivered, knowing that Bennington would hurt him. He said nothing.

"What's the matter, punk? Cat got your tongue?" Duke reached over and, with a hard thump, tweaked the end of Sam's nose contemptuously. "Speak up, double ugly, or I'll knock your head off."

Sam's nose stung, telling him that if he stood there long, more pain was on the way. When Duke reached for him again, something snapped inside the little boy. Fear flip-flopped into rage. Instinctively Sam believed that throwing the first punch was everything. From out of nowhere, Sam swung at Duke's face with all his strength, catching the jerk square in the nose. Blood instantly spewed in every direction.

Bennington grabbed his face and moaned in pain. Before he could react, Sloan kicked him hard, and the older boy toppled over on the street. Sam leaped on top, whaling the daylights out of the boy. Bennington rolled over, crying, and ran for his apartment building. The fight didn't last a minute, but it had changed how Sam reacted under pressure. Unexpectedly, anger became his dominant thrust, propelling him past any obstacle . . . particularly ones that were a head taller.

Sloan blinked several times and looked down on Colorado Springs again. He didn't like the fact that his anger still exploded violently every now and then, usually getting him into trouble. Still, the fact couldn't be escaped. Two people seemed to live inside his head: on one side, an angry street warrior with the capacity to whack an aggressor in a second; at the same time, a kind, sensitive Samaritan, caring about people and what happened to them.

Sam took a deep breath and started back down the hall again. After turning two corners on the long hall, Sloan opened the door to the interrogation room, stopped in his steps, and blinked several times. An enormous man sat in front of him, hunched over the table. Stringy hair hung over his forehead, across his ears, and down the man's shoulders. His sagging massive shoulders made the huge guy look like a tired, worn-out wrestler. The worn green T-shirt appeared smudged with grease, and the overalls badly needed a run through a washing machine. His nose looked as if it must have been broken several times.

"Can I help you?" Sloan asked hesitantly.

"Need to talk about somethin'," the man grunted nervously.

"Okay." Sloan slipped down at the table across from the mountainous man. "What's your name?"

"Barnes." He peered up through slit eyes. "George Barnes is on my birth certificate."

"Yes?"

"But everyone just calls me Ape. Picked up the name somewhere along the way, and now that's how they run me down." Barnes smiled, revealing missing side teeth. "Ape's good enough for me."

"Ape?" Sloan raised his eye brows.

"Yes, sir?"

Sloan pulled out an identification form used to gather information in interviews. "I always begin by getting some basic data on the person." Sam smiled easily. "Helps us locate people later. I'm sure you don't mind."

Ape nodded. "Sure. Fine."

Sam began asking the usual questions about name, address, and background. As he finished the first page, he said, "I always advise people of their rights as simple standard practice. I'm sure you will agree."

Ape pursed his lips. "Sure."

Sam read the facts about a right to legal representation casually, as if it were nothing. His nonchalant attitude always discounted what was in fact a potential obstacle to suspects divulging information.

Barnes shook his head and took a deep breath. "Got somethin' I need to say, sir."

"Sure. I'm here to listen."

Ape's face darkened and his thick neck began turning red. "Big problem." He ran his hands through his hair nervously. "Really big." Ape turned toward the closed venetian blinds and shook his head. "Biggest one I ever got into."

Sloan stared, saying nothing.

"I don't know if you know anything about murder, but I need to talk to someone about a killin'. Got to get it off my mind before I leave for California."

Sloan's eyes narrowed and he rubbed his chin. "*A murder?*"

"I'm needin' to talk to somebody about what I know."

Sloan pulled at his upper lip and rubbed the end of his nose. "I'll listen to whatever you want to tell me." His voice flattened and didn't convey any hint of emotion.

"See." Ape scratched his head. "See, I'm on my way to California and I just want to get this out on the table before I leave. Don't want the murderer ridin' in the front seat with me."

Sloan's eyes narrowed. "Riding with you?"

"Just a matter of speech." Ape rolled his eyes nervously. "Talkin' about my feelings, you know."

"Yeah."

"They ain't got no motorcycles . . . no car . . . no nothin'. Just a bunch of punks. That's all. Just rotten little punks. That's how I figured them to be."

Sloan held up his hand. "Who are you talking about?"

"Jester," Ape said dogmatically and shook his head. "These people are all in Jester's gang." He rolled his tongue around under his lips. "They're a bad lot, sir."

"Jester?"

"Yeah, that's the name this dude used. Only name I ever heard. Him and his wife . . . well, his common-law wife." Ape scratched his head and rolled his eyes as if searching for a name. "Alice!" Ape shook his head. "Yeah. That's her name. Alice. Anyways, they was leadin' the gang. The motorcycle gang."

"You're telling me about a motorcycle gang, but no one in it even owns a bike?" Sloan turned his head slightly and looked hard. "Am I getting you right?"

"Yes, sir. Yes, sir. Indeed."

"No motorcycles but they were a gang?"

"Uh-huh." Ape shook his head. "See. That's how I got into it with these people. They wanted to pay me to take the whole load of 'em up to Lincoln, Nebraska. Weren't goin' to pay me much, but that's how they got a hold on me was payin' me."

"And these people were living here in Colorado Springs?"

"Yeah." Ape hooked his fingers over the straps in his overalls and settled back into his chair, abruptly appearing to relax. "See, they hung out around here. Lived on the town's square. Acacia Park. In an old house. Sorta general-class nobodies that got their kicks by hangin' out together. Causin' trouble and all. Stuff like that."

"And you live here too?" Sloan scooted around in his chair, looking for another angle from which to view Barnes.

"Not really. I'm sorta a drifter. Monrovia, California, is my home, but don't hang around there much. Kinda like the Springs."

"But you met these people here?"

"Out there on the square. Just ran into 'em. Hangin' around down there. Doin' nothing. Smokin' pot and all."

"You said there was a murder?"

Ape stiffened. He pulled at his long shaggy beard and shook his head. "Yes, sir. Those people killed a young man."

"Know his name?"

"Jester said the boy's name was Al. Al Henry."

"A boy?"

"Well, this guy was seventeen years old, Jester said. Sorta a boy . . . sorta a man. You know, kinda in that in-between stage, but I guess he was more like a man. Good-sized boy."

"Al Henry?"

"No question about it, sir. That's the name old Jester gave me. Said it several times. Burned it into my mind."

Sloan leaned over the table and stared Barnes in the eye. "If you're fooling around with me, you could be in a significant amount of trouble. Do you understand that?"

Ape nodded and his eyes widened. "Oh, yes, sir. I know what you're tellin' me. I ain't givin' you no bull."

"No nonsense?" Sloan raised both his eyebrows.

"Sir, I came in here on my own. Nobody sent me. I just don't want to be carryin' none of this garbage with me no more."

Sloan settled back in his chair and stared. The man's fat cheeks and hairy face covered much of his normal expressions, so he wasn't easy to read. Not much to see except around his eyes, but Barnes's voice didn't seem to convey or betray deceptive intentions. He sounded sincere.

"Maybe you'd like coffee." Sloan stood up. "I'll get you a cup."

"Sure thing, man. I could use a little somethin' to wet my tongue."

Sloan walked to the other end of the room where an automatic coffeemaker sat on a table. The pot was almost empty, and the coffee looked black as coal. Sloan poured the dregs into a Styrofoam cup. "How many of them were there?"

"As far as going to Lincoln . . ." Ape started to count on his fingers. "Jester . . . his wife—I mean common-law wife, Alice—and three others." He took the coffee from Sloan. "More of 'em hung around the gang here in Colorado Springs." Ape took a big drink of the coffee and grimaced. "Kinda strong, ain't it?"

"How much were they willing to pay you for the trip to Lincoln?" Sloan eased back down to the table again.

"Fifty bucks plus my personal costs. You know, gasoline and all." Ape took another sip of coffee and blinked his eyes. "Yes sirree, that's strong coffee!"

Sloan leaned back in his chair and gaped at the man. While he had seen few people who looked any stranger, the man seemed to be making sense. In his disjointed way, his account hung together and appeared to be consistent. The name Al Henry sounded realistic. Maybe this strange character really was on to something that needed a full investigation.

"Anything more?" Sloan probed.

Ape raised his eyebrows, rolled his eyes, and looked benevolently at the floor. "That's my story."

"Where'd you leave those people?" Sam pushed.

"Ya know, that's the problem. Can't remember. Sometimes my mind works funny."

Sam rubbed the back of his neck. "How come you're dragging into the station house at this late hour of the night, Barnes?"

Ape scratched his head and shrugged. "Hard thing for me to do. Real hard thing. Didn't want to come. Worried about it all day. In fact, I thought about it all afternoon and nearly drove off to California." Once more he pulled at the massive beard. "Guess my conscience wouldn't let me leave town. Took me all day but I had to come in. I couldn't wait any longer."

"And who *exactly* is this Jester character?

"Good question." Ape shook his question. "Honest to God. I don't know. Just don't have a clue."

3

Speeding down Twenty-third Street, Sam knew that he was showing up at home three hours later than he'd told Vera he would be there. This crazy Ape guy had only thrown another log on an already hot fire. Fortunately, he'd finally told the gorilla to come back early in the morning. Vera simply wouldn't put up with Sam coming in any later that night.

Sloan's mother and father often fought because his old man constantly came home late at night. Unfortunately, Jack Sloan's problem had been drinking. After a hard day pushing steel around on construction jobs, Jack liked his beer, which quickly turned into the heavy booze and staying too long down at the corner bar. By the time he wandered into the house, Alice would be livid, he'd be loaded, and the battle was on.

In time, Sam came to see their warfare as only a reflection

of what he saw in the streets and heard on television. Blacks and whites had a war going on in the South while Americans shot it up in Vietnam and the kids protested in the streets against the government, parents, whomever. Didn't seem to be anyplace in his childhood where somebody wasn't duking it out with everything from fists to M-1 rifles. By 1974, he'd lived through the sad end of the Vietnam struggle and the resignation of Nixon, as well as the assassinations of Martin Luther King Jr. and the Kennedys. Anger seemed as omnipresent as oxygen.

And that's what got Sam into boxing. One afternoon a tall, muscular guy rolled into his neighborhood. Sent by the Salvation Army, Jack Robbins had come to recruit boys for the boxing team down at the army's gym. Robbins had the big arms any kid naturally admired. Sam had certainly taken enough punches and learned how to throw them back. Robbins was looking for kids like him. The match fit perfectly.

Sam turned the corner off Twenty-third Street and knew his house would be three blocks ahead. He could smell smoke rising from people's chimneys and wondered if some of that steam might be coming from his place. He stepped on the gas pedal.

Jack Robbins had proved to be quite a friend. He could pull a punch with the best of them and would beat the socks off any street brawler. Sam couldn't believe the difference that training and discipline made in how well Robbins used his hands. He'd taught Sam that the important issue was not to be aggressive as much as defensive. "Yeah, there's a time to hit first but let the opponent take the lead," Jack always said. Counterpunching was Robbins's thing. He'd let the other guy swing wildly and then lower the boom. Before Sam's eyes, a completely different strategy of life opened up. Don't hit first; make sure you hit last. Sloan's new style became that simple.

But it wasn't that simple, Sam thought. *Jack Robbins eventually changed my entire view of the world, adding a new dimension that I hadn't previously recognized as existing. Robbins believed that the vastness of the world could be reduced to a flat playing field where every day, good and evil faced off for a struggle to the death. The issue isn't simply that some people do terrible things to others; the problem I have to face is the collision of the spiritual army of righteousness and debauchery fighting to the death.* Sam shivered. *A horrible combat I must face virtually every hour of the day.*

Sam turned the corner and slowed down. Their home wasn't far away. But he couldn't help thinking about what he'd heard at the police station before he left. If there had ever been an example of right and wrong locked in conflict, Ape's strange story laid the struggle out on his desk. No matter what young Al Henry had ever done, he didn't deserve to be murdered by these criminals. No question about it. Here was another one of those classic wars with evil sucking Sam in. The feeling was not pleasant.

Sloan pulled in his driveway and got out. He looked at the snow around the lawn. The crisp smell of winter signaled that cold days were ahead. Maybe even another snow would fall that night. Taking a deep breath, he hurried up the front steps.

"My, my," Vera clipped as Sam walked in. "You decided to come home tonight." She tossed her red hair and crossed her arms defiantly over her blue sweater. "What a surprise."

"Sorry." Sam smiled. "Got detained."

Vera's blue eyes narrowed, and she glowered at him. "Just like last night? The night before? Like you do every night?" A shadow descended over her striking face. Although small, Vera could fight with fierce determination. Jack Robbins would have been impressed.

"Honest." Sam kept forcing his smile. "Some big guy wandered in just as I was leaving, and I was the only detective there to talk with the man." He felt anger boiling but fought to stuff it down.

"The other officers were smart enough to have already gone home." Vera's red hair almost seemed to sizzle. Her words were hard. "I guess the other policemen respected their wives enough that they left at the regular time like normal people."

Sam slid in next to her on the couch. "Really, dear. That jerk on the front desk dumped this clown on me. I got trapped in the interrogation room."

"Seems like you do that about every other day."

Counterpunch, Robbins had said. *Let them take the fight to you.* Sam kept smiling. "Please, I do apologize." He reached for her hand. "I'd rather be with you than anyone else in the world." She pulled back.

"The world?" Vera's heart-shaped mouth turned upward slightly, signaling that she might not be as angry as she sounded. "I thought you loved those criminals more than anyone around this place."

"Let me tell you about this bizarre huge man." Sam sidestepped her last jab. "You'll find this man's problem to be a fascinating situation."

Vera looked down at the floor and pursed her lips. "Honest, Sam. I truly get tired of sitting here looking at the television by myself. In that back bedroom, you've got a ten-year-old daughter sound asleep. She went to bed wishing her father was here to tuck her in and say her prayers with her." She pulled at his shirt. "Do you understand me?"

Sam ran his hands nervously through his hair. Vera had hit the one button that stopped all of his mental machinery. His daughter, Cara, forever remained the soft spot in his heart, and he knew Vera was right. He couldn't think of anything to say.

"The child adores you and simply wants a little attention from her dad."

"I know." Sam hung his head. "I'm very, very sorry. I simply don't know what else I can say."

Vera abruptly reached over and took his hand. "I know that you don't mean any harm, but you need to do better, Sam. Much better."

The pain in her voice touched him. Sam only shook his head.

Vera stood up. "Come out in the kitchen and let me fix you a cup of coffee." The change in tone meant that she might not want to talk much more about his being late. "Okay." She shook her head. "Tell me about this person who dropped in." She walked with the easy swing that accentuated her attractive figure.

Sensing his opportunity to change the subject, Sam launched into a long, detailed description of Ape, telling Vera of his unusual appearance. "Strangest thing. I sensed that this monster of a man actually had a strong conscience. He seemed to be deeply upset and wanted help in getting this murder off his mind."

"It happened here?" Vera poured him a cup of coffee and set it down on the kitchen table. Her long, graceful fingers held the cup gently. "In the Springs?"

"Apparently so."

"Someone found the body earlier?"

"That's just it." Sam sipped his coffee. "There's no body. At least not yet."

"A murder without a body?" Vera's blue eyes widened. "You've got to be kidding. Sounds like an empty coffin."

"Like I told you. I need your thoughts on this case."

Vera frowned. "How can you chase a murderer when there's no body?"

"Happens like this infrequently." Sam pulled at his chin. "You believe a crime happened but you can't find the victim."

"And the man's coming back in the morning?"

"Uh-huh." Sam looked at his watch. "If we hurry back to the living room, we can get the ten o'clock news. Maybe there'll be something on the tube that will throw some light on this case."

Vera shook her head and raised an eyebrow. "Sure." She shrugged. "Okay." She picked up her cup. "Let's see what's on."

Sam followed her into the living room, thankful the war zone had turned into a truce. He flipped on the television and sat down next to her on their old green couch. "Sure is nicer when you're happy." He put his arm around her.

For a second Vera's eyes flashed. "I'm always nice except when I have a *good reason* not to be. You understand me?"

Sam set the coffee cup down. "Of course." He gave his wife a kiss. "I love you."

"I love you, Sam. I just don't like your job very much."

Sam kissed her again. "I'll do better," he promised.

"That's what you always say."

Sam leaned back against the couch. "I tell you what. Why don't you come down to the station and we'll have breakfast tomorrow."

"You planning to be at your desk?" Vera asked cynically.

"We'll go wherever you'd like."

"Sam, I swear. You play me like an old fiddle."

"I'm serious, dear. Why don't you come down around 8:00 after Cara goes to school, and we can find someplace nice to eat."

Vera shook her head. "Oh, Sam, you know that I love to eat out." She turned and looked him in the eye. The serious look returned across her face. "But you've got to do better."

"I promise." Sam held up his hand as if swearing an oath. "I promise."

"Okay," Vera said. "I don't have anything that would keep me from coming down to the station house. I'll be there."

"Wonderful!" Sam kissed her on the cheek. "Let's see what the Thursday night news tells us." He settled back in the chair. A slight grin crossed his face.

4

FOR MORE THAN TWENTY YEARS PANCHO'S
Mexican restaurant had been wedged between a man's haber-
dashery and an office supply house. Long ago Sam learned he
could use Pancho's as leverage in his arguments with Vera. She
enjoyed eating in the taco palace enough that he'd often win by
dangling supper at Pancho's before her eyes. A trip down
Mexicali Lane always ended up in her heart.

Growing up in rural Shelton, Iowa, Vera had missed the
offerings of exotic restaurants. Her maiden name of Leestma
signaled she was a card-carrying member of the local Dutch
ghetto that stretched back to dairy farmers in the Netherlands.
Farm life had proved to be simple and basic. Her father's view
of trips to restaurants "in town" was on the order of silly and a
waste of money. Consequently, Vera Leestma grew up with an
inordinate desire to eat in all of those "newfangled" restaurants

her father despised. Throw in the chili, jalapeños, and spices and the result was a Tex-Mex addict.

Vera hurried down Nevada Street toward Pancho's. Sam's office was only a block and a half away. The only thing better than eating in a Mexican restaurant by herself was eating in an enchilada city with Sam. The combination of her husband and a south-of-the-border grease shack had inestimable worth in Vera's mind. She saw the yellow, red, and blue front of the restaurant ahead and walked faster.

Still, breakfast or no, Sam couldn't be allowed to run free without her holding at least one of the reins. When he started working for the police department, Sam seemed to become like a young man coming home after the war. He'd found the work for which he was created and loved every minute of pounding the beat. When they promoted Sam to the rank of detective, he thought they'd made him president of the United States. Sam could work at that confounded police station twenty-six hours a day.

Nothing about the Nevada Street bureau appealed to Vera. The place smelled funny and gave the appearance that maybe it should have been recycled twenty years ago. Terrazzo floors reminded her of the sterile offices in the courthouse, and the walls never got clean. Why Sam liked being around that worn version of a cowboy sheriff's office left her completely mystified.

And yet . . .

Vera found Sam's murder cases to be intriguing. She loved thinking about the whodunits on television and remained fascinated with how Sam solved difficult problems. That *one dimension* enchanted her more than she'd ever let Sam know. If he knew she was on the hook, no telling what Sam might finally do with his time!

Vera hurried inside, believing that she'd beat Sam to the restaurant. Sure enough, no Sam.

"*Buenos días*, Senora Sloan." The short, heavyset waitress recognized her immediately. "*Mi amiga.*" The woman hugged Vera.

"Maria!" Vera squeezed the woman's pudgy warm hand. "Good to see you." She hugged Maria back.

"*Sí.*" She smiled and gestured toward a table for two next to the wall. "A special place for you and your hubby today."

"Sure. Sam will be here shortly." Vera giggled. "We're having a little breakfast out this morning."

"*¡Muy bien!*" Maria winked at her.

Vera didn't have to look at the menu. She always got the same thing, even early in the morning. Soft tacos with beans and rice, and a Diet Coke. Still, Vera studied the sheet of paper as if she might change her mind today.

Vera knew the Martinez family that ran Pancho's Restaurant. Good Roman Catholics. They went to church every Sunday, and that pleased Vera. She hadn't been reared to have sympathy with Romans but time had changed her attitude.

When she was twelve, her family had bundled Vera up and sent her off to a rather routine straitlaced church camp. If nothing else, the lodge was a reprieve from the farm, and she'd go anywhere to get out from under the laborious routine that the farm placed on every day of Vera's week. Church camp had to be better than chores starting at the crack of dawn.

To Vera's surprise, the summer camp experience had turned out to be far more than a diversion. During the evening chapel time, Vera had been challenged to make decisions that changed her life. She moved from being a difficult, demanding little girl to a young woman operating out of a faith center. Whatever else would prove true about Vera Leestma, time demonstrated that she remained true to this fresh start.

In recent years, her church helped the Martinez family during a critical period when their house burned down. Helping Maria and Gomez brought Vera into contact with how their faith shaped and guided this good Mexican family. The bridges that the Sloans and Martinezes built during those days between the Dutch and Mexican worlds made everything different for both families.

"Hey, I'm here," Sam called from the door. Several people turned and looked at him. "How about a few tortillas?" His brown sport coat and tan pants gave him the look of a local businessman.

Vera grinned. "Late as usual."

Sam waved at Maria. "Darn it. I got wrapped up in trying to find this kid who was supposed to have been killed. Can't find a trace of him."

"This is the case you were talking about last night?"

"Yes. The adolescent's name is Al. Al Henry. Nobody seems to have ever heard of him."

"Maybe that strange Ape guy misled you."

Sam nodded. "Yeah, that's a good assumption, but I can't understand why this character would take the time to come to see me and then mislead me. The whole case doesn't fit together."

Vera pushed the menu in front of him. "Take a break, Detective. Figure out what you're going to order from Maria."

Sam made a quick survey of the familiar menu. "Going to do something a little different today," he spoke more to himself. "Think maybe I'll go for a little tortilla soup. Something light. Yes, that'll do it." He smiled at his wife.

"Very nice to be here," Vera said. "Just like *normal* people."

"We *are* normal people."

Vera kept smiling. "Not really, Sam. Regular folks don't eat out just to patch up a dispute. They live a routine, well-regulated life. Know what I mean?"

Sam took a big breath. His eyes carried a flash of fire, but he kept the smile on his face. He was trying.

"I want to thank you so much for inviting me out today." Vera kept talking.

"Sure. My pleasure."

"Now the next step is for us to bring Cara along."

Sam's artificial smile faded. "Vera," he said sounding serious, "you know that I would love to have Cara with us. I'm probably more partial to her than anyone in the world." He scratched his head. "Unfortunately . . . sometimes . . . business . . . police work . . . gets in the way of the best-laid plans."

"I understand." Vera forced a smile. "But you also have to exercise the discipline of *saying no* as well."

Sam stiffened slightly. "Periodically, matters over which I have no control get in the way. You know how that happens."

Vera could feel her blood starting to heat up. "Yes," she said slowly, "but you also know that you don't do your best to drop a pair of pliers in the gears when the machinery is grinding in your direction."

"I *do my best*." Sam sounded defensive. "What more can I say?"

Vera studied his eyes. He was nearing the edge. She'd hit this button before and watched him explode. An emotional upheaval wasn't what she had in mind.

"We've been over this problem many times." He picked up the menu again. "Somewhere along the way *you* have to develop an understanding attitude." Sam stared at the menu.

Oh boy, Vera thought. *Looks like the party is over.*

5

"YOU HAVEN'T SAID MUCH DURING BREAK-fast," Vera said.

Sam pushed the empty tortilla soup bowl back. "Forgive me." His voice sounded more professional than sincere.

Vera sipped her Coke for a moment. She wasn't trying to agitate Sam. Far to the contrary, Vera really wanted him to know how much she cared and desired everything to go well. All she wanted were a few adjustments that seemed minor to her.

"I'm sure you've been thinking about the problem of locating this missing person. You said his name was Al Henry?"

Sam pulled at his chin and rubbed the tip of his nose as he always did when thinking. "Strange." He frowned. "No one seems to have even heard of the guy. We couldn't even find any bulletins on him as a missing person. The whole situation doesn't fit together. Something's wrong."

"Like a machine that doesn't work right?" Vera smiled earnestly.

"Yeah." Sam stared at the table. "Something like that."

"You truly care about these people, don't you, honey?"

Sam blinked several times. "Yes. Sure."

Vera nodded. "Why? Why do you have such a strong interest in these characters that are bottom-of-the-barrel types? Really, Sam! You work with a truckload of losers. Why?"

Sam looked up slowly. His face had taken on the serious, thoughtful look Vera had come to recognize when he probed for the truth about a person or what had happened in a situation but only came up with consternation. The "Sam-Wham" gaze, Vera called it. He could be smiling one minute and the next be more introspective than a philosopher.

"You want to know?" Sam raised an eyebrow. "Really?"

"Sure."

"It happened a long time ago," Sam began quietly. "When I was a boy. A boy in Chicago." He looked out the window thoughtfully, almost as if watching a scene on a television set.

"I don't talk about the situation often. The whole thing happened where I lived. In that old apartment building. Remember that scar over Dad's left eye?"

Vera nodded and leaned forward, watching her husband's eyes. His entire countenance had changed. Sam's brow furled and his eyes narrowed. A streak of pain shot across his face. Vera listened, not saying anything.

"Dad always looked like one of those losers you're talking about. Just another immigrant worker. Let me tell you about that evening. My father had been home from work for maybe an hour. It was one of those rare evenings that he hadn't stopped by the bar." Sam smiled. "Yeah, Dad was truly being a good boy that evening." He looked out the window again and took a deep breath. "Mom was very contented.

"I was sitting on the living room floor watching late-afternoon television when I heard a hard rap on the door that scared me. A harsh voice yelled for us to open up. Said they were police. Mom ran for the door.

"She hadn't even opened it a crack when these two big cops knocked it against the wall. Pushed her aside like she was a piece of lumber. The creeps rushed across the room and leaped on my father like they were capturing an escaped animal from the zoo. Knocked him to the floor. Ready to kill him."

"Your *father*?" Vera's mouth dropped. "What in the world had he done?"

"You know that Dad wasn't an easy man to push around. He jumped up and knocked one of the cops on his butt and took on the second one as easily as two wrestlers lock it up on Saturday night." Sam took another deep breath. "Unfortunately, the man on the floor came up swinging his club and smashed my father across the forehead. The nightstick slit his head open above his eye. Knocked him out cold."

"That's how he got the scar." Vera squeezed her hands together. "I just assumed that he'd been injured at work."

Sam shook his head. "The police never even told him or us why they'd broken in like an attack from the marines. My mother started screaming and beating on the cops. I was a young boy and couldn't do anything, but I tried. These policemen were mean and tough."

Sam looked at his fingernails for a moment and rubbed the backs of his hands. "They hauled him down to the station house. Mother and I followed them in a cab. Turned out that a lady downstairs had been raped and someone saw my father going up the stairs at an unusually early hour. They put two and two together and came up with five. Jack Sloan had been identified as the rapist for doing nothing more than coming home on time!"

Vera reached across the table and took Sam's hand. "You've never told me this horror story. How terrible!"

"Not proud of it," Sam quipped. "Not proud of it at all. My father stayed in jail for a month, then the police came up with the man who committed the crime. Turned out it was the woman's brother-in-law and she was actually protecting him for that entire long month. The jerk came back and bothered her again. That's when she told the full story to the police and they nabbed him.

"Something interesting happened, though, that I wouldn't ever have expected. My father didn't even sue the police. They ended up shaking hands, and the cop that hit him apologized."

"You're kidding!"

"Nope. My father believed the police were only doing their jobs. Just made an error. He believed that people can make mistakes trying to do the right thing." Sam shrugged. "The old man simply went about his business, and in time the problem died down. Cooled off."

"People forgot?"

Sam shook his head. "Not really. I heard cracks at school and got in a few fights. Having your old man in jail for a month was no small problem in those good ole days. Every now and then someone living in the apartment building made some remark that set me off. Of course, I'd come out swinging first. I knew that my father got the same thing. Had to be painful for him."

"And it was all a mistake?"

"That's what stuck in my mind. I realized that poor people usually end up getting the brunt of someone else's errors. They need a little extra help because other people aren't as likely to believe them." Sam took a big breath and his chest swelled. "As a boy, I guess I decided that if I ever got the opportunity to help people like my father, that's what I would do."

"So that's why you have such a strong concern for these people?"

Sam nodded.

Silence settled between them. Sam seemed to be still thinking about what had happened. Vera's mind focused somewhere else. Maybe this was the time to level with him. He'd obviously told her a difficult private story. Possibly that was what she ought to do in turn.

"Honey," Vera began tentatively, "the story about your father helps me understand why you work so hard."

Sam looked at her stoically, his face portraying nothing.

"I've been thinking about this snit that we keep getting into over your working so much." Vera stopped and took a deep breath. "I want you to know that I support everything you're trying to do."

Sam's eyebrows raised.

"It's that I simply don't seem to be part of your life . . . at least in the ways I want to be. I want us to be a team."

"A team?"

Vera stopped. The word had slipped out without her meaning to say it in quite the way that she had, but *team* still sounded good to her. She nodded.

Sam puckered his lips and pulled on his chin. "I'm not sure I'm following you."

"Maybe if I was part of helping you work on these tough cases, we wouldn't have these problems over your working such long hours."

Sam frowned. "The police department wouldn't stand for you being involved in solving these crime cases. I mean . . . after all . . . people have been killed fighting these wars. Shootings happen. People get slugged, zonked, beat up! You could be in danger."

His threatening words tickled Vera's ears. The thought of a little risk or unpredictability sounded very good in her routine life that was more than a tad too close to growing up on that Iowa farm. She smiled. "I'm not afraid."

"*Afraid?*" Sam frowned. "You should be!"

"Look, Sam." Words began slipping through her lips as if they had a life of their own. "I'm not talking about riding in a police car with you or coming down to your office. Heaven knows, I'd go a mile out of my way to avoid walking through that Nevada Street station! I'm describing being your buddy at home. Your unofficial partner that you share the intimate details with."

Sam rubbed the entire side of his face. "I don't know," he more mumbled to himself. "Never thought of anything like this . . . before *now*."

"You know that I'm good at asking the right questions. Every now and then I come up with an important insight. Why not make me the wall that you bounce thoughts off of? You might find that I'd really surprise you with what I'd discover."

Sam kept pulling at his chin. "I'd have to think about this one a while." His voice sounded so far off that he wasn't easy to hear.

He glanced at his watch. "I've got to get back to the station. Got several people waiting for me to make their reports on this

Henry kid." He started scooting out of the seat. "Let's talk about this later."

"How about tonight?"

Sam blinked several times. "Sure." He reached over and kissed Vera on the cheek. "See you later." Sam left money for the check on the table and hurried out of the restaurant.

Vera watched him hurrying up the street. "For once, I've won!"

Sam was always putting her behind the eight ball with little maneuvers like lunch at Pancho's. This time she'd scored so big, he'd be worrying about this idea all afternoon long. That Sam-Wham look covered his face. She laughed again.

Vera didn't move but sat at the table sipping the Coke for another fifteen minutes. She thought about this strange idea that had oozed out of her mouth. Being a team fascinated her. What might it be like to work seriously with Sam? To come up with ideas? To help him think through placing the pieces in one of these crime puzzles? The idea sounded so totally fascinating that Vera felt captured, entranced by the thought.

She set her drink back down on the table and slipped out of the chair. For the first time in months, something gripped her mind that gave new snap and direction to her life. Not only could this idea help Sam, but it would grant her new purpose and meaning. Maybe she could even do research at the library, gather up data for Sam. Who knew where it might lead?

Vera walked through the red-and-blue door back out onto the street. The cold wind from the mountains swept down Twenty-third Street and made her pull her coat closer to her neck. She glanced to the mountaintops and could see that it must be snowing up there.

"Sure not cold down here!" Vera said to herself as she hurried to the car. "No sirree. I'm as warm as a piece of toast!"

6

AT AROUND 9:30 ON THURSDAY NIGHT, AN old man stepped out of his rented 1920 one-story house on one of the backstreets in Lincoln, Nebraska. Shingles on the sagging roof looked windblown and in need of replacement. The white-haired pensioner glanced up and down the street several times. Chilly night air caused him to pull his collar up tightly around his neck. Cigarette smoke spun up into the dark night from the butt hanging out of the corner of his wrinkled mouth. After looking around again, he gripped his cane and hobbled with a creaking limp down the street.

Twenty-six years earlier, Raymond Bench lost his leg in a railroad accident and that meant all future walking would have problems. Actually, the "accident" had been his own fault. The drifter had a predisposition for hopping trains as they pulled out of towns. Of course, his joyrides left his wife behind and that always felt good. He'd jump on and ride to the next stop, no matter how close or far the ride proved to be. Sometimes the freight trains would roll on for hours. At other times, the ride proved to be only fifteen to twenty minutes. Being half-drunk didn't slow Bench down, but it did make the first leap on a flat-car a mite bit harder. In the hustle to get on a flatcar in 1974, his hand slipped, and Bench fell under the cold metal wheels that clipped his leg off just below the knee.

Raymond Bench hated trains after that accident. He found walking around on crutches to be completely despicable and eventually picked up a wooden leg that never fit him well. As a result, the pain from the "happenstance" amputation never completely left the old codger. Passing years only made matters worse because walking agitated the pulsating nerves that never completely shut down until Raymond went to sleep at night after a few drinks. The good news was that the aching gave him an excellent reason to keep on drinking day after day, night after night.

Bench pulled his stained felt hat down over his eyes and tucked his left hand into his pocket, the cigarette bobbing up and down on the edge of his lips. The liquor store should be only a couple of blocks ahead. At this hour of night, they'd be closing up and shouldn't pay much attention to him wandering in. Raymond figured in a matter of seconds he could get a pint of whiskey in his coat without anyone catching a thing. Once the pint was stashed, he'd amble out the door as if nothing interested him and sidle up the street like the cold night was mighty fine. Perfectly simple and an easy way to get a little sleeping tonic to put him on ice for the rest of the night.

A couple of cars whizzed past, but nobody looked his way, which was about what Bench expected. At sixty-six years of age no one looked at him anyway. Raymond didn't have anyone who paid any attention to him. Well, of course, except for his girlfriend, who was close to being a dog. His current wife had left a couple of weeks back for who knows where, taking the boy with her. The new girlfriend liked him because he'd spend money on her, but there hadn't been much between them except a little fooling around. He had to keep appearances up.

Headlights of another passing car shot in Raymond's face, but the vehicle didn't slow down. He kept limping down the street. Halfway down the block Raymond saw the advertising lights of the corner liquor store. *José's Liquors* flashed on and off in bright red neon lights. He didn't come into this place often, and no one would recognize him. Shouldn't be hard to get in and out quickly. He pulled his hat farther down over his eyes.

Bench studied the front of the building and then cursed. "No cars!" he grumbled under his breath. "Thought there'd be at least one customer in the place about now." He pulled at his wooden leg and walked slower, using the cane to steady his gait and make the limp stop for at least a few moments.

At the corner where the store abutted both streets, Bench studied the building more carefully. He couldn't see anybody inside. With a flip of his thumb, Raymond tossed the cigarette in the gutter and edged closer to the glass front door. He slipped the cane under his overcoat and hooked it to his belt so no one could identify it later. Still nobody was in sight. Inhaling deeply, he opened the front door of José's Liquors and slipped inside.

The blast of warm air felt good to his cold face. Bench slowly started down a side row, knowing the heavy stuff sat on shelves near the back.

"Can I help you?" a hard voice called out. A man popped up from behind the counter near the entrance.

Bench shot a look out of the corner of his eye and recognized the black-haired manager. He cursed under his breath. "Naw, just looking." Bench edged farther down the aisle. "Can help myself."

"Don't hesitate to call me if you need any assistance locating any of our products."

"Don't worry," Bench grumbled. "Just checking your stock." He watched the man return to a sheet of paper that he was writing on. The manager appeared totally occupied.

Bench stopped at several shelves and looked quickly back and forth up the aisle to make sure no one had come up behind him. He didn't see another person in the store. Good.

＊＊＊＊

Johnny Gonzales had managed José's Liquors for three years. Although he'd seldom had people steal from the store, Gonzales had a suspicious streak and paid close attention to anyone entering his domain. While he finished tallying the day's sales, he kept watching a television monitor located under the counter where he could see what the customers never suspected. The camera was old and the picture quality poor, but at least he could see people walking around. The old man in the back was acting funny, limping down the row as though he was hiding something.

Gonzales had noticed the old coot hanging around outside the first time he'd showed up. The limp had made him easy to remember. Besides looking rather shaggy, the old-timer had constantly looked up and down the street, which made him appear questionable. Gonzales immediately noticed the guy when he sauntered into the liquor store.

The surveillance camera perched above the front door made a clear sweep of the entire store. Once the derelict started down the aisle, Gonzales had the jerk in clean, clear view, although the old man had no idea that the camera was following his every step. He watched the television monitor under the counter intently.

Bench turned the last corner and slipped near the shelf lined with pints of whiskey. Gonzales watched the old man take another quick look around and knew exactly what he was about to do. Without making a sound, Johnny quietly slipped his shoes off and walked out of the cashier's cage. He stealthily and silently slipped up the center aisle of the store, hurrying to the back where the old man was rifling the whiskey. As he reached the end of the last row of shelves, he heard a tiny clink of glass and figured the theft had occurred. Now was the time to act.

"What's going on back here?" Gonzales said roughly and stepped out from behind the shelf.

━━━━

The loud voice resonating only a couple of feet behind his head shook Bench so completely that his hand slipped and the bottle missed his pocket, crashing on the floor and shattering in a thousand pieces. Raymond stared at the whiskey surging in every direction. His heart started beating like a drum.

"Just what I thought!" The manager reached out and grabbed Bench's coat. "Back here stealing my booze!"

Bench's heartbeat leaped again, and he panicked. The old

man knocked the manager's hand off his coat. "Get your mitts off me," he growled.

"Thought you'd slip a few bottles in your pocket, huh?" The manager reached for Bench again. "Let's see what the police say." The manager started dragging him forward.

Raymond knew he'd have to act instantly or surrender. He impulsively reached for a large Gallo wine bottle behind him and swung it at the manager. The bottle broke against the manager's head with a splattering sound as red wine splashed everywhere. With a backhand sweep, Bench brought the broken handle back across the manager's face with a final massive swing and then slung the broken bottleneck across the store. The remains of the razor-sharp bottleneck scattered against the far wall.

For a moment the manager stood in front of Bench with wine and blood running down his face and across his shirt. Blood spurted wildly in every direction. His eyes slowly rolled back in his head as he dropped to his knees in a large puddle of red wine and brown whiskey.

Bench stared, realizing for the first time that his back-handed thrust had slashed the man's throat. The manager made a strange gurgling sound, then abruptly fell face forward on the floor. Blood splattered on Bench's pants and shoes.

"Oh, no! No!" Bench grabbed his hat and pulled it down farther over his face. For a moment he watched blood pump out of the man's throat in wild fury, merging into the pool of booze. Across the gray tile the strange blend of colors and consistencies oozed in a weird surrealistic shape. Like a puff of smoke from a campfire, the bizarre smell of a "whiskey cooler" jolted the old man into running.

"Gotta get out of here," Bench said to himself, clutching his cane tightly. Without looking back, he rushed through a small door at the rear of the store. "Don't got no idea how to get out!"

In the dimness of the back room, Bench saw the outline of a door. He hit the metal door hard and bounced off, knocking himself to the concrete floor. For a moment, he tried to get his breath and sputtered. After a struggle with the artificial leg, Bench barely managed to get back on his feet and finally unlocked the exit door. He pulled out his cane and quickly hurried into the black alley, hustling as fast as his artificial leg would take him.

Bench turned instinctively toward his rented house, hurrying but unable to move fast. He could feel the wetness of his blood-soaked pants. All he could think about was that strange sight of wine, whiskey, and oozing blood running together.

Bench hoped that the manager was still alive . . . but he didn't think so.

7

Detectives trudged in and out through the downtown Colorado Springs police offices, as they always did on Friday morning with the start of the weekend bearing down on them. Getting started on the day's assignment proved difficult for the few men and women still standing around the coffeepot, sipping and talking as though they had all day to get their work done.

Sam Sloan stared at the pile of paperwork on the corner of his desk, left over from last night.

Hate these bureau reporting forms. I swear I won't let the pressure keep me at the office tonight like it did yesterday. No more fights with Vera because of getting the paperwork accomplished.

Sam pulled the papers forward. His phone rang. "Sloan here."

"Hello, hero," the morning officer at the front desk sounded crisp and smart-mouthed. "Ready for excitement?"

"Yeah," Sloan answered dryly.

"Got a friend of yours up here. At least this guy says he is."

"Look like a gorilla?"

"Sam? What an uncomplimentary thing to say." The officer laughed. "Yep, sure. You got the guy. Calls himself *Ape*."

"Have an officer put him in the interrogation room, and I'll be there momentarily."

"Want me to put a leash on his neck and tie him to a chair?" The officer snickered.

"Funny." Sloan hung up. *Ape's arrived. Didn't think he'd get here this early.* Sloan stood up and pushed the files and papers to one side. *Let's see what our boy has on his mind this morning.* He started down the hall.

Dick Simmons turned the corner in front of him. "Hey, it's my main man. How ya doing this morning, Sam?"

Sloan glanced at the big detective standing in front of him, dressed in his usual natty tie, looking more like an executive at the bank than a policeman. Simmons had the square jaw, the crew cut, the thick eyebrows of a hard-nosed cop, but he still dressed like a business administrator with the look of a first-class operator. Always a class act.

"I'm set for another big day, Dick."

"Good." Simmons slapped him on the back as he passed by. "We always get one down here on Nevada Street." Simmons hurried on down the hall. "Take care of yourself on the sharp turns."

Sam walked on down the hall and turned into the observation room with the transparent mirror to take a quick look at George Barnes before he started the interview.

The big man sat slouched over the table with the same uncomfortable look on his face he'd had the night before. Ape looked like he might have slept in his van the night before or at least hadn't taken off that dirty old T-shirt. His hair was more pulled back than combed. The dizzy look on his face made him appear ready to talk. Sam turned away from the mirror toward the hall.

"Morning, George," Sam said, shutting the door behind him.

"Ummph," Ape grunted.

"Trust you slept well." Sloan sat down at the table.

Ape shook his head and looked at the floor dismally.

"Too bad." Sloan leaned back in his wooden chair. "Sorry to hear it. Appreciate your coming in first thing."

"Didn't have anywhere else to go."

Sloan pulled at his lip, thinking about where to begin. How to start. The big brute kept looking at him, saying nothing. Waiting on Sam to speak.

"Last night," Sloan started slowly, "you were describing this . . . you called them a gang . . . a motorcycle gang, I believe."

Ape nodded.

"Didn't sound like much of a motorcycle gang to me."

The big man cleared his throat and shook his head again. "Ain't much of anything except they were sure capable of killin'." Ape ran his tongue around the inside of his mouth. "Yup. They thought they were somethin' else, but truth of the matter is that they didn't own nothin' outright."

"Last night you said they'd paid you fifty bucks plus expenses to make the run in your van over to Nebraska. Fill in the details for me."

Ape rubbed the back of his neck. "See, Jester and his common-law wife Alice had this child with 'em. Some little feller about two or three years old, I'd guess. But Jester had another kid back there in Nebraska."

"Wait!" Sloan held his hand up. "What is Jester's actual name? His birth certificate name?

"Got no idea."

Sam leaned forward. "You must have obtained something. A last name? More of a moniker than just Jester?"

Ape nodded. "Never heard nothin'. Nothin' at all."

"You mean you're telling me that some guy with no name other than a nickname is the killer?"

"Uh-huh."

Sloan slumped back in his wooden chair. "Little hard to run down a crook with nothing more than a weird name like *Jester*. Right?"

"That's all I got." Ape shrugged.

Sloan studied the man's drooping eyelids, which turned his eyes into narrow slits. The scars around his cheeks had probably been picked up in a fight. Barnes's nose was flattened by one too many punches, but his voice still sounded sincere. This strange-looking guy seemed to be telling the truth.

"Honest." Ape's eyes widened. "At the time I didn't want to know anything more about Jester. He scared me."

"Big man?"

"Oh, no. Probably wasn't five foot six, but the man had a mean, tough way about him. He is the sorta guy you walk on the other side of the street to avoid. Good with a knife. Little on the crazy side, ya know."

"And Jester had to go back to Lincoln for some reason?"

"Had another young'un over there," Ape rambled on. "Some sort of legal problem with this other son living over there in Nebraska. I didn't find out much about them until we started our trip. See, Jester began really talkin' after we started down the road a-ways out of Colorado Springs."

Ape stopped and pulled out a pack of rumpled cigarettes and flipped one out the end of the packet. "Mind if I smoke?"

Sam raised an eyebrow but shook his head. "No. Go ahead."

Ape flipped a cheap plastic Bic lighter and took a long draw, blowing smoke above his head. "Truth is that the gang seemed more interested in gettin' out of town than arrivin' in Nebraska. They all wanted to be a-movin' on. Ya see, as we went rambling down the road, ole' Jester started talkin', tellin' stories and all. Sure enough. They was all on the run."

"And that's when the murder story spilled out?"

"Yes, sir." Ape nodded firmly. "Yes, sir. Indeed. Ole Jester started a-tellin' me how they got to go outta state to check on some legal business about this other boy of his. He talks on and on and then gets off on this story about killing a seventeen-year-old boy here in the Springs."

"Al Henry?"

"Yup! The boy I told you about last night."

Sam made a note on the pad lying in front of him on the table. "You never saw Al?"

"Nope. Long gone before I came along."

"And Jester told you he killed this person?" Sam's voice raised slightly.

"Ole Jester was a-puffin' on a joint and high. That's why he was a-talkin' to me." Ape said with a grin. "Think he was dumb too."

"Dumb?" Sam's voice raised slightly. "I reckon! Why did Jester kill the boy?"

Ape suddenly grinned for the first time since he'd come into the Nevada Street police station. "Oh, I got that story. Seems that Jester's gang had this little rule they lived by. Sorta like communism. Everything is held in common and you don't own nothin'. Ya gets what ya needs but there ain't no stealin'." Ape raised his heavy eyebrows, looking menacingly across at Sam. "Well, that's where young Al went wrong. He stole from the gang. That was the big no-no and the boy went and done it wrong."

"The boy stole money from the gang?"

Ape shook his head emphatically, sending his bushy long hair wiggling in every direction at the same time. "Heavens, no! Nothin' big like slippin' cash out under the table. Poor ole Al apparently stole some clothes, a few patches, decorations, some little stuff."

"Wait!" Sloan held his hand up. "You're saying that Jester killed this boy over his stealing clothing? That's all?"

"Sure." Ape shrugged. "It's the principle of the thing. Ya see, Al violated the code of the gang. That was the heavy thought on Jester's mind. Got to keep order with the troops."

"And there were how many people in this gang?"

"Sorta came and went, but I took Jester, Alice, and three other gang members with me to Lincoln. Of course, that count was plus their little boy. Sometimes a couple more people hung around the gang. Maybe eight or nine at the most."

Sam pulled at his chin again and studied George Barnes carefully. The basic story seemed to be rather simple. The Jester character killed like other people threw trash into a city-owned waste can. Killing meant nothing to the man, so Jester would do it again without regret or second thoughts. Somebody had to stop him.

"Of course, I got frightened by the time I dropped the gang off in Lincoln. Maybe ole Jester would decide to kill me!" Ape beat on his chest. "I mean that little man ain't a-feared of killin' nothin'. I may be big, but a knife will stick just as deep in me as it did in poor little Al. That's what's been worryin' me. Jester might come back here to this town and start lookin' for me."

"You never saw Al Henry? Don't know what he looked like?"

"No, sir."

Sloan kept studying the man. Obviously, Ape wasn't bright, but he seemed to have the problem clearly in focus. Ape didn't seem to realize his own strength and probably ran off of fear much of the time.

"Ape, you're afraid of Jester. What else scares you?"

The man gestured aimlessly. "Nothing, really."

"How about the law? You been in trouble with us before?"

"Did a little time in California." Ape wiped his mouth nervously. "Got caught up in a burglary heist. Big mistake."

"What else?" Sloan's voice lowered to a growl.

"Got caught with a little pot once."

"No such thing as *a little* when we put our hand on you."

Ape nodded. "Yeah, done a little time on that one, but I'm here to tell ya that I'm clear. Slick as a whistle. Ain't done nothin' in years. Wouldn't be here talkin' if I was in trouble."

"Ape, I've already checked your record. I know about those terms in prison." Sam pulled at his lower lip. The big man was probably lying somewhere. "You're really *afraid* of Jester, aren't you?"

Barnes cursed. "You bet I am. Jester can kill as easy as he can slice bread."

"I'm going to need to check on some items before we talk further," Sloan said as if thinking out loud. "I want to be able to find you. Where can I run you down?"

"Don't got no place to stay. Just sleep in my van."

"Where you keep it parked?"

"Usually around Acacia Park. Down there around the back where I can find an empty free parking space. You know. I just sorta bum around."

"Don't plan to leave town for a while." Sam pointed at Ape's chest. "You settle in here until I get some questions answered. Understand?"

"Yes, sir."

"I'm serious. You go running down the road, and we won't have a hard time finding that crazy van of yours. You just sit back and take life easy here in Colorado. We may need your help."

Ape pulled at his shaggy beard. "Most of the time I'll be down there somewhere around the park." He stood up. "Don't you take too long now to find them things out. I don't got much money on me."

Sam nodded. "Try washing dishes."

Ape raised one eyebrow menacingly but started for the door. "I'll be a-goin' now if that's all right with you."

Sloan stood up. "Like I say, don't be hard to find."

Ape nodded and shuffled off, looking slightly depressed.

Sam watched him slouching down the hall, then the detective moved over to the window, parting the blinds. Ape kept walking in the direction of his parked van. People moved aside as he clomped past with his heavy leather motorcycle vest blowing in the breeze. No one wanted in his way.

"Ape, you are a sight to behold," Sam said to himself. "Got to find out if you're really telling the truth." He turned around and shut the blinds. "Let's start by finding out about Al. Al Henry. Does anyone know anything about this guy?"

8

FRIDAY AFTERNOON WOULD BE OVER IN less than thirty minutes. Not an easy week. Sam felt emotionally stretched out of shape by the swirl of unexpected events. The encounter with Ape remained a mind bender. Saturday morning ought to give him a little reprieve to sleep late and recoup some energy. He felt drained.

"Sam, don't get in any trouble over the weekend," Dick Simmons called into Sloan's office. "We all know about those drinking sprees you go on every weekend."

Sloan snorted. "Right."

Simmons strolled in carrying a manila file folder in his hand and sat down across from Sloan. "Don't you ever do anything you call bad?"

Sloan grinned slyly. "Not what *you'd* call bad, Dick."

Simmons laughed. "You're a strange guy, Sam." Dick's

normal joking disposition suddenly shifted. "I've seen you operate meaner than a junkyard bulldog, then turn around and be as gentle as a lamb."

"All part of the job."

"Come on, Sam. Ain't nobody down here functioning like that but you. You're Mr. Nice Guy, who can be tougher than Dick Tracy. Why do you tick like that?"

"I don't," Sam said dryly. "It's all in your imagination."

"No, it's not." Simmons's voice shifted again, sounding more serious and concerned. "I've never asked you this question before but I'd truly like to know. How can you be kind and gentle but still be rough and tough?"

Sam studied his friend for a minute. Dick Simmons had been on cases with him for years. A good man. Little on the frivolous side occasionally but basically a good, dependable professional.

"You really want to know, Dick?"

"Absolutely."

Sam leaned back in his chair. "I don't think that we're simply chasing criminals." He shook his head. "We're part of a spiritual warfare where some of the people on this planet have decided to line up with evil. If we don't stop them, there's no end to how much havoc they'll create. When the battle is on, good people have to be tough or they'll get run over."

Simmons squinted, running his tongue around inside his cheek. "Hmm, that's a different idea."

"Good people must stand up in the spiritual battle, or the forces of evil will grind them into the ground." Sam smiled. "I don't have any choice, Dick. I'd like to be a nice guy with everybody, but many of these people eat good folks for lunch."

Simmons sprawled out in the chair and laid his file folder on the desk. "You bet they do! We see that every day of the week down here."

Sloan shrugged. "We're players in the game. We have to stop the forces of evil before they invade our communities. If we don't prosecute them and put these characters behind bars, they'll turn our normal world into hell."

Simmons pursed his lips and rubbed his mouth. "Ask a serious question, get a serious answer."

"Makes your job a little more important, doesn't it?"

Dick stood up slowly. "Makes me feel like I ought to go to church on Sunday."

"Not that a visit wouldn't be good for you." Sloan laughed. "Make sure you sit near the back so the roof doesn't fall on your head."

"Ahh." Dick waved him away. "They're not even sure which side I'm on most of the time." He strolled out into the hall.

Sam grinned and started closing up his desk. "Funny guy," he said to himself.

Vera hurried around the kitchen, glancing at the wall clock. "Your daddy will be home soon. Got to get supper ready."

Cara sat at the table, looking out the kitchen window at what had been the summer garden. The freeze had turned most of the grass white, and the bright flowers were gone now that fall had come. Patches of snow lay scattered around the yard. "I like this time of year, Mommy."

"Why, dear?" Vera pushed a pie into the oven.

"Everything changes and the snow comes," Cara said

"You like changing clo—"

Cara grinned broadly. "I do, Mommy. I love having a new set for every season of the year. Maybe we need to get me a few new things."

Vera laughed and set the dial on the kitchen stove. "We'll have to have this pie done before your father comes home. It's his favorite." She ignored the ploy for another trip to the clothes store.

"Mommy?" Cara patted the top of the table. "Would you sit down and talk to me for a minute?"

Vera stopped and turned around. "Talk to you?"

"I want to ask you something." Cara didn't sound like she was talking about buying more clothes.

Vera studied her daughter, realizing that she didn't talk to her often enough. Cara was ten years old and wouldn't be a child much longer. Her blond hair had always given her the appearance of having a halo around her face, assuring Vera that Cara truly was the angel she always thought she was. She stared at her daughter, recognizing that Cara would be considered a beautiful child by anyone's standard.

"Something is wrong, Mommy?"

"No, dear." Vera glanced at the clock again. "We don't have much time, but I can always make a few minutes to talk with my daughter." Vera sat down opposite Cara.

Cara's broad smile stretched a tad farther, and she raised her eyebrows. "I love to talk to big people."

"You consider me a big people, huh?"

"Sure. You and Daddy and my schoolteacher are the biggest people in the world. I listen to everything that you say."

"That's good, Cara. Very good."

Cara's smile changed, and a frown covered her face. "My teacher always talks to me." She raised one eyebrow. "And you always stop to listen to me, Mommy."

"Sure, dear."

"Then why doesn't Daddy talk to me more?"

"What do you mean, Cara?"

"He's always flying around here like he's run out of time." Cara tilted her head. "Know what I mean?"

"Of course, Cara, but unfortunately your father is a very busy man. His job at the police department demands a great amount of his time."

"I know that's so, but even when he's not hurrying off to his job, I don't think he really listens to me."

"Cara, your father loves you more than life itself."

"I know that, Mommy, but I'm thinking about his listening to me carefully. I always get the feeling that he's working me in between his cases."

Vera took a deep breath and looked out the window for a few moments. "I understand," she finally said.

"I only want to have a few moments for us to sit down and talk. You know, talk like I do with my friends."

"Yes," Vera answered.

"Do you think I'd be asking too much for some time that Daddy and I could talk alone?"

Vera looked at her daughter again. Cara had always been a bright child, on the edge of precociousness. Her innocence didn't conceal emotional sensitivity. Cara wanted her father to listen like he understood and cared about her thoughts. Sam needed to open up and let her walk around inside of his head for a while. Surely Sam could try to allow her to come in.

Vera reached over and squeezed her daughter's. "No, Cara, of course there's nothing wrong with talking . . your father, and I know that he'd like to spend much more time with you."

"Really?" Cara grinned.

"Yes. Much more time."

Cara stood up and hugged her mommy. "That would be so wonderful!" She hurried out of the kitchen. "I'll be back in my bedroom, playing until Daddy comes home."

"Okay," Vera called after her.

Cara needs to know her father's values, she thought. *The words need to come out of Sam's own mouth. Please, Sam. Please sit down and listen to your daughter. She's a wonderful child, and you need to know her much more intimately.*

9

THE TWO BUSINESSMEN HUDDLED AROUND the news rack, waiting silently for the delivery man from the *Lincoln Daily Sun* to slip in his latest Saturday morning newspapers. A third man in a worn coat leaned against the corner light pole, watching the scramble to get the morning paper and listening to the conversations as the two men picked up their papers.

"Nasty murder last night." The first man in a dark blue suit stared at the blaring headlines. "Looks like somebody slashed the throat of the liquor store operator."

"Heard it on the television news this morning," the second man in a sport coat answered. "We haven't had a barbaric attack like this one in years."

"Doesn't look like a robbery attempt," the man in the blue suit said. "Sounds like some kind of attack by the mob."

"Here in Lincoln?" The second businessman's voice raised. "Naw. We don't have organized crime around here."

"I don't know." The man tucked the paper under his arm and hurried up the street. "Can't ever tell," he said over his shoulder. The second man disappeared in the opposite direction.

Raymond Bench straightened up, but held on to the light pole. He shook his leg slightly and hobbled closer to the newsstand, peering through the wired glass cover on the rack. He cursed under his breath when he read the headlines: *Murder in Liquor Store.* He slipped in a quarter and bought a newspaper.

"Police need to start shooting these creeps," a feminine voice said behind Bench. "Kill them on the spot."

The old man turned and saw two women only three feet behind him, looking at the same paper. He watched them carefully.

"Yeah," another woman's voice said. "I hope they catch this jerk and hang him from the nearest tree." The two walked off, talking to each other.

Bench pulled his hat down more carefully around his face and started hobbling up the street. The whole town seemed to be irate about the killing. Lord, he didn't mean to kill the liquor store operator. Everybody had assumed the worst. Big mistake. "An accident," he mumbled under his breath, "nothing but a stupid accident." He kept meandering up the street, thinking about how bad he needed a drink right now. Bench hadn't had one since last night and was long overdue. He licked his lips.

Fortunately, the television security camera pictures were of exceedingly poor quality. The paper said they didn't get his face, which was about the only lucky thing that happened the whole evening. The television news also said the camera didn't shoot over the top of the back row very well, so it missed getting his face. Hiding the old brown cane certainly paid off. Going out the back door kept them from getting a shot that would have identified him. Another lucky move. Apparently no one could identify him. So far so good. The old man took a deep breath and kept hobbling up the street, cursing and mumbling to himself.

+⇥━⇤+

The Lincoln Police Department had been built close to the court for obvious reasons. When a trial was on, the cops had easy access to the courtroom and could get in and out of the courthouse quickly. Although business always seemed to be brisk around the station, seldom had the Lincoln police been faced with a crime of the scope of Johnny Gonzales's murder. Every cop on the force had been called in to work the case. The gruesomeness of the murder of the liquor store manager left a chill in the air that the police could still feel when the sun was high overhead. Nothing about the man's death seemed to make much sense.

"Look at those pictures!" Sergeant Fred Pile held up the photos of Gonzales's body sprawled on the floor. "He's slashed from ear to ear."

"Yeah." His assistant peeped over Pile's shoulder. "Really nasty."

The sun streaming through the window threw Pile's shadow across the wall. A tall man, the sergeant had shoulders that stretched broadly along the wall, giving him the look of a guard on a professional football team. The detective's neck proved to be equally thick and strong, adding to the man's ominous appearance. Pile's bald head topped an obvious and easily identified appearance. Everyone in town knew he was a cop.

"Just can't make out why anyone would want to kill Johnny," Pile concluded. "The guy wouldn't hurt a flea."

"Everyone knew him," the assistant added. Jack Downs usually functioned more like a yes-man, but the assistant did know the town well. "If Gonzales got his hands into something dirty, we'd have heard about it by now."

Pile put the photo back into the pile of pictures taken at the crime scene. "I think someone came into the liquor store with a grudge against Gonzales or possibly the owner of the store. Probably angry about a past confrontation."

Downs nodded. "Could have been a teenager or a young person," Downs ventured. On the slender side, Jack Downs had just turned thirty but looked ten years younger. He stayed skinny enough that crooks didn't take him seriously in a raid. Downs knew that the sergeant used him as a partner because he was always the first one the bad guys would hit. Every now and then the thought made him shudder. "You know," he added, "a juvenile delinquent."

Pile shot him a dirty look. "This is a murder, Downs, not a Halloween prank. Doesn't fit the sort of thing a kid would do. We're talking big-time killing here."

"Yeah? What about those two characters that shot up Columbine High School in Littleton? I'd say those boys could have pulled off a killing like this one."

"I don't see this throat slashing as similar in any way, shape, or form," Pile fired back.

"Nothing was stolen," the assistant ventured defensively. "No money gone out of the cash register."

Pile bit his lip. "Why would a kid attack someone and not take the money?"

Downs scratched his head. "What if the guy was only stealing booze? Maybe Gonzales caught a kid trying to sneak out a bottle of whiskey."

"Did that guy in the security camera pictures look like a teenager?" Pile crossed his arms over his large chest and glared at the assistant. "Or an older man?"

"Could the kid have been wearing a disguise?" The assistant sounded even more tentative.

"This is starting to sound like a conversation between the Three Stooges," Pile grumbled. "Come on, Downs. Get your head in the game."

The assistant held out his arms in a questioning gesture, then walked off.

Sergeant Fred Pile watched the young man walk away and shook his head in disgust. Once again he picked up the photographs and thumbed through the file, stopping at the head shots.

"I don't care *who* did it," he said to himself. "I'm going to find this guy if it kills me. We ain't going to have these kind of murders in this town as long as I'm running the detective squad around here, so help me God!"

⊹══╼═╾══⊹

Raymond Bench came to the end of Main Street where Mac's Bar made the transition into the lower end of town. The quiet dark interior of the tavern made as good a stopping place as he'd find. He walked in quietly and slipped up on a stool near the bar. Only three other men sat around the room. Two guys in back kept shooting pool. The place looked safe.

"How you doing, Mac?"

The bartender eyed Bench for a moment, then smiled. "Making it okay. How about you, Ray?"

"Little slow today. Need a beer to put a little fire in my engine."

"More like quietness in your mind, ain't it?"

Bench snorted. "Whatever. Make it a draught Coors."

The bartender picked up a glass. "Hear about the big killing last night?" He pulled the lever down and the beer poured out.

Bench froze. "No . . . no."

"Someone whacked the manager over at José's Liquors."

"Oh?" The old man scratched the back of his neck. "Humph."

"You ain't going to do that to me, are you?" Mac laughed and shoved the beer across the counter. "Wouldn't shoot your old buddy, now would you, Ray?"

Bench didn't say anything.

"Yeah, somebody killed the guy but didn't even steal a dime." Mac shook his head. "Strange killin'."

Bench took a big drink, still staring at the bartender. He didn't make any comment but wiped his mouth with his sleeve.

"Come on, Ray," Mac persisted. "Give me your take on what happened."

"Maybe it was an accident." Bench's voice sounded raspy and low.

"Accident?" Mac laughed. "I knew you'd have some bizarre twist on this story. Raymond, you're a funny old coot. Just drink your beer."

Bench looked away in disgust.

10

SAM AND VERA SLOAN SAT CLOSE TO each other as they always did in Sunday morning worship services, with Cara sitting next to her mother. Cara had grown up in that church, and everyone in the congregation knew her. The minister usually delivered a stimulating message, and Cara listened well. Sam normally paid attention to whatever came from the pulpit but was struggling this morning.

Not that the sermon wasn't intriguing, but Sam's mind hadn't settled in on much happening in the sanctuary. He kept fighting distractions and feeling worried. Two cross-currents ran back and forth, confusing his thinking and clouding his mind. No one in the Colorado Springs police force had any idea who Al Henry was. It was not so much that the guy had gone up in smoke as he seemed to have never landed on the ground. Sam couldn't find a trace of the man Ape claimed

Jester had murdered. The name Al Henry didn't ring anybody's bell. More than a little disturbing.

From the other side of his brain a different message rolled
in. Vera wanted to be a *team,* whatever that was. His wife had
called Sam's cards. He didn't want to offend her, but how in the
world could he live with the thought of telling Vera everything
about a case? Moreover, the police had ethical standards, and
talking about a case could get him in a great deal of trouble.
Sharing facts and evidence with Vera would be walking a difficult tightrope. The entire idea made him uncomfortable.

"I want you to consider a text from Jeremiah, the thirty-sec-
ond chapter, the twenty-seventh verse," the pastor said. The
forty-five-year-old minister stood behind a massive wooden pulpit that looked like it had been carved by hand at least a century
earlier. The front of the church had a European drift with decorations cut from dark-colored wood about the same shade as
the preacher's hair. He cleared his throat and looked out at
maybe four hundred people. "Speaking through the prophet,
God declares, 'I am the LORD, the God of all mankind. Is anything too hard for me?'" He walked from behind the wooden
edifice and smiled. "Interesting, isn't it?"

Sam heard the words but his mind didn't click in to listening mode.

*I bet the Lord could say that because He didn't have a wife who wanted
to be His partner. Would that twist have proven even too hard for Him? At
least it would have slowed Him down more than a tad.*

"We serve an amazing God," the pastor proclaimed. "I
want to explore some of the dimensions of the meaning of His
sovereignty this morning." He held his hand up in the air.
"Let's consider what they mean for *you.*" The minister pointed
at the congregation.

Sam kept thinking about the Al Henry problem. The police received missing persons bulletins from all over the country, particularly when they expected lost people to show up in Colorado. He'd had several officers and a secretary check everything that had come through their offices for a couple of years. Several "Henrys" had turned up, but one happened to be a child and the other was a woman. No adolescents named Henry had come through the station house in the entire period.

Could Ape be misleading me? And why would he create such an obvious problem? Might he be covering up some other crime? But the man doesn't hardly sound like that type. He doesn't know Jester's legal name, but he sounded dogmatic about Al Henry. Must have said the name a dozen times. If Ape is lying, he's certainly more clever than he looks and sounds . . . and they seldom are.

"Since God remains all-powerful," the pastor preached, pacing back and forth, "we have a resource of greater capacity than anything else in this world." He stopped and looked at the choir. "When He offers His help to us, the possibilities are extraordinary." The preacher turned back to the congregation. "The promises of Scripture are based on God's character and His overwhelming capacities."

Sam blinked. The preacher certainly hit his button. "I need some help," he mumbled under his breath.

"What?" Vera leaned over. "You said something?"

"No!" Sam whispered. "Nothing."

Vera frowned at him, then turned back to the sermon.

"Thanks." He glanced upward.

"What?" Vera asked again.

Sam shook his head. *Keep my big mouth shut. Everything gets too complicated. Okay. Okay. I get the point. Pay attention to the sermon.*

"We see amazing examples of the power of God demonstrated in Old and New Testament stories." The preacher turned back to the choir. "Most of us don't think of these incidents as occurring today, and that's probably one of the reasons why we don't recognize what God is still doing in our own time." He looked back at the congregation. "It's time to wake up!"

Sam took a deep breath. He couldn't see any semblance of how Vera wanting to be part of a team could be an example of God doing something wonderful and marvelous today. In fact, the whole idea remained distasteful and a bit depressing. She certainly wouldn't let this thought set, then eventually blow away; he'd seen her eyes light up like someone had thrown a 220-volt switch located in the middle of her back. He was going to have to deal with this idea some way, and trying to kill the suggestion wasn't the road to take.

"Therefore, I admonish you to be people of an even greater faith than you've ever had before." The minister raised his voice as he headed for the home stretch. "You are living in a historical moment that requires a greater exercise of faith than any generation has known in the past!" His voice trembled and he pointed toward the sky.

His conclusion couldn't be far away.

Need to pay attention, but I can't get my mind off what Ape told me. I simply can't believe the man lied to me. Don't often miss on these things, and Ape doesn't seem to be intent on running me around the building. Pieces are missing. That's all. Something simply isn't in the right place. That's what I've got to figure out. What's not here?

Vera slipped her hand into his. Sam felt the warmth of her palm and gentle squeeze. She smiled at him, then looked back at the preacher. He loved that little twist at the side of her mouth when Vera smiled. Sam knew she looked happier today because she'd found the path to work her way into his world at the office. No question about it. The team idea wouldn't float out the back window and disappear.

The choir stood, and the congregation started to sing. He'd missed the last of the sermon, but had the gist of it clearly in mind: Trust God more today than before and start now. Expect Him to do great things. He certainly could use a large dose of that medicine. If the minister said he should, then Sam was ready for the big try.

The entire congregation sang joyfully, "The Church's one foundation is Jesus Christ her Lord." Sam knew the words so well he didn't have to look at the hymnal. Vera's and Cara's voices joined into one harmonious blend but Sam's drifted to the inaudible side of the congregation.

"She is His new creation by water and the word," the hymn continued on, but Sam's mind was gone. His thoughts were out there in Acacia Park, where Ape probably sat on a bench right now, puffing on a cigarette. Sam was sitting on the same bench, asking the big man hard questions, not singing in church.

Maybe Ape didn't know the right name. What if the guy got something wrong? After all, the conversation was casual. Shooting the bull while cruising down the highway. Possibly he simply didn't put something together right. Happens to people all the time, and this guy is far from bright.

One thing was for sure. Sam needed to talk to the hulk as quickly as possible. The entire police department might be running down the wrong trail. Church would be over momentarily, and they'd be going out the front door. Sam knew what he needed to do as quickly as possible.

The congregation started filing out of the worship service toward the front. The minister stood there shaking hands with the members. Sam knew that a firm handshake and a word of appreciation were always necessary to complete morning worship. The reverend's perfunctory response wouldn't be insincere, but more a part of the ritual. The "howdy's" and "how are you's?" simply came and went with the day. At the least, Cara liked shaking his hand and exchanging a few kind words.

Out on the street, Sam waited for his wife to finish a couple of conversations. He kept thinking about the team idea and finally decided that he didn't have much of an alternative but to be honest with Vera.

"Ready to go home?" Vera waved good-bye to a friend. "Or would you rather eat out today?" Her eyes sparkled.

Ah, the perfect edge! Sam smiled. "How about trying the Glass Jar? You like that restaurant."

"Good move!" Vera reached out for Cara's hand. "You like that suggestion, dear?"

"Sure." Cara rolled her eyes. "I like to eat out on Sunday."

"Vera"—Sam sounded tentative—"I think that would also solve another problem."

"Problem?"

"Yeah." Sam switched into his serious, all-business look. "I'm going to need to run an errand after lunch and eating out will—"

"Make life easier for you." Vera cut him off. "What is it this time?"

"Shouldn't take long."

"Long?" Vera's face fell. "Don't tell me. You're off on another of those blasted police investigation trips that suddenly spring up like weeds in the grass." Her voice sounded hard. "And the little excursion takes *all* day."

Lunch on Sunday wouldn't quite cover it.

"I shouldn't be gone long. Just got to clear up a problem."

"Oh, *a problem?*" Vera raised an eyebrow. "Well, don't you forget that I'm a part of the team now."

"The team?" Sam took a deep breath. "Of course. I'll tell you all about everything that happens."

"You bet you will." Vera sounded determined.

11

AT ONE O'CLOCK SUNDAY AFTERNOON, Raymond Bench woke up in his dingy rented house on the edge of downtown Lincoln. Walls of the dull brown building hadn't been painted or repapered for years. Several worn places on the carpet exposed the wooden floor underneath. The residence felt cold, like someone hadn't set the thermostat at a decent temperature. Bench's head felt awful. The hangover made him feel like an 18-wheeler had run over him . . . and Bench was still thirsty.

Fear and apprehension had fairly well devoured his emotional stability. He constantly worried that the police would come flying in out of nowhere and raid him. The anxiety created one big, mean thirst. Saturday night felt like the right time to satisfy it. Bench had gotten drunker last night than he usually did, and the nasty aftereffects were hanging around his neck. He lived off of his Social Security check, which never stretched far enough to cover his binges.

Bench struggled to get out of the worn wing chair but couldn't seem to make anything work. He slowly began to realize that he didn't have his artificial leg strapped on and had been trying to stand up on a leg that was gone. He finally reached for his crutches, but fell on the floor. Getting up wouldn't be easy.

Ten minutes later, Raymond's thinking started to clear slightly, and he managed to plop down on the couch on the other side of the room. Newspapers lay scattered all over the couch and on the floor. Obviously someone had read the paper much earlier in the morning. Looked at it. Dropped it all over the floor. Left. About par for the course for the visitors that came and went through the house.

Bench didn't mind these people staying here. Actually they provided a little noise that made the house sound more livable. The problem was they didn't take care of anything. Everything just landed on the already cluttered floor, only adding to the messy look.

With considerable reluctance, Raymond picked up the front page of the morning paper and glanced at the headlines. Sure enough, the murder made the top story again. He started scrutinizing the text.

Sounded like the police were running down everything that walked. They'd already called in about a half-dozen suspects and given them intense interrogation. The story made their scrutiny appear to be rough, tough going. Bench shivered and put the paper down.

For several minutes he thought about the times that the cops had picked him up for drinking. Getting DWIs had become almost a hobby until the penalty got so stiff. Another arrest behind the wheel, and he'd be off to the state pen. Not a trip he had any intention of taking in the near future.

Raymond shook his head and picked up the funny papers, looking at them until he let himself go back to the front page story again and start over reading the story about the murder of Johnny Gonzales. The article said Gonzales had a wife and three children. Made it sound like they didn't have much money. Bench cursed. He didn't have much either.

What was he supposed to do? Get sad and call the cops? Make a big confession about cutting the man's throat? Bench cussed like he'd just hit his finger with a hammer. After all, the killing had been nothing more than an accident. He'd never killed nobody in his entire life.

Well, some old geezer had gotten out in front of his car once and he'd run over the wandering fool. 'Course, that was an accident! Had to leave his car in the garage for two months, letting that little problem cool off. Nobody saw the jerk wander out in front of his car, or at least that was the best he remembered about the accident 'cause he'd been out of his mind drunk when it happened. Just one of them unfortunate things that happened along the way.

Bench finished reading the article and threw the paper across the room against the wall. His head ached bad enough without having to read such garbage. If Gonzales hadn't decided to become Mr. Kung Fu, he'd still be alive today. It was his own fault that he'd jumped on Raymond, forcing the old man to defend himself!

Bench pushed and pulled until he got back on his crutches and hobbled out to the kitchen. Breakfast dishes still covered the kitchen table. Raymond pushed the dirty cups and glasses in the sink aside, looking for a clean glass. None seemed to be anywhere. Raymond remembered that he needed his eye-glasses for distance.

"Fools! Idiots!" Ray suddenly shouted to himself. "I told 'em they could stay around here a while if they'd clean up after themselves. Can't even wash their own dishes!" He slung a dirty plastic glass against the wall.

Raymond rinsed out a cup and took a drink of water before swinging around and going back in the living room. With his same reluctance, Bench picked up the inside of the paper and read a second article on the liquor store killing, which reported that the person in charge of the investigation was Sergeant Fred Pile.

Bench pulled the paper closer to his face. "Oh, no! Not Pile!" He cursed again.

Fred Pile and Raymond Bench had a long history. Pile had only been a cop on the street the first time he picked up Bench for drunkenness. As the years went by, Pile ended up being the cop that picked up Bench several times. At first, their con-frontations remained simply business as usual, until one night when Bench was in a foul mood. Without any warning, Raymond grabbed a pipe and cracked Pile over the head, knocking the cop to the sidewalk in a daze. The second officer leaped on Bench, and the fight turned into a big-time nasty knock-down-drag-out. From that moment on, Sergeant Fred Pile never forgot Raymond Bench. The policeman even devel-oped the habit of hauling Bench in when they put out a drag-net for everything from robbery to rape.

Bench rubbed his mouth nervously. "I hate Pile. Ain't seen him for a while, but I know he sure remembers who I am." He pushed the paper aside and stared around the small living room.

"If Pile gets a whiff of a one-legged man entering that liquor store, I'm dead meat. He'll be over here faster than a greased pig running through a bar filled with fat old ladies."

Thinking about Pile bothered him. A lot.

Bench finally got up and wandered back into the kitchen. Moving around helped. Let the nervousness subside. He finally sat down at the kitchen table and looked at the dirty dishes. No question about it. He needed something to steady his nerves. The Pile situation had raised the ante. If there was anybody out there on the street to worry about, the sergeant was it! Now he'd have to stay in the house even longer. Big-time bad luck.

Raymond had problems that he needed to attend to, and that made keeping out of sight all the more difficult. First of all, his wife and grandson would be back before too long, and the boy required care. Shouldn't have taken him on in the first place. Then all these crazy people showed up, and that added another log on top of the pile. Nothing, absolutely nothing, was easy.

What he needed, Bench decided, was a drink. A good stiff shot of whiskey would turn everything back down to normal. He licked his lips. A bottle had to be around the place somewhere.

The question was where?

After ten minutes of rooting through his usual hidden stashes, Raymond was about to conclude that he'd made the fatal mistake of drinking the entire house dry. Not one of the normal hiding places had even the shadow of a bottle. He slammed the door under the sink and started back into the living room. At that moment, he remembered.

Bench swung around on his crutches and headed for the back door. Out on the screened-in porch, a sleeping bag sat unrolled against the back of the kitchen wall. November coldness had settled in on the back of the house, and Raymond knew the temperature must be in the forties.

He kept hobbling across the floor and out the back door, pushing his memory. He had a habit of hiding whiskey, then forgetting where he'd stashed the booze. Drinking had affected his memory. Sure enough. The old bucket that flowers once grew in sat right there where he'd placed the urn the last time that he put a bottle down in the bottom. Bench jerked a dead geranium out and plunged his hands into the soil. The bottle was still there!

With the pint of Jack Daniels in his pocket, Raymond shuffled back into the kitchen. He set the bottle on the table and grabbed the glass he'd used for water. Bench downed the drink in a burning gulp. For a moment he grimaced, then sighed. Actually felt good after the whiskey settled a bit. Bench poured a second glass.

The hot fire of the whiskey roared in his empty stomach and Raymond knew that he needed to eat something, but maybe a snack could wait just a while. He sipped the Jack Daniels and thought some more about what he ought to do. No question. Staying out of sight would be important.

In a few minutes, Bench poured a third glass and kept sipping, slowly but persistently. The edge faded from his frightening thoughts, and he felt much better. Needed to remember to put another bottle out there in that flower bucket.

Ten minutes later, Bench had downed three glasses of whiskey and was just getting started.

12

ACACIA PARK SPRAWLED ACROSS THE middle of Colorado Springs, down a couple of blocks from the Nevada Street police station. On the south corner, a bronze statue of General Palmer, the Englishman who helped settle and form the town, marked the beginning of the large green park that adults and children loved to walk through during the summer. Big pines and tall oaks lined the edges where small bushes formed green lines. By late November, little patches of snow dotted the landscape, and the tourists were long gone. A few hangers-on floated here and there, but it was easier to find anyone walking around the area. The Sunday afternoon sun left a gentle warmth that made Acacia Park feel unusually inviting for a stroll.

Sam Sloan got out of his car and started making a slow survey of the park, looking for George Barnes. The big hunk of a man might be holed up in his van somewhere taking a nap. Wouldn't be hard to spot that rattletrap if the vehicle was near the park. Sam started strolling out across the grass, looking in all directions.

After walking about ten feet, Sloan saw a large man stretched over a park bench, taking a nap on the outer fringe of the park. His belly stuck up like one of the mountains behind the city. Had to be George Barnes. Nobody else in town laid out like Santa Claus on vacation.

Sam hurried across the park toward Barnes, who was sleeping like a hibernating bear. Ape had covered his face with half of a newspaper and sprawled out with his feet up on the other end of the bench. Fortunately, the man had changed clothes, putting on a new pair of buckled overalls and a clean green T-shirt. Sam stood back and took a second look. With the beard and the hair hanging down off the sides of the bench, the big man looked like an ancient gold miner who had wandered down from the top of Pikes Peak and was resting up from the long trek.

Sam picked up the newspaper, letting the sunlight hit Ape's eyes. "Wake up!" he said loudly. "Day's hardly started."

Barnes bolted up like someone had hit him with a club. He swung a big meaty fist in the air, aiming at whatever might be out there. "What the . . ." He blinked a couple of times and looked at Sloan in a disconnected gape before a look of recognition settled in his eyes.

"Hey, it's the middle of the afternoon," Sam said.

"Ain't that the time when people take their naps?" Ape sat up and rubbed his eyes. "Normal people, I mean."

"Got a point there." Sam sat down. "Been sleeping long?"

Ape glanced at the plastic-strapped Casio watch on his arm. "Longer than I thought."

"How about a little talk?" Sam turned to one side of the bench to see Barnes's every movement. "Thought maybe I'd put a little joy in your Sunday afternoon." From the side he could study Ape's face.

"Got enough already." Ape groaned. "Enjoyin' a good dream."

Sam raised his eyebrows but said nothing.

"You found out where Al Henry come from?" Ape glanced at Sam with a naive sound in his voice.

Sloan studied the man carefully. Barnes didn't seem to be smart enough to feign such a question. If he was acting, Ape was the best act Sam had seen in his entire life.

"No," Sam said. "I haven't found any leads."

Ape frowned. "Should have been able to turn up a-somethin' by now."

"That's exactly what I figured, and that bothers me."

Ape turned and puckered his lips. "Surely the boy had some relatives. Ya know, Al was only seventeen years old or so."

"As you said." Sam pulled at his chin. "Said you never saw the boy?"

Barnes nodded vigorously. "That's right."

"Never even talked to him on the phone?"

"He's dead before I come along."

"Yeah." Sam pulled at the tip of his nose. "Maybe Jester was misleading you in that little conversation as the two of you cruised down the road."

Ape scratched his head. "Now why'd do somethin' like that?"

Sam's eyes narrowed. "Possibly he was only telling you a story. Spinning a yarn. Pulling your leg?"

Ape didn't answer. He looked around the park at a couple of boys who had started tossing a football back and forth. After several moments, he turned and looked up at the mountains behind them. "Why'd you think I come in to talk with ya?" he asked.

Sam hadn't expected such a twist in the conversation. Ape's eyes looked serious. The fearful look that he came in with on Friday night had been replaced by a sudden acquisition of boldness.

"I'm not sure," Sam said.

"Didn't want nothin' on my conscience. I told you that Jester started unfoldin' this story like a fisherman telling about a big catch. Might be exaggeratin' here and there, but no, sir! I don't for a minute believe he was a-makin' this one up."

Sam leaned back on the metal bench and let what he was hearing soak in. At the least, Ape believed he was telling the truth. The man might have a little this or that wrong, but Barnes truly believed that someone named Al Henry had been killed by Jester and his gang.

"I ain't the brightest guy in the world, Mr. Sloan, but I knows when someone is stringing me along, and that bulldog told me a story that was like betting on the sun coming up tomorrow morning. Whatever weren't right, Jester killed a kid."

Sam knew he'd run his first approach to the ground. He needed to turn the conversation in a different direction, had to try another angle, look behind a different bush. "Pieces are missing in your story, Ape. I don't understand why Al Henry hung around here after they beat him up the first time. I'd think he'd leave town. Move out. Get out of Dodge."

Ape nodded. "I sure would have. Remember, I know only what the Jester man told me, but I got the impression that Al Henry did disappear for a while. At the least, Al holed up until he got healed from that royal beatin' and all. I imagine ole Al stayed out of sight for a couple of weeks or so."

"Hmm." Sam rubbed his chin again.

"Mind if I have a smoke?" Ape reached inside his bib pocket. "Smokin' makes me a mite bit calmer."

"I'm bothering you?" Sam pushed.

Ape lit up a cigarette. "Nothing personal. Cops always make me nervous."

"That jail time you did out in California had a few lingering bad aftereffects?"

Ape nodded but didn't say anything. Sam watched but didn't respond. For a full minute and a half, no one talked.

"Tell me some more about what Jester said in getting you to take him to Lincoln, Nebraska." Sloan crossed his arms over his chest.

"'Course at the beginnin', I didn't know about this killin', which was the big reason they wanted out of town," Ape said slowly. "Nobody's goin' a-tell me about that murder number at first. You understand that turn of the screw?"

"Sure."

"When Jester asked me to haul them outta town, he said there was legal troubles of some kind. Best I can remember is that he had an older boy. The court took this boy away from Jester when he got in trouble on a burglary charge. Seems as if Jester'd done a number of these house breakin'-ins, but somebody nailed him to the floor one night. Think he got into a place where a man kept a gun under the bed."

"The court took his child away?" Sloan asked slowly. "The Lincoln court?"

"I guess. Best that I can tell was that Jester's father ended up with the boy that he's a-lookin' after until some other time when Jester would try and get the boy back. That's why we was a-goin' up there—to see about this legal business."

"And now Jester had a woman with him? A common-law wife?"

"Yes, sir, and them other three characters, plus the little bitty guy that belonged to Jester and this here woman named Alice. I swear that's the only name I ever heard. Just plain Alice."

"Something's not in here, Ape. A piece of the puzzle hasn't turned up. You're not telling me something important."

Barnes rubbed his eyes. "My mind gets a little fuzzy now and then, ya know. Sorta slips off the track. You got to help me get back on the road."

Sam searched for what the big man hadn't told him yet. "Let's go back over why Jester and his buddies picked up Al Henry a second time. How come they found Al Henry again and went to work on him?"

"Wel-l-l," Barnes drawled. "Started with a problem from this Ginny woman. Big Gal. Never quite got the whole name but do remember they called her Ginny once. She had someone steal from her. Broke the code of the gang, ya know."

Sloan nodded.

"Ginny's first thought was that the stuff had been stolen by a local street boy named John-boy Walton. Part-time male prostitute. Hear of 'im?"

Sam nodded. "Sure. I know who he is. Hangs around on the streets. Sells hot dogs not far from here."

"That's 'im. Well, Ginny was sure that John-boy had gotten into the house and stolen some jewelry, clothes, a coat, and some kind of crazy patches." Barnes leaned and wiggled his finger like giving a lecture. "Ginny's one mean woman, you understand. Seems to like pain."

"Uh-huh."

"Ginny and Jester and some other jerk in the gang ran John-boy down on the street. They dragged him into their car and took Walton back to their place. Hauled ole John-boy into the broken-down house and tied him to a chair. The three of 'em started beatin' John-boy. Whacked on him until he said Al Henry's name. Spit it out like gettin' rid of teeth and blood."

"Walton fingered Henry?"

"That's how it started," Ape insisted. "Yes, sir, that's when Jester's crowd started lookin' for the boy again."

"Must have taken them a while?"

"I guess at least a week went by, but one of 'em spotted Al goin' down the street one day. Just like they done to John-boy, the gang pulled up alongside and whisked Henry away like stealin' a dog out of somebody's front yard."

"This is the last time that Jester's people captured Henry?"

"Yes, sir," Ape said politely. "To the best of my knowledge, at least. You understand that I ain't doin' nothing more than repeatin' what I heard?"

"They beat Henry?"

"'Spect so." Ape hung his head. "Guess they beat some kind of confession out of him, then took the boy up into the mountains somewhere around here. Left his body tied to a tree."

Sam stared at Barnes.

"Yes, sir, them mountains is big ones. Poor ole Al could be out there anywhere. Just got no idea."

Ape hadn't previously told Sam the last part of the story. Obviously the big man hadn't realized that he'd left out the final component. Sam felt he had no choice but to trust Ape. Somewhere out there in those high mountains around Colorado Springs, a dead man lay tied to a tree. The problem was that neither Ape nor Sam had the slightest idea where the body might be hidden. Years from now someone could stumble onto a pile of bones and never know what they'd found.

13

THE COLD WESTERN WIND SWEPT ACROSS Acacia Park, and Sam realized that neither he nor Ape had said anything for more than ten minutes. He glanced at his watch. Three o'clock meant that he didn't have that much time left before he'd have to get back home to Vera and Cara. Ape sat there staring straight ahead as he must have done in the past for hours alone in that park. Sam sensed that the man wasn't going to say anything more until asked the right questions.

A magpie flew down on the grass in front of them and hopped across the lawn. Ape didn't say anything, but his focus shifted to the bird. The agile white-and-black creature walked along the grass, pecking at pieces of debris.

"Did you ever see anything that once belonged to Al Henry? An object? A piece of clothing?"

Ape shrugged. "Ah, the gang had some stuff they been a-carryin' around with them. Junk and all."

Sam's eyes widened. "Really?"

"Yeah, they seemed to pass the trinkets around like souvenirs picked up on a vacation."

"Give me some examples."

Ape scratched his head. "Well, Al had a backpack that Jester stole from him. Just an old knapsack. Henry used that to keep his things in."

Sam gestured. "Keep talking. What do you mean by *things?*"

"Best that I can tell, they'd taken some of Al's clothes. Like a T-shirt, some patches or another, a jean jacket. I believe I saw a broken knife in that mess of junk."

"Broken knife?"

"Now it comes back to mind. Jester and Jack seems to have stabbed the boy to death. Guess they broke that knife's blade off in the fight. At least that's what Jester claimed."

Sam leaned forward. "And you saw all of this material?"

Ape jutted his lip out and nodded. "Yes, sir."

"And you saw the backpack?"

"Uh-huh."

Sam pulled at his chin. "What'd they do with the backpack?"

"Strange thing." Ape settled back on the bench and put his hands behind his head. "Ya see, when we was just outside of Lincoln, one of them women started gettin' nervous and all. Seemed to be afraid the police would catch us or somethin'. We stopped at a little restaurant, and she got to creatin' a stink that we needed to get rid of the backpack. Jester didn't agree, but finally decided that she might have a point."

"You haven't told me any of this before," Sam said. "How come it didn't come out earlier?"

Ape rolled his eyes. "Guess it just didn't come to mind none."

"Don't stop now," Sam insisted. "What'd Jester do about that backpack?"

"Well sir, got to be a big discussion. A real debate amongst 'em. Nobody paid me no attention. They just jawboned the subject until Jester said we'd throw it away at the first good place we saw. With that, everybody got back in the van and we started off again."

"Toward Lincoln?"

"Yeah, we was not far from the city. I was buzzin' down the road a little ways, and there was one of them rest parks. Jester had me pull over, and out there behind a park bench was one of them old-fashioned outhouses that they keep out there in them places. Ole Jester just runs over there and dumps that backpack in one of them outhouses. *Boom!* It's gone."

"The backpack was there in that rest stop? How far is that from Lincoln?"

Ape scratched his head again. "The place is out there on Interstate 80 west of town I'd guess maybe a mile or so. Ain't nothing else there like it."

Sam put his arm on Ape's shoulder. "You're telling me that material should still be out there?"

"Seems so to me."

Sam could feel his pulse starting to pick up. This data was the first solid evidence Ape had given him. He had a lead to take back to work in the morning.

"Hey," Barnes said abruptly. "I bet I can find that house where I picked 'em all up. Ya know, the old house where Jester and company beat poor ole Al up the second time." Ape pursed his lips. "Yes, sir. Come to think of it. I bet I could even run down Henry's house where the beating happened the first time."

"All right!" Sam slapped him on the back. "Now you're talking, Ape. Just took you a while to get here."

The big man rubbed the back of his neck. "See, them psychedelics kinda messed my mind up. I flip out every now and then. Can't get my head workin' right. Things get all goofed. Know what I mean?"

Sam nodded. He'd heard it before.

"I don't remember things sometimes." Ape looked Sam in the eye. "But I don't lie none, understand?"

"Sure." Sam smiled. "Let's find that apartment where Jester and the gang lived."

Barnes stood up. "I'll tell you what. You follow me in my van. I'll have to do some lookin' and seein'. When I gets there, I stop. How's that sound?"

"I'm with you." Sam started walking backward. "Give me time to get behind you."

Ape lumbered off to one side of the park, and Sam trotted over to his car and quickly circled Acacia Park. Within minutes the two cars drove down Nevada Avenue in the opposite direction of the police department. After four blocks, Ape turned down an alley and went up a block. In the middle of the back alley, he pulled in behind an old white garage. Ape jumped out of the van and signaled Sam to follow. Sloan pulled in and turned his car off.

The area looked like a dilapidated second-rate section of Colorado Springs. On the other side of the garage, a parking lot of Jake's Car Repair Shop had the outside space filled with broken-down and banged-up vehicles. The two men walked down a weed-covered cement walkway around to the street door of an old rental house in front of the garage. On the other side of the building, a tattoo shop looked closed.

"Yes sir, boss." Ape pointed at the front porch. "Up there is where Jester and his people started beatin' on Al Henry."

Sam started walking carefully up the front steps, looking at the wood on each of the steps. He stopped and got down on his knees, running his hands gently across the wood. In a few moments, he started up the side of the wall with his nose only inches from the worn white painting.

"What ya a-seein'?" Ape kept looking over his shoulder.

Sam said nothing but kept examining the wall and a narrow handrail along the wall.

"Found somethin'?" Ape stayed with him.

Finally Sam stood up. "Yeah." His voice stayed flat. "Blood-stains."

"I knew it!" Ape clapped. "I knew this was the place!"

"See them?" Sam pointed at spots on the floor. "That's dried blood. I'll have the laboratory people out here in no time. At the very least, we have evidence that a man was beaten on this porch."

Ape smiled broadly, exposing an empty space on the side of his face. "For some reason I didn't remember about this place earlier, but now it's clear. I parked out there in that street." He pointed toward the curb. "Yes sir, that's where I picked up the whole patch of them when we left town."

Sam pulled a cell phone out of his pocket and quickly punched in the number of the police station. "How soon can you get a crew out here to check out a house for me?"

Ape quit listening and started looking in the empty windows. "Still some stuff in there."

Sam kept giving instructions and keeping an eye on Ape. He finally hung up the phone.

"I think we might find other junk inside there." Ape pointed into the house.

"Oh, we will. Don't worry. Our boys will come prepared to enter the place."

Ape jammed his hands down in his pockets. "Sorta touches me," he said, his voice taking on a sentimental sound. "All this killin' talk bothers me." Tears formed at the corners of his eyes. "I done some bad things along the way but never hurt anybody. Ain't in me to be a pain to nobody. Just get myself in trouble."

"I understand," Sam said.

"When this Jester guy started laying this killin' talk on me, he thought he was making himself sound like a big man. Not so with me. Only made me upset. Don't even like to think 'bout them murdering that poor boy."

Sam studied the wrinkles under Ape's eyes. The man was simple, but down there under a bundle of bad experiences lay a good heart. Any questions about Barnes lying were gone.

14

WHEN RAYMOND BENCH WOKE UP, HE
was still sitting at the kitchen table. Dirty dishes and half-empty
plates looked back at him. He had to check his watch several
times before he grasped the fact that it was 7:00 in the evening.
He felt sick, and his head hurt worse than it had when he first
awakened in the afternoon. The smell of the dirty kitchen
worked its way into his nose like a crowbar prying a stuck door
open. For several minutes he sat at the table, afraid that he
might vomit. Raymond had to turn and get a breath of fresh
air. Slowly the pangs of nausea subsided enough that he finally
got up, pushed his crutches under his arms, and wandered back
into the living room.

"Got to stop doing this," Bench muttered to himself. His
tongue felt thick and his mouth dry. "Drinkin's goin' to kill me
one of these days." His crutches quivered when he dropped

down in a worn living room recliner. "Shouldn't have gotten started again." He looked around the cluttered room and shook his head. "No more. No more!" Raymond caught his breath. "Least not tonight."

With his head thrown back against the soft chair, Bench closed his eyes and tried to get a good deep breath. The entire room seemed to start moving slowly. Shutting his eyes stabilized the motion of the living room and got things back on an even keel. He remembered stuffing the bloody pants and shoes in the back of his closet. Eventually he felt himself drifting off to sleep again.

When the back door slammed, the crashing noise echoed through the room. Bench sat upright in the padded chair. "Who's out there?" he screamed like an angry bull charging at his tormentor. "Who are you?" He started trying to find the crutch to use as a weapon.

"It's me," the voice said. "Cool it, I just got back."

Raymond shook his head. Maybe he was dreaming. "Who?"

The man cursed. "Your son! Who else you expecting?"

Bench blinked his eyes. "My son?"

A short man in his late twenties walked into the room. "I came back to get a coat." The man's cowboy boots looked dirty, old, and battered. His ruffled hair appeared as though he'd just gotten up or been riding a motorcycle. "It's getting cold out. Got a problem with that?"

"Cold?"

The young man's face turned angry. His hard dark eyes abruptly appeared mean and unrelenting. "What else? It's fall. Fool."

Bench stared at him, trying to grasp the gist of the conversation.

"Fall!" the man hollered back. "Get it?"

"Don't yell at me. I can hear you."

The man started to walk across the room but stopped. "You've been drinking again, ain't ya?"

Bench didn't like the accusation and cursed.

"Don't you be cussing at me, you old coot. I can smell whiskey on you like you was a usin' it for aftershave lotion. Takin' a bath in it."

Bench jutted his chin out and looked away.

"I swear to God that you've been drunk all day. Right?" He started walking around the chair. "Probably started just after we left this morning. Been nipping all day." He swore. "Where you hiding this worthless rotgut stuff?"

Bench looked in the opposite direction; he didn't feel like a brawl. More than anything else, he wanted the noise of the young man's loud yelling to stop from behind the chair. The shouting only made his headache worse.

"Never saw nobody that could put away the booze like you do." He circled the chair without stopping and spit on the floor.

Raymond looked hard at the boy. He could fly off the handle and go into a rage at the drop of a hat. He'd seen Junior nearly beat the face off another kid. Back then Raymond thought it was funny. Not now. No point pushing him. "Sit down," he finally said.

"Who are you to tell me what to do?" The young man straddled the front of Raymond's chair. "You never done nothing for me, anyway." He held his fist in the air. "Don't you ever tell me anything I gotta do."

"You and your worthless buddies stayed here last night."

"Whee! Big deal. You let your son come home for an evening and spread out in an empty bedroom." He started clapping. "Never seen such overflowing generosity in my whole life. My, my, but the ole town drunk's done gone and got a touch of goodness."

"I let those worthless cronies of yours come in with you."

"Oh, add more marks to the scoreboard. Dear old Dad's done let my wife in, too."

"You were always an ungrateful rat," Raymond hissed.

"Ungrateful? Suppose I should bend over and kiss that one worthless foot of yours."

"Now, son," Raymond's voice started rising, "you got no respect for nothing living." Bench could feel that his anger was about to pop. No telling what would come next. "No sirree, you don't even have decent respect for your old man."

"Don't call me *son*," the young man hissed. "Use the name that everybody calls me or keep your mouth shut."

"Oh, don't they call you Raymond Junior like your birth certificate says? That's what you're telling me? Call ya that stupid name them little thugs that runs with ya uses?"

With a sudden thrust, the young man reached out and grabbed Raymond by the shirt, holding him up in the chair with his one good leg on the floor. "*The name is Jester.* That's what they all call me. Don't got any other name anymore and don't want one." He shook Raymond. "You understand me? Sure don't want to ever hear that worthless name of Junior again!" He cursed and dropped Raymond back in the chair. "Next time you do it, I'll knock your head off."

Raymond's heart started to pound, and he kept thinking about punching Junior in the face. A hard right hand straight to the nose. After all, he'd killed a man just days ago! Of course, his worthless son might just smash Raymond's own face in.

"You think 'cause that worthless court took custody of my little boy away 'cause of that little heist that you got some kind of special edge?" Jester poked his finger within inches of Bench's nose. "I come back to get the child of mine. That's why my friends come with me. Get it, brick head?"

"I'll tell you what I got," Raymond's voice raised. "All I got to do is walk into that courtroom and tell 'em you're still a worthless little toot whistling around the country with some no-good woman that you call——"

Jester grabbed his father by the shirt again, but this time he yanked him up on his one good leg and suddenly hit him three or four times across the face with his palm and the back of his hand. "How you like that?" The young man hit Raymond in the stomach, sending him crashing back into the chair.

Bench leaned back, gasping for air. The torment in his stomach shot through his entire body. His head spun and for several moments, Raymond was sure he would pass out.

"You think I wouldn't break your neck?" Jester growled in his ear. "Old man, I've killed men that could wad you up and stick your body in a garbage can. Hear what I'm saying?"

Bench groaned. He could feel that the skin on the inside of his mouth was broken. Probably bleeding.

"Don't you ever in any way, shape, or form threaten me about trying to stop me from getting the boy back." Jester put his hand around his father's throat. "'Cause if you do, I'll snap that skinny neck of yours as easy as poppin' a twig."

Raymond felt the strength of the fingers squeezing his windpipe. Wouldn't take much to strangle him. Junior had always been half crazy, and that bad half certainly was in the driver's seat right now. His anger turned into cold fear.

Jester leaned closer. "You call my woman *Alice*, hear me?" He kept shaking his finger at Raymond. "Alice. That's enough. Good enough. You sober enough to understand me?"

Bench looked up into teeth grinding in front of his face. The boy had always looked like his mother, Bench's first wife. Same pointed nose and dimpled chin. Those thick dark eyebrows that dominated his face hadn't been bad lookin' as a child, but age didn't do much for him. Got in too much trouble. Somewhere along the way he picked up that vicious streak. Put him in a fight and no telling what he'd do.

"I said, do you understand me?"

Bench nodded.

"Now we got our own little one, and you'd best treat that boy well too. Got me?"

Bench nodded one more time.

"Now, where is my boy?"

Bench took a deep breath and tried to get himself composed. "My wife's gone for a trip. Went to her mother's. Took your boy. Don't know when they'll be back."

"'Cause of your drinking?" Jester sneered.

"None of your business."

Jester reached out but stopped with his hand in front of his father's face. "Want to try that answer again?"

"I said she'll be back in a week or so."

Jester stood up straight and put his hands on his hips. "Better be. I want to go down to that courthouse and get this thing settled. I want my boy back. You got me?"

Bench nodded again.

"And I'm warning you, old man. Keep the police out of this. Ain't nothing going to get your head torn off like calling the cops."

Raymond looked away. "Don't worry none about that. Ain't got no interest in touching the police. No, sir, that's one thing you can count on. No cops is coming around here by my invitation."

15

VERA SLOWLY HUNG UP THE TELEPHONE. At least Sam had called to say that he was meeting a lab crew at some house where he'd found bloodstains. Not much, but a little progress there. At least he'd phoned.

She looked around his small office where they kept one of the telephones. Tonight that office looked smaller than it ever had before. The whole house seemed to shrink in size when Sam wasn't there, and Vera hated the feeling.

She decided to make a quick check to be sure that Cara was still back in her room and everything was okay. Vera walked down the hall and pushed the door open.

"Everything fine?" Vera stuck her head through the door.

"Sure, Mom." Cara laid her book down. "I guess Daddy got into some business again, huh."

Vera caught the disappointment in her voice. "He called me

just a bit ago," Vera said, trying to sound casual. "He'll be home in a little bit." She glanced around the room that had been carefully decorated and trimmed. It looked like a little girl's room, but Cara wouldn't be small much longer. She was growing quickly. Things would change in the not-too-far future. "Okay?"

"Oh, good!" Cara smiled and went back to her book. "I hope he gets home in time for us to talk before I go to sleep."

"I'm sure he will, dear." Vera backed out and started to pull the door closed behind her. "At least, I know that he wants to be here."

Vera turned away and walked back to the kitchen. She poured herself the umpteenth cup of coffee of the day and sat down right there, looking out into the dark evening. She could see the stars twinkling in the sky. That afternoon the hours had seemed to drag by.

Vera loved Colorado Springs. The town had always been a dream come true. No more of that flat land in Iowa. Every morning the beauty of the mountains floated down over her house, and the blue sky made all the other colors appear more bright and beautiful. The towering majesty of the high peaks never ceased to thrill her. Moreover, the Springs had always been a great place to live. Not far down the street was the old Colorado City part of the town that had been the capital of the entire state decades ago. Of course, that was before the town of Colorado Springs swallowed up everything around it. The quaintness and old western look of the entire city pleased her. And Vera liked the cold winters that reminded her of the days when she was a little girl. No question about it. Fall was a good time of year.

The only problem was Sam's all-absorbing job!

Maybe this time Sam would let her inside, and something new could start between them. One thing was for sure: Vera wasn't about to spend her life with a husband who only came home when it pleased him, in the middle of the night. She wanted a real marriage, and that meant a man in her life who cared more for her and their children than he did for his work controlling the city's criminal population! No matter what it took, Vera wasn't going to put up with the nonsense she and Cara had experienced in the last several years.

Vera took a long sip of coffee. At the very, very least, Sam let her know that he'd found new important clues and he'd ask her to help him think about where someone might stash a body up in the mountains. Okay. Maybe he was only placating her, but at least he'd taken a couple of bigger steps than she'd ever seen him take before.

Vera got up and pushed the small kitchen window open. A cold chilling breeze rippled across the room. The sudden frosty jolt felt good and made her feel more awake. Vera shook off the lethargy that had settled around her. The briskness reminded her of the nights in Iowa when the pond froze over and she'd wake up to find the lawn covered with snow.

"Where would some nut hide a body up in the mountains?" she asked herself out loud. "Only in probably a million and one places! Oh Lord, help us see what only You can see."

The vast national forest reserves covered countless acres. A human body could be anywhere from stuffed in a culvert to buried under a pile of dirt. It'd take an army of men with nothing to do for months to run down all the possible trails around the Colorado Springs area. Obviously an impossibility.

Vera shivered and got up and closed the window. She glanced at her watch again. *Come on, Sam. Don't make this investigation take all night.* She looked into the half-empty coffee cup. *Certainly don't need any more of that stuff.* Vera looked around her kitchen with all the little doodads they'd picked up over the years. Kitchen magnets on the refrigerator door from places like the Grand Canyon and the Black Hills of South Dakota. A small notepad she'd once purchased in a store in Wyoming. Everything was exactly in the right place . . . the *too-right* place. Vera must have worked on that kitchen six times that afternoon. She arranged and rearranged. Of course, everything was perfect!

She abruptly got up and went back into the living room. With a tap on the television monitor switch, she turned the set on, but at the same time pressed the mute button. Didn't seem like the right thing to do to listen to the noise right now. After all, today was Sunday. Sunday should be special. A family time. A quiet time for rest, for worship. That's one of those quaint things that her father had always said a million times, which she agreed with.

Vera reached across the coffee table and picked up her Bible. She flipped through the pages to Psalm 101 and read out loud, "'I will sing of your love and justice; to you, O LORD, I will sing praise. I will be careful to lead a blameless life . . .'" Vera stopped.

I want to lead a blameless life. And I believe Sam does. He certainly is committed to justice. No question about that. But we need to walk this path together. More than anything else in the world we must step in the footprints that the Lord has already laid down. That's the only way we're going to make this journey work.

Vera laid the Bible back on the end table and pulled her knees up under her chin. She folded her hands and pushed them against her chin.

"O Lord, please hear my prayer tonight. I want to be blameless, to have the best marriage in the whole world. I want to be a helpmate to my husband, and I believe that he tries to do everything he can to please You. Maybe I'm not seeing things right, but I do believe that You want us to walk this path together.

"You know that I get angry and say more than I intend. Of course, I wouldn't divorce him, but I do get awful angry with him. We desperately need Your help."

For a moment Vera opened her eyes and looked around her house. The room was nice, the furniture still had a new quality. Their blue rug didn't even show much wear. Just as she wanted the house to be . . . except Sam wasn't there. She closed her eyes.

"Gracious God, thank You for everything You've given us. You've provided so abundantly and fully for us. We're thankful. We love our daughter and want to raise her right. Don't get me wrong in what I want to ask You to do. I don't overlook the fact that You've given us a wonderful abundance. I just want to have a marriage in which I can be a part of what my husband does.

"Could You help us? Maybe just a little bit. We sure don't seem to be doing so great by ourselves. We need Your assistance. Okay?" Vera waited a moment, then said, "Amen."

She unfolded her legs and stretched them across the floor. She felt better, much better. Maybe these things would work themselves out. She hit the mute button again on the television monitor, and sound filled the room. Noise seemed okay now, but she didn't really listen to the program as much as she drank in the peaceful quiet that she now kept feeling.

Fifteen minutes later, Vera heard a noise in the driveway. A car door slammed. She scooted to the edge of the chair and heard a key turning the lock on the front door.

"Hey, honey, I'm home!" Sam called out. "You here, baby?"

Vera leaped to her feet.

16

AT 8:00 ON MONDAY MORNING, SAM hurried into his office at the Nevada Street precinct. The first day of the week had a different ambience than it did the last Friday. Ending the week always had a flurry of getting caught up on everything that needed to be completed before the curtain dropped. Starting the week had more of a feel that someone called out "show time!" and everybody was running to get in place.

"Hey, Sam!" Dick Simmons stuck his head in the door of Sloan's office. "How was your weekend?"

Sam laid his pencil down. "Excellent. I think I've got a breakthrough on this murder case I was worrying about last Friday."

"Over the weekend?" Simmons laughed. "Don't you ever let it rest?"

Sam grinned out the side of his mouth. "Crime doesn't take a vacation."

"Really?" Simmons raised his eyebrows. "But I do. See you later." He hurried on down the hall.

"Keep running," Sam called after him. He turned back to his desk. "Al Henry is probably an alias," Sam mumbled under his breath. "Bet the kid took another name. Maybe he'd run off? Hiding from something he'd done. Needed to try a new town."

He reached for the telephone. "Mary? This is Sam over here in homicide."

"Good morning, sir. How can I help?"

"Remember that Al Henry guy we tried to run down as a missing person last week without much success?"

"Certainly."

"Let's try another angle. Forget the name and assume Al Henry was only a cover. Let's try looking for a seventeen-year-old boy from California who wandered into town recently. I'm sure there's a million of them, but maybe we can put something together."

A sigh buzzed over the receiver. "I liked working on the Al Henry angle better than this one," Mary said. "Pseudonyms are tough. Let me see what I can do . . . I'll call you back in about an hour."

"Thank you, Mary. I deeply appreciate your help." Sam hung up the phone.

He got up from his desk and walked over to a large wall map of the Colorado Springs community that stretched back into the high mountains. He ran his finger quickly across Fort Carson up to Manitou Springs and on to the Ramparts Range Road winding into the Pike National Forest area.

"Huge," he said to himself. "Incredible number of caves, valleys, culverts." Sam looked closer to town, studying Ute Valley Park, Woodstone Park, and north toward the Air Force Academy. "Naw, they wouldn't have stopped so close to such a thickly populated area. Had to go way out into the trees. Could have gone beyond Woodland Park or even out toward Wilkerson Pass." He scratched his head. "Heaven help us if they drove out into that Tarryall Creek region."

"Can't find a file folder." Dick Simmons's familiar voice called from the door. "Didn't leave one in here?"

"No." Sam turned to the door. "If you'd killed somebody, where would you dump their body around here, Dick?"

Simmons laughed. He had on another of those ties designed to make him look like a special assistant to the mayor or a manager of a factory in the area. "Guess I'd go out there and drop them in the lake by the Broadmoor Golf Course. Or maybe over in the Mesa Reservoirs. Give 'em a little touch of class. Send 'em to the bottom with the best."

"These people I'm chasing don't know the meaning of the word *class*," Sam said. "I think maybe they're a little on the crazy side."

Simmons squinted. "You serious?"

"Yeah, I think I've got a genuine murder case with no corpse."

"That's a little on the difficult side."

Sam nodded. "The coffin that I'm looking for is somewhere out there in more than several thousand acres of land."

Dick rubbed his jaw. "Snow's already started falling up high. The white stuff won't help your problem any."

"I may need you to assist me on a wild-goose chase through those mountains." Sam tapped on the map. "Think you and some of the boys might need a little exercise?"

Simmons's face twisted. "That's not my idea of exercise. You're talking pain. Stomping through the mountains is quite different once the snow starts falling. Man, that's old-fashioned hard work."

"An executive like you?" Sam chided. "Ah, come on! The experience would be good for your waistline."

Simmons turned toward the door. "I was just leaving for the

Bahamas. Call me and my waistline in the spring if you don't find this body by then."

Sam laughed. "I'll keep your name at the top of my special list." He watched Dick leave and shut the door behind him.

Sitting alone in his office, Sam stared at the form on his desk. Obviously he needed to report formally what he'd learned from Ape the day before. Everything on this bizarre case had happened so quickly that he'd not had time to follow his usual methodical procedures. As strange as it seemed to the rest of his fellow cops, one of Sloan's normal policies was to pray about his cases. When one of the men saw him praying, the ribbing went on endlessly. To keep from being obvious, Sam generally tried to find a secluded, solitary place to pray silently. So far, he'd missed that significant step.

Sam leaned forward and dropped his head into his hands. He waited a moment for total quietness to permeate his office and then took a deep breath.

"O Lord, everything seems to suggest that a young man has been killed. Brutally murdered. And I know that justice is important to You. Finding this person and doing what's right by him is significant in Your sight. Please help us. The broken pieces of the puzzle seem to be too large for us to fit together. We need Your touch, Lord. Could You give us a little nudge here and there so we'd be able to work out the situation with this boy? Sure hope You hear me. Amen."

"Let's see what happens," he said to himself and rubbed his temples for a moment. Time was pressing, and he had to get his work done.

Sloan picked up a group of files on his desk and decided this would be a good time to file this material and get the papers off his desk for a change. He walked across the room and stuck two files in his cabinet. To his amazement, the file Simmons had been looking for was on the bottom.

"How'd this thing get in here?" Sam shook his head. "Simmons leaves his stuff all over creation." He put the file back on the desk to give it to Simmons the next time he came down the hall. The phone rang.

Sam straightened up and grabbed the receiver. "Hello."

"This is Mary down here in statistics. I tried a different approach on locating this person you're trying to find."

"Yes?"

"I did some cross-file checking, jumping forward some, and discovered that a missing person bulletin came in about a week ago on a guy named Allan Hammond. The initials of the two persons match."

Sam leaned forward on his desk. "Sounds significant! Good job, Mary."

"I did a little further checking in our adolescent unit and found that a guy named Allan Hammond had gotten into trouble, a scuffle of some sort that required police intervention. No one was arrested, but the file report says that Hammond worked on the street at a hot dog stand. Got ten bucks a day and all he could eat. Some deal, huh?"

Sam held the phone more tightly. "Can you get me a copy of those reports?"

"Already sent them over to you. A courier will be there any moment."

"Mary! How can I ever thank you? Tremendous job."

"Buy me lunch someday, but don't tell anyone. I'm just doing my job."

"Bless you. Thanks!" Sam hung up the phone.

"Fantastic!" Sloan hit the palm of his hand with his fist.

"We are moving this baby right along!"

Sam again picked up the phone and dialed the lab unit. "Sloan here," he said. "I had your people come out to a house and run a check for me yesterday. How's the work coming along?"

"We're working on it right now, Sam. Tell you one thing. Those blotches were certainly bloodstains. We've got that part of the tests nailed down. Yup, somebody got pounded on the steps of that old house."

"Excellent work. Send me the report as soon as it's done."

"Sure thing." The laboratory technician hung up.

"Yes! It's coming together!" Sloan put the phone back in the cradle. "Great."

"Detective Sloan?" a woman asked from the doorway.

"Yes?"

"I have a report from Mary Edwards for you." She held out a manila envelope.

"Thank you. Appreciate your speed." He quickly opened the file. When he looked up again, the woman was gone.

Sam sat down at his desk and stared at the pictures. One must have been taken several years earlier. The other looked like a school picture. Bushy, thick brown hair gave Allan Hammond a hippie look, but his eyes, face, and mouth didn't have the tarnished appearance that criminals often take on. He didn't appear to be mature for his age. More like a kid out on a lark.

The particulars said Hammond's place of residency had been Huntington Beach, California, living at 32321 Oak Drive. Ran away during his junior year in high school. No reported record of drug abuse. Had two older brothers. Must be a divorced family, as only a Wilma Hammond had been listed as his mother. No father's name was given. Could be dead. Sam read the report three times before laying it on his desk.

Nothing sounded abnormal from a thousand other runaways who drifted through the Springs every day. Simply kids not happy at home, who thought they'd find something different out in the mountains. Little boys wanting to take on the big world with no idea how many crazy, dangerous people wandered down those same streets looking for the naive to devour in a single gulp.

Sloan wondered how this boy had stumbled into Jester and his gang's world. Maybe by selling hot dogs out there on the street? Could have been nothing more than a chance conversation out there in Acacia Park. An unsophisticated kid with no idea that he was talking to a dangerous sociopathic killer. *Boom!* Hammond crossed the web and became the fly in the spider's trap.

Sam got up and went over to pour himself a cup of coffee. He wished that the missing person's sheet had included a picture of Hammond's shoes. Shoes helped. They told a story and revealed a unique view of the victim. As Sam studied their shoes, they seemed to speak to him, spinning their own tale about who the person had been. He studied them, thought about, prayed over, and even dreamed about them, wondering what they might tell him about the person.

Where had the victim come from and where was he going when the fatal moments unfolded? Every victim had been a person walking down the street like all those other people out there before someone ended their life. Sometimes the shoes had mud of a definite hue, a soil sample that told its own story. Occasional bits of straw, grass, or debris had stuck on the soles. Of course the quality, the cost of the shoes, said something about the values of the owner. Shoes gave important clues about the nature of the wearer. The turn of the toe or the wear on the heels had a story. The leather, the shoestrings, the soles, each part of the footwear said something about the thoughts and ideas of the victim.

Sam tried to slide into the victim's last thoughts and feelings through studying what the leather might say or hint. His intuitions let any impulse out there come flowing in. He tried to stand in the dead man's shoes and let any possible clues surge out of the leather.

And sometimes they did.

Sam had often found that hunches and premonitions bubbled up from his contemplation of the victim's shoes. He'd develop feelings that caused him to look in new directions or reconsider some aspect of the case that hadn't struck before. Some of his fellow detectives thought his preoccupation with shoes was too mystical, but Sam knew the difference that a few minutes with a pair of old gnarled shoes could make.

"Wish I could see his boots, sandals, whatever," Sam said to himself. "Just a few minutes with that boy would answer so many questions. What caused Hammond to leave home? Something must have exploded."

At that moment another face came to mind. Sam could see the small lovely face of his daughter, Cara. Innocent. Good. Kind. Thoughtful. Nice person. He could see Cara's shoes. All the things that Allan Hammond had once been. But there hadn't been a father, a strong male figure who cared for Allan. Apparently, the boy floundered around and for some reason decided to leave home. No guidance, a little problem, and Allan was on the road. In his wildest dreams, Sam couldn't imagine that ever happening to Cara, but what parent could? The issue was always where a kid's shoes took them.

Sloan set the cup of coffee down on his desk. *I need to give my daughter more attention. Much more time. Long talks. Let this be a harsh reminder: Spend more time with Cara.*

17

SOMETIME AFTER 4:30 ON MONDAY AFTER-
noon, Sam Sloan picked up the telephone and dialed the
police department in Lincoln, Nebraska. Although he might
be on the early side, the time had come to see if the Lincoln
Police Department could get in the act with him. He had
enough hints that would probably turn into hard evidence.
Everything suggested that this Jester character and his gang
were probably still in the Lincoln area. The Nebraska cops
could help.

"Lincoln Police Department," a woman said.

"This is Detective Sam Sloan in Colorado Springs,
Colorado. I am calling on official business."

"To whom may I place your call?" the woman asked.

"I need someone who works investigations."

The woman paused. "Unfortunately, Sergeant Fred Pile is

107

not in the office right now. His staff people are also out on a case. You could leave a message and I'll make sure he gets it."

Sam frowned. "I need to talk with him personally. Would you please have him call me in Colorado Springs?"

Hate to miss him. Needs to be a conversation. Guess I have no choice but to wait for him to call back. He gave her the phone number.

"Thank you," the receptionist said. "I'll relay the information and phone number to Sergeant Pile."

Sam hung up. *Hope that guy doesn't take until Christmas to call me back.*

Once more Sloan picked up the pictures of Allan Hammond and studied them. "Has to be Al Henry," he said to himself. "Too much fits." He put the pictures back in the folder and picked up the telephone to call Vera.

"It's me. Your lover man," he said when she answered.

"Sam!" Vera's voice danced. "Good to hear your voice. I've been thinking about this Al Henry case all day."

"Figured out where he is up in the mountains?"

"No," Vera said slowly, "but I'll bet they took him up very high. Possibly on some remote road that gets near the top of a peak."

Sam blinked several times. "Why? Why are you suggesting that?"

"Because he wouldn't be likely to be found far up on the top of a ridge or a mountain. Doesn't that make sense?"

"Yes," Sam answered thoughtfully. "Makes very good sense."

"See! I'm already helping you."

Sam wasn't sure what to say. Her idea had been excellent. "Well . . . uh . . . uh . . . I was wondering if I came home right now, if it would be okay with you for me to take Cara out for a little ice cream before supper?"

"This early?" Vera sounded surprised. "Sure. You bet!

Listen, anytime you can come home early and spend time with Cara, you can buy her anything you well please."

"Be home in a few minutes."

"Dear, I can't tell you how much this pleases me."

Sam hung up the phone and made arrangements to have any calls from this Sergeant Pile person forwarded to his home. He looked around his desk. The job was far from done but he felt better than he had on Friday afternoon.

═══

"Let's try the Baskin-Robbins over on Unitah Street in the Colorado City area," Sloan suggested.

Cara beamed. "Daddy, we haven't gone out for a special treat like this in a long time."

"Too long."

Sloan pulled into a parking place in front of the store. He followed Cara inside and listened as she ordered. "I'd like a two-scoop hot fudge sundae, please."

"I'll take the same," he told the high school kid working behind the counter. "Put a little extra whipping cream on top."

They sat down near the large glass window overlooking the street.

"Cara, I can't believe that you are ten years old. Seems like only yesterday you were crawling around on the living room floor."

Cara grinned. "Surprises me, too, Daddy. Do you realize that I'm in the fifth grade this year?"

"Fifth grade? My, my."

"Yes, and the teacher promoted me into the accelerated math class. Isn't that good?"

"Excellent!"

"Un-huh. I really like math. I think it's my favorite class in the whole school."

"Accelerated?" Sam shook his head. "Quite remarkable. Must have inherited that ability from your father."

"Daddy!" Cara reached across the table and poked at her father. "That's exactly what Mommy said you'd say."

Sam laughed. "Caught me in the act. What more can I say?"

Cara ate her ice cream silently for a while. Finally she looked thoughtfully across the table at her father. "Daddy, we don't talk often enough."

Sam pressed his lips with his fingers. "I know. Cara, I'm sorry that my job takes so much time, but things happen, and in police work, sometimes you simply can't put actions off until later."

"I understand, but I still like to know what you think about things. School problems and stuff like that."

Sam pushed the ice cream dish back and leaned against the wooden seat. "Never thought about sharing much before," he said. "I guess I didn't think that a little girl would be interested in a grown man's reflections."

"Of course I am!" Cara beamed.

"Really?" Sam smiled. "I don't remember thinking much about my father's ideas on things when I was your age."

"Well, you were a boy and . . ." Cara leaned forward and spoke softly, "Did your daddy ever tell you things? Secret things?"

"No. No, I don't remember having many special conversations with my father." Sam cleared his throat. "No hidden mysteries in any of our talks."

"That's your problem." Cara raised her eyebrows. "He didn't talk to you."

Sam chuckled. "Dear, you make a lot of sense. I'm sorry that you never met my father. Even though we didn't talk together much, I think you'd have liked my dad. He certainly would have liked you."

"He died when I was little?"

"Yes." Sam looked out the window. "It was an accident. Unfortunately, a steel beam fell on him." He hadn't thought about the tragic accident in a long time but the remembrance was still painful.

Cara frowned and shrugged. "Since I can't meet him"— her voice brightened and she smiled—"I guess I'll need to spend double time with you. Right?"

"Absolutely, dear."

"Daddy, I have something to ask you."

"Sure."

"I'm only ten, but sometimes I think about doing things that will make you happy." Cara looked at Sam sideways. "Daddy, what makes you happy? You can think about your answer for a while if you wish." Cara went right on eating her ice cream.

"Give me a moment." Sam fumbled and scratched his head. He smiled at Cara, but found himself pushed. Surely Vera had told her about the birds and the bees. Why hadn't she included a dissertation on his personal likes and dislikes?

"Of course, we go to church," Cara suddenly added. "I know that you like those things we learn in Sunday school and think they are important."

Sam nodded. "Sure."

"Now, what else do you want me to do that makes you happy?"

Sam took a deep breath. "You know that we believe in always telling the truth. Honesty is up there near the top of the list."

Cara nodded. "Sure."

"We want you always to know that your mother and I highly value your being a kind person. That trait is important in a young lady."

"Okay. That's what I'll always try to do." Cara took one more bite. "But I also want to know something you've never told me before." She looked very thoughtful. "Why do you put such importance on what they teach us at church?"

Sam looked down at his hands. Both knuckles and fingers looked worn beyond their years. The bumps and cuts remained as little remembrances from old struggles. "Cara, I grew up in a rough neighborhood. Fighting seemed to be the way of life. Know what I mean?"

"I've read about places like that in books."

"Today we'd call people like my parents poor folks but we were honest and hardworking. The neighborhood simply proved to be a difficult place in which to survive."

"And you got in lots of scrapes?"

Sam smiled. "Afraid so, until I met a man named Jack Robbins. Because of what he did, Jack truly saved my life."

"Saved your life?" Cara's eyes widened. "His name is just like the owners of this ice cream store, Baskin-Robbins?"

"Sure is, dear. Same name."

"Fascinating!" Cara's eyes got larger. "What'd he teach you?"

"Jack said that I should learn to love people."

Cara giggled. "Well, sure. We all know that's right."

"But nobody in my neighborhood lived that way, and it seemed weak to me until I came to understand what Jack believed. We got into the boxing ring one afternoon, and I was determined to prove he was wrong about fighting defensively. I came out swinging like a merry-go-round, and Robbins beat the fool out of me. Simply flattened me."

"Daddy, I didn't think anyone could defeat you!"

"Jack certainly did. Then he sat down with me and told me the most amazing story." Sam laughed. "I can still hear his voice. Apparently Jack Robbins's boxing style had been developed from studying the ideas of the Bible. Can you believe that? In boxing?"

"Are you serious?" Cara frowned.

"Jack reasoned that Jesus' way wasn't to hit people first but to do everything he could to defend the down-and-out. I realized I didn't have any idea about who in the world he was describing, but slowly I began to recognize what the Bible meant. Cara, that afternoon changed my life. Everything that I've done since then has been conditioned by my encounter with the Scriptures."

Sam reached out and took Cara's hand. "Dear, I don't think there's anything in this world more important than trying to walk each day with love in our hearts. I believe God's the most important friend a girl your age can have."

⊹⟞⟝⊹

The day had long since passed when Sam began to get ready for bed. He unbuttoned his shirt thoughtfully, thinking about his time with Cara. He'd enjoyed every second of their being together. Maybe what he'd told her could make some difference and keep her from ever going down the path that led Allan Hammond to disaster. He hoped so.

Sam laid his billfold on the dressing table and put his keys next to a pile of coins. He kept his shoulder holster and pistol in the closet out of sight. Sam slowly slipped out of his shoes and sat down on the edge of the bed.

I hope that Cara heard something she'll always remember from what I said today. An idea that will affect her thinking as the years go by. I hope I made an impact.

"Dear," Vera called from the bathroom as she combed her hair, "thank you for taking Cara out this afternoon. I know it meant a great deal to her."

"I trust so."

"Sam, you have no idea the difference you make when you're simply being yourself."

"Think so?"

"I know so."

Sam nodded thoughtfully. "I'll try to do it more often."

"How about *me* next week?" Vera stuck her head out and winked at him.

18

LIGHTS IN THE BACK OF THE CAT BALLOU bar on Lincoln's A Street had been turned down so low that anyone coming in the front door wouldn't have an easy time identifying a person huddled next to the back wall. Standing behind a long bar, the bartender dried glasses and kept an eye on whatever happened in the dingy dive. The thirty-year-old place looked decrepit and the tables worn. Two women and a man talked in the darkest corner at the back.

"I never trusted the little pimp," Ginny Creager growled. "Could see in his eyes that he was a snake." Tall and big-boned, street woman Ginny Creager's face and severely tied-back hair looked hard. Her black leather vest, decorated with a skull and crossbones, gave the appearance of a motorcycle gang member. Most of Jester's gang called the lusty woman Big Gal. She had the reputation of not being afraid to trade blows with a

man, and her calloused knuckles looked as if they had. "I knew
he was stealin' from us." She glared at the other two.

The Asian woman sitting across the table nodded. "Henry
never was more than a punk, a jerk." Koo Mae had always
been of small stature and still didn't break five feet as an adult.
The Japanese-American kept an attractive face, but had long,
pointed fingernails that looked threatening even when she was
in a good mood. "Hated him the first time I saw the creep."

"He kept looking at my motorcycle jacket," Ginny continued. "I could see immediately that the little squirrel might try
to rip me off."

Koo Mae reached across the tabletop and took Jack Alban's
hand. Both Koo and Jack looked in their early twenties, while
Ginny Creager had to be in her late thirties. Koo wrapped her
hand around the top of Jack's hand. "You didn't trust Al either.
Did you, Jack baby?"

The young man shook his head. "I knew he lied. Could see
it in his weasel eyes that kept dartin' back and forth. I knew he
had itchin' fingers."

Jack picked up a pack of cigarettes off the table and lit one.
A bandanna had been pulled down over his head, making him
look something like a pirate and only hinting he had blond hair.
Small and on the slight side, Alban always wore gloves, sug-
gesting that he was ready to slug anyone who irritated him.
When he was sober, Jack's eyes had a strange groveling look.
Otherwise, he walked around with a dazed, silly stare. Which
was most of the time.

Koo reached up and took the cigarette out of Jack's mouth.
After a long draw, she blew smoke in the air and put the cigarette back in his mouth. "My baby don't take nothing off
nobody."

"I bet," Big Gal said cynically out the side of her mouth. "Let's get down to the real business in this conversation. I'm worried about what Jester told that big Ape, driving the weird van. Did you get the drift of their conversation?"

Jack looked nervously at Koo. "What do you mean?"

"I'm talking about what Jester told the big hunk while we were coming up here in Ape's van," Big Gal said. "You understand me?"

Jack glanced at Koo again but didn't say anything.

"You'll have to be more precise," the Asian woman answered.

"Look!" Big Gal leaned over the table. "I heard Jester tell Ape what happened to Al Henry. Beatin' him to death. Don't tell me you didn't hear him."

Koo looked at Jack for several moments, then back at Big Gal. "Yeah, we heard what he said. How could you miss it? Jester was talking so loud."

"That means the empty-headed fool is driving around out there in Colorado Springs with information that could put all of us in jail," Big Gal hissed. "You get the picture? Time in the big house! Maybe the electric chair!"

Alban looked anxiously around the bar to make sure no one was listening. "The big tub of lard has his brains scrambled. He probably doesn't even remember the conversation. They were both smoking dope. Big deal!"

Big Gal suddenly grabbed Jack by the shirt. "But what if he does remember what Jester told him? That's a *big deal.*"

Alban looked down at her fist hanging onto his shirt. "Let go of me."

"Maybe I'll let go of you over the edge of a cliff," the large woman threatened.

"Okay." Koo reached over and put her hand on Ginny's. "Let's not get rough. What do you have in mind?"

Big Gal let go of Alban's shirt. "I think we need to go back to Colorado Springs and kill the Ape."

Jack's eyes widened. "That mountain of flesh is big enough to break all of us sitting around this table in half at one pop."

"I didn't have in mind a wrestling match." Big Gal bristled with anger. "Shooting him in the back of the head was more what I was thinking."

Jack caught his breath. "You serious?"

"Look, meathead," Big Gal fired back. "You helped kill Henry. You can help kill Ape."

"The action with Henry was different," Jack objected. "He stole from us."

"You're a fierce little whacker, Jack," Big Gal taunted. "A real Hannibal Lecter meets a Mac the Knife type." She laughed hard and mercilessly. "Look. You wouldn't have done nothing that night you ran Al Henry down on Fifth Street if Jester hadn't made you."

Alban's face began turning red. "That's a lie!"

"Jester pounded the little man out there on the sidewalk," Big Gal insisted. "Not you. You looked like a gambler trying to figure out who to bet on."

"You're lying!" Jack insisted.

Creager took another drink of beer. "Jester stretched out Henry on the heating pipes in the basement under our place. *Not you, wimp!*"

"How'd you like me to smash you in the mouth?" Alban doubled his fist.

"Try it and I'll cut you up for fish bait." Big Gal's expression went flat. She looked capable of killing Jack.

Koo waved her hand with a gentle soothing swing. "What do you think Jester's going to say about this idea of killing Ape?"

Big Gal lifted her eyebrows cynically. "I didn't plan to discuss it with him. We shoot the big guy and that's all there is to the story."

Koo and Jack exchanged a look of consternation.

"It's your choice," the big woman said. "Help kill Ape or spend the rest of your life in the pen." She abruptly stood up. "I don't intend to kill him by myself. You two are in whether you like it or not." Big Gal stood up and walked toward the door.

Koo Mae and Jack Alban didn't move. Ginny Creager marched out of the bar like a determined warrior. Alban picked up the last glass of beer on the table and swallowed it in a couple of gulps.

"Be cool," Koo said. "Just stay cool."

+=—=+

Wearing his black leather motorcycle jacket, Jester slouched in the old recliner chair where he'd found his father sitting the day before. The Sunday newspaper still lay scattered over the floor, and the house remained a mess. Window shades had been pulled, and the old white curtains hung limp around the windows.

Koo and Jack walked into the room and sat on the floor.

"Where you been?" Jester asked caustically.

"Down at the Cat Ballou bar," Jack said. "Drinkin' a little beer."

Big Gal sat on the other side of the room, glaring at Jack and Koo.

"You're late!" Jester cursed. "Nothin's comin' together like it should have by now."

Ginny Creager nodded. "How come your court appearance thing fell apart?" The big woman sat on the edge of the chair with her jeans drooping over the top of her combat boots. Her tight knit T-shirt did nothing to conceal her big bustedness. Big Gal wore weight lifter's leather gloves. "I thought the hearing was set."

Jester cursed again. "Turns out that it wasn't. I went to the courthouse, and they told me I'd have to come back and talk to the assistant D.A., but the jerk won't be available for a few days."

"Sounds like they're giving you the runaround," Jack said. Alban's slight build made him look younger than he was. "Think those stupid attorneys are simply running you around the courthouse?"

Jester shrugged. "Could be."

"Look." Koo Mae's Asian eyes narrowed. "We're stuck here in this crummy town without a car." The Japanese woman looked slowly from one person to the other as if taking a vote count. "You really want to stay around this dump?"

"Yeah," Jack added. "Man, it's hard to get around this burg without wheels."

"I'm afraid about that Henry boy you knocked off the other day," Alice suddenly spoke up. "Maybe the cops are now looking for him." Alice's stringy blond hair hung down her neck in a straight line. Like Jack Alban, Alice stayed on the thin side. Although her bare arms looked unfashionably malnourished, Alice's face still had a pretty look. "Even as we speak, the police might be searching for him."

Big Gal raised one eyebrow but kept staring at Jack and Koo.

"We need to go back to Colorado Springs."

Jester shook his head. "That loser hung around Colorado Springs like a toilet waiting to be flushed. Nobody out there is paying a hair of attention to 'im being gone."

Alice raised her eyebrows. "Maybe he was lying to us. What if he has family right there in the Springs that was waiting for him to come home?" Alice smiled at the others. Although she never wore lipstick, her grin remained one of her best attributes. "Could be, you know."

Everyone looked at Alice without saying a word. For a full minute no one spoke. Finally a little boy toddled through the room. Jester and Alice's one-and-a-half-year-old son, Georgie, walked across the room toward the kitchen, wearing only a diaper.

"Don't think so," Jester said. "I believe Al Henry drifted in from out of state. One of them hippie runaways that settled down around Acacia Park. Naw, the guy wasn't no more than a bum."

"Yeah, but he dressed well," Ginny said. "Dressed too good not to have someone out there somewhere looking for him. I don't think Al Henry was Mr. Nobody."

Jester didn't say anything but kept staring straight ahead.

"We left him up high on that mountain," Koo added. "Nobody could find that body in a million years."

Alice kept her simple smile in place. "Can't ever tell. Some hiker might stumble by. Maybe a hunter."

"This time of the year?" Koo objected. "The jerk's got to be covered with snow by now, or animals probably had old Al for breakfast a week ago."

"Isn't this hunting season?" Alice sounded innocent. "Hunters could be up there shooting deer." She had a way of asking questions that sounded naive, when Alice knew perfectly well everything that was going on around her in a conversation. "Can't ever tell about them hunters." She smiled again.

Jester turned and looked at Alice with a hard stare. She'd obviously hit his button. He gave her a "cool-it" glance.

"Got something there." Ginny nodded enthusiastically.

"Come on!" Jack objected. "Ain't nobody going to be up there in that part of the national forest clompin' around. We tied that boy to a tree like he was a hostage in one of them John Wayne cowboys and Indians movies. Naw, he's so far back in them trees that nobody'd ever run him down."

"The truth is that nobody likes Lincoln," Koo said abruptly. "The town stinks. Since we're not accomplishing anything, I think we want to get on our way to somewhere else."

"Like back to Colorado Springs," Big Gal insisted.

"Maybe," Jester said, "but we've got to make sure that it's safe to show up down there."

Alice held up her hand tenuously but spoke in a definite tone. "I'd suggest that we give this place a few more days, extra time to discover exactly what has to be done legally before we go elsewhere. You don't want to have to come back. Right?"

Silence again settled over the group.

"Sure," Jester finally said. "We want it settled and done before we leave town."

"Therefore, we agree to stay here longer?" Ginny asked. "Several more days?"

"Sounds about right to me," Jack said. "After that we split."

"The question is, where are we going," Koo pushed on. "We need to decide what part of the world we want to settle in."

"I always liked the Springs," Big Gal pushed.

"That's where we might be hot," Koo objected. "I think we need to think about going to some other location." She stared at Big Gal.

"I don't agree with simply heading off into nowhere." Big Gal glared back at Jack and Koo.

"Okay!" Jester held up his hand. "Maybe the time's come

to consider some new place out there like Montana or maybe Wyoming."

"Wyoming?" Big Gal's voice turned shrill.

Jester's face remained deadpan. "Wyoming," he repeated. "Something wrong with your hearing, Big Gal? Yeah, I'm suggesting that maybe we give some thought to one of those empty countrysides where there ain't many people floating around. We might just do real well out there in one of those wide-open spaces where there ain't nothing but coyotes and cows."

Ginny crossed her arms over her chest and glared.

Jester got up. "Nothing's for sure yet. Understand? We're just talking, so don't nobody get excited or heated up none. We'll simply play our cards one at a time. See what tomorrow brings and then the next day." He looked around the circle. "Anybody got a problem with that approach? Who knows? Maybe we'll go back to Colorado Springs."

No one spoke. Ginny suddenly smiled, but Koo and Jack looked worried. Alice didn't move, but kept smiling with the naive-appearing twist in the corner of her mouth.

Jester started toward the door. "Then that's the way we'll go. Don't sound like anyone's getting hurt none." He slammed the front door behind him and stood out on the front porch.

The wind had picked up, and flakes of snow blew across his face. Coldness drifted in under his leather jacket, and he could feel the temperature dropping. Winter would be setting in big time before long.

"Florida doesn't sound bad either," he said to himself. "'Course, I don't have any idea how we're going to get a car, a van, a whatever."

19

S AM WALKED INTO THE POLICE STATION THE
next morning after his ice cream outing with his daughter,
thinking about the night before. His ten-year-old child had put
her finger on the center of Sam's problems in dealing with his
family. He had not grown up experiencing the right approach.
Jack Sloan certainly didn't give extra thought to his family's
emotional needs. Not once had Sam's father talked with him
about his dreams and hopes. The vacuum wasn't easy to fill.

Sam sat down at his desk and started getting ready to take
on his responsibilities. He picked up reports that had been filed
the day before on a couple of cases developing near the Air
Force Academy and glanced through the evidence, assessing if
he'd be needed to work on these problems. The telephone rang.

"This is Sergeant Fred Pile in Lincoln, Nebraska."

"Ah, Sergeant Pile! I appreciate your returning my call so

quickly." It'd only taken Pile the rest of the afternoon, all night, and the next morning to get around to it. "Thank you."

"What can we do to be of help to you, Detective Sloan?" The sergeant's voice sounded gruff and to the point. All business.

"We're working a possible murder case here in the Colorado Springs area." Sam determined to be equally factual and sounded more like a radio reporter talking. "We think that you've got some vital evidence related to this case over there in the Lincoln area. We need your help. Our problems are rather strange. I've got a killer named Jester with no last name, who killed a man we've not found."

"Hmmm." Pile laughed. "I'd say you got a big-time quandary down there."

"But we feel certain that our killer is now in Lincoln, Nebraska."

"Really?" Pile's voice changed. "Could this guy kill someone running a liquor store?"

"We think this character might kill anybody. A nut case. A psychopath."

"We're working around the clock on a strange murder in a local liquor store. Maybe we're both chasing the same dog. Our killing happened last week."

"That's about the time Jester would have been pulling into Lincoln."

"Possibly we're on to something worthwhile here. Certainly sounds like a parallel," Pile replied. "Can't ever tell about these strange killings. Lots of times some varmint comes wandering through after creating chaos elsewhere. Your Jester might fit the bill we're trying to fill here."

"We believe this guy can kill with little provocation. What we're trying to track down is the death of an adolescent around seventeen years of age. I think our man's got the potential to beat, knife, shoot, whatever."

"Our killing is equally strange," Pile added. "A liquor store owner got his throat cut. Sounds like your boy could have done it. How big is this Jester guy?"

"Medium to small. We think around five foot seven, eight, somewhere in that range. Not heavy."

"We got a shot from a security camera in the liquor store, but it only got the back side. However, we know the man wasn't large. The size certainly seems to fit."

"Excellent." Sloan took a deep breath. "Sounds like we're both traveling on the same track, but we've got no idea of the killer's legal name."

"At least I got a body!" Pile's laugh had a crude twist. "Yes, sir. At least I got his workmanship. Except we've already buried the dead man."

"What I'm after is evidence," Sam said, slowing down. "Some rather difficult collaboration that could tie everything together."

"Yeah?"

"We think there is an important source of a . . . a . . . let's say, *material* out on the edge of Lincoln."

"Material?"

"You know Interstate Highway 80 west of Lincoln?"

"Sure."

"There's a little roadside rest area just a short distance before you come into Lincoln. Maybe a mile to five miles or so out there . . . Recognize the place?"

"Yeah. Certainly. There's only one of those places out there on Highway 80. Every now and then we get a little rough stuff going on at that stop on the road."

"Good." Sam smiled. "We're both on the same wavelength. I think that rest area has old outhouses. Is that right?"

"Outhouses?" Pile exclaimed. "It sure does!"

"That's why I need your help."

"To locate outhouses?" Pile's voice raised.

"Unfortunately we believe our suspect threw important evidence in one of those facilities."

"You mean *down inside*?"

"Afraid so."

Pile's end of the phone went silent. After several moments, he said, "So?"

"I'm calling to see about you going out to that rest stop and checking out those outhouses to see if what we need is down at the bottom."

Pile cursed.

"We believe this evidence will tie everything together and make our case."

Pile cursed once more.

"Unfortunately, we see no alternative but to get inside those facilities and find out if a backpack was dumped in there, which was filled with some clothing and motorcycle gang patches."

"And you want us to go out there and dig into the bottom of those receptacles?" Pile's voice kept rising. "You're talking one nasty task."

"I'm afraid so, but I don't see any other way to get at it. We're reasonably sure that Jester threw this knapsack, which held the effects of the boy he killed, into one of those facilities."

"Heaven help us!"

"We believe it's got to be checked out at once or someone will make the rounds, then we'll have a real big-time problem."

Pile cursed a final time. "Not sure how we'll do it, but I guess we'll come up with something."

"Probably help both of us," Sam threw in as a final motivator. "Who knows? We may kill two birds with one potty search."

"Very funny," Pile said. "Times like this make me wonder how I ever got in this business."

"We'll owe you one," Sloan added.

"You bet your bottom dollar you will. Describe again what I'm looking for."

Sloan smiled to himself. He'd won this one and by that evening ought to know if Hammond's stuff had been found. Round one to the local boys.

⊰═══⊱

Fred Pile hung up the telephone and turned around to his assistant. "I need your help."

Jack Downs looked up at him with a quizzical gaze. "Huh?"

Pile scratched his bald head. "Got a job for you to do, Downs." Pile stretched his broad shoulders to try to look more massive. "I need you to run out there on I-80 and check out a location for me."

Downs pulled at his ear and listened much more carefully. He'd seen the broad-shoulders act before. The approach usually meant that Pile was laying down some sort of problem or trap for him. Always bad news and a revolting assignment.

"We're looking for some lost items out there in that rest area just west of the city." Pile's voice took on a more professional tone. "We need to find a backpack that might solve two murder cases at the same time. Could solve the liquor store murder." He cleared his throat. "An important assignment."

ROBERT L. WISE 129

Downs knew the professional sound, part two of the dump-it-on-Jack syndrome. "Yeah?" he said in his most disinterested voice.

"I need you to go out to that roadside park and find a knapsack that is filled with a jean jacket, patches for a motorcycle gang, and possible other debris. Maybe a knife handle or a blade in there."

"Where is it? Not many places to hide something in a roadside rest stop."

Pile stopped and rubbed the back of his large thick neck. "Not exactly sure," he lied.

Jack rubbed his chin. "Let me put it this way. *Exactly* where did the guy on the phone say that this stuff would be?"

Pile pursed his lips and took a deep breath. "In an outhouse."

"Just what I thought!" Downs slammed his pencil down on the desk. "I can tell you one thing, Sergeant. I'm not going out there without you. You can fire me if you want, but I'm not taking on some old toilets without you standing there sticking your own hands into the same mess."

Pile eyed his assistant as if he wanted to break his neck, but on the other hand, nobody was going out there into that stinking toilet without a struggle. Downs didn't sound defiant often, but when he did, there was no moving the guy off his position.

"Okay," Pile said slowly. "I hear you."

"No, sir! I'm not about to run around turning over toilets without you being part of the entire operation."

"I got you the first time." Pile turned away. "Call the fire department and see if they've got a gaff or something long—and I mean long—and pointed we can use to go after the inside of those toilets."

Jack shook his head and picked up the telephone, reluctantly dialing the local fire station.

By midafternoon, Sergeant Pile, Jack Downs, and two men from the fire department as well as Shorty Crawford from a local sewage management company gathered at the rest stop.

"Shorty," Fred Pile spoke hesitantly, "I don't see any way of getting at this problem than to have you stick the hose from your pump truck down in the hole and pump the thing out."

Crawford squinted at the outhouse. "Ain't my favorite sort a work to do, but I can certainly drain that place clean."

"The next step will be to squirt what you pump out back over the grass so we can check out what's down inside."

Shorty shook his head. "You're serious?"

"We're here on police business," Jack Downs said with an air of self-importance. "Has to be done."

Shorty eyed Downs with a look of contempt. "Well, why don't *you boys* just do the job then?"

Pile nudged Downs and gave him a "shut-your-mouth" look. "Sorry. We simply don't have the equipment. We really need your help, Shorty. Of course, we'll pay you right."

Crawford shrugged. "Okay. Hang on, boys," Shorty said. "This ain't gonna smell nice." He walked back to his large truck and started attaching the hoses.

For the next fifteen minutes, Crawford pumped the outhouses, then backed his truck around into an open field, where he reversed the process. Pile, Downs, and the men from the fire department began searching through the debris with long gaff hooks, while Shorty Crawford stayed downwind, watching.

"Hey!" Downs pointed to the ground. "I think that looks like a backpack down there. Who-eee! The thing must have gone down to the bottom."

Pile covered his eyes from the sun. "Yes, sir! No question about it. You've found a backpack. Think that's it?"

"Don't have many people leaving their shaving kits down there very often," Shorty Crawford said caustically.

Pile took a stick and pushed the backpack open. "Sure enough! We've found what Sloan is looking for. Hot dog!"

Jack Downs covered his nose. "Don't see any knife blade anywhere. Guess it isn't here."

Pile pursed his lips. "Run back to my car, Downs. Look in the backseat. Bring that large magnet back over here."

"Magnet!" Downs's eyebrows rose.

"We ain't quite done yet, boy." Pile crossed his arms over his chest. "No sirree! But I bet we find that blade before we quit!"

Twenty minutes later Sergeant Fred Pile dialed Colorado Springs from his cruiser. "Give me Detective Sloan."

In a few minutes Sloan answered.

"We found it!"

"What?"

"This is Sergeant Pile in Lincoln, Nebraska. We found the backpack!"

"Really?"

"Yeah, your source was correct. The bag was in the bottom of one of these receptacles. Had to sort through all that excrement, but we found some of the stuff that had fallen out. The motorcycle patches were laying down there on the bottom. We also finally found a broken knife blade."

"Excellent!" Sloan pounded his desk and the thump echoed over the phone.

"I think this is the man we're both looking for," Pile said.

"Problem is, we don't know his true name," Sloan answered. "We're looking for someone wandering your streets with nothing more than the name of Jester."

"Jester, huh?" Sergeant Pile smiled. "Shouldn't be too hard to run down such an obvious alias."

"We'll keep working our end," Sloan said. "Let us know as soon as you get any solid leads."

Fred Pile laughed. "You boys find that body you've lost while we locate this man. Don't worry, we'll get right after it." He ended the call and stepped out of the car.

"Hey, Downs! Ever hear of anybody named Jester making the bar scene around town?"

20

Vera was standing at the sink peeling potatoes when Sam came in the back door. Her day had gone by relatively quickly.

"I'm home." Sam stuck his head around the door. "Back from the war."

"Wonderful." Vera dropped a potato in a green bowl. "How'd *our* case go today?"

Sam caught the inflection. He'd been thinking about the fact that Vera's involvement could end up getting her called to testify in court if the defense attorneys got wind of the fact that Sam had discussed the case with her. The idea bothered him, but at this point there was no reason to hedge anymore. Vera was now part of the operation regardless of what he thought. He might as well give it up and lay the truth on the line.

"We had a big breakthrough. The police in Lincoln,

Nebraska, found the boy's knapsack in an outhouse. We've got hard evidence that completely supports Ape's story."

Vera hugged Sam. "Excellent!" She sat down at the kitchen table. "Sit down, Sam. Let's talk, because I've been thinking about this murder all day."

"Some way to spend your time."

"Sam, I really have!"

Sam looked at her sparkling eyes. No question about it. Vera had stayed in a better mood over the last week than he'd seen in a long time. Things were certainly better between them.

Vera continued, "I've been thinking about that old house where you found the bloodstains. Who owns it? I'd think we could run down Jester's legal name if we knew who rented the house to them."

Sam raised an eyebrow. "Not bad, dear. As a matter of fact, I checked that angle this afternoon."

"And?"

"Turns out the place was rented by a woman who paid cash on a monthly basis but wouldn't sign a lease."

"Why would anyone rent on that basis?"

"The place is a total wreck, and the landlord isn't exactly a member of the local country club." Sam chuckled. "Had to run the man down. Turned out that the guy was simply another old codger floating around town."

"But did he come up with a name?"

Sam smiled. "You're certainly chasing down the right trail, Vera. He actually heard a gang member call the woman Ginny and said she was a large woman, probably in her twenties or early thirties at best. Thought she'd had a last name like Conger or Cratcher. Something along that line, but he couldn't be more specific."

"Doesn't put us much closer to identifying Jester, does it?" Vera rubbed her hands together.

Sam held a finger up in the air. "Don't go past this evidence so fast. We've established an important link to this character. Ginny Whatever-Her-Name-Is might turn out to be someone we'd pick up here in town, or she might be captured with Jester; then they'd both be tied to the house." Sam winked at Vera. "Every piece of evidence helps."

"I see what you mean. Hmm. Ginny Conger? Ginny Cratcher?" Vera shrugged. "At least you've added another name to Jester's file." She frowned. "Anything on where this poor boy might be hidden in the mountains?"

"No." Sam shook his head. "Haven't picked up any leads on that problem at all."

"I thought about that poor seventeen-year-old boy all day. How terribly, terribly sad."

"Yeah," Sam answered. "I'm almost certain that the boy's name is actually Allan Hammond and he's a missing person from California."

"The boy surely had a family of some sort?"

Sam nodded. "Had a mother. Two brothers."

"They must be out of their minds worried about the young man. Think what it would do to us if Cara disappeared."

Sam flinched. "I wouldn't even want to speculate on that possibility." He raised both of his eyebrows. "Too frightening to think about."

Vera shivered. "If nothing else, I can feel how someone loved that boy and deeply cared what happened to him. Even if Allan Hammond had been in some sort of trouble, he still had people who cared about him."

Sam took a deep breath. "I thought about this boy while I

was working yesterday, wondering about his shoes." Sam held up a hand to ward off her obvious question. "I know this sounds strange to you, but I often look at a victim's shoes to see if I can find clues about where they were going or had come from. Many times I'll sit at a crime scene and do nothing more than think about what their shoes tell me."

Vera tilted her head and looked thoughtful. "Interesting. I wouldn't ever have thought of such an approach."

"Shoes can tell you many things. Many, many things."

Silence fell between Sam and Vera, and no one spoke for a full minute.

Vera finally said, "You maintain a marvelous concern for characters to whom I wouldn't give the time of day."

"Don't give me that line." Sam snorted. "You care about every dog and cat that wanders across the front yard, as well as these people who drop into our lives. Why, Vera, you've done nothing all day but worry about a young man you've not even seen."

Vera laughed. "Well, I'm helping you with a problem . . ."

"And you're worrying about what became of a street person! See what I mean?"

Vera smiled and reached for her husband's hand. "I love you, Sam. You're funny."

Sam looked more intently. "And you're a very bright woman!"

⊹━━⊹

At that same hour in Lincoln, Nebraska, Raymond Bench sat in a street-corner restaurant not far from his rented house, thinking about his problems. He didn't like being around the place when Raymond Junior's gang floated in and out. They had proved to be the most inconsiderate, thoughtless group of bums he'd ever seen. And Raymond Bench had seen truckloads of bums.

Bench wasn't about to start calling his son "Jester," a stupid name! Moreover, that worthless woman he slept with wasn't any better. She walked about the house all day with an ignorant grin on her face, chasing that idiot child of theirs. Never put any clothes on the baby. The little guy hopped around the rooms all the time with a dirty diaper hanging down, looking really stupid.

No sirree! Raymond Bench wasn't about to get close to that baby they called Georgie. He'd gotten emotionally involved with the first boy and was still paying the price for that kid's care. No more being nice to little children that Junior came dragging in with him.

Bench sipped his coffee and stared out the restaurant window. He could see the front of José's Liquors two blocks down the street. The business was running again, with the owner watching over the place. Apparently he'd taken Johnny Gonzales's place, and the newspaper said he'd put in even more security equipment. No more sneaking a bottle of whiskey out of that place.

Raymond worried about the constant police pursuit of the killer. He could see cops coming and going out of José's all the time. The Lincoln newspapers kept a story running nearly every day. Raymond couldn't understand why the whole town was making such a fuss over this dead Mexican. The world seemed to be full of 'em. In fact, more Mexicans had poured into Lincoln than Raymond ever believed would live in that town. Why make a stink over one jerk who accidentally got his throat cut?

The front door of the restaurant opened, and a heavyset middle-aged woman walked in. Her low-cut red dress looked both too tight and too short. She glanced around the place as if to make sure that nobody recognized her, then walked straight over to Bench's booth, wobbling on high heels.

"How ya doin', doll?" Bench gestured to the other side of the table. "Good to see you, baby."

The woman winked, and the whole side of her pudgy face moved. "The old lady's still out of town?" Maria Phillips suddenly looked serious. Her dress probably had been close to style a decade and a half ago. "Don't want no surprises."

"Yeah, she will be out for, maybe, a couple of weeks."

Maria Phillips's face slid back into a smile. "I don't know why I put up with you, Raymond. This running around to avoid getting caught by your wife gets old."

"'Cause you love me." Bench winked.

Maria blushed. "You silly old man."

Bench laughed, then broke into a bad cough. "First time I've laughed in days." He picked up a smoldering cigarette and took a long drag. "Been tough."

"How come?" Maria frowned.

"My son's come back with a pack of wild, illiterate friends. Ain't no fun havin' that gang of fools parked in my bedrooms."

"Kick 'em out," the girl friend growled. "My son kept coming around looking for a handout until I kicked his behind out the front door. Haven't had no trouble since."

Raymond puffed on his cigarette. "I think Raymond Junior could have gotten himself in some big trouble. He's acted weird in the past, but now he's even stranger."

Maria ran her tongue over her front teeth and opened her purse. The heavyset woman took out a cigarette and lit up.

"Raymond?" she said, smoke floating out of her mouth. "Sure isn't any of my business, but I'll ask you a question if you don't mind."

"Of course." Bench shrugged.

"You ever beat that boy when he was a young'un?"

Bench twisted nervously in the seat. "He got what he had coming a few times. When Junior didn't behave right, I had to get him back into line some way. You know, hitting them is the only method that works, if it's done properly with enough pain."

Maria took another deep puff off her cigarette. "When I say *beat,* I mean, did you go beyond spanking the child and really knock the daylights out of 'im?"

Raymond pursed his lower lip. "Few times."

"More than a few times?"

Bench cursed. "What are you trying to prove, Maria?"

"I'm trying to determine what this boy of yours is capable of. That's what. You say he might have been in trouble. Well, I'm thinking about what he could do to you." Maria raised both eyebrows and stared across the table at Raymond.

For a few moments Bench looked down at the table, then frowned. "You know that I tell you everything," he said. "Ain't no secrets between us."

"I'd say that's an understatement."

Bench smiled. "I'm afraid that I'd have to admit to beating the boy. Seemed like that was the only way I could keep him under control. 'Course, my old man beat me royally when I was a youngster and didn't harm me none."

Maria shook her head. "I saw this Maury television show about childhood beatings, and they said it had long-term bad effects on some children. Your boy might have a significant vicious streak running down his back. Know what I mean?"

Bench sipped his coffee and didn't say anything for a while. "Yeah, I know what you mean." He puffed on the cigarette again. "Sure." He looked across the table with as much straightforward honesty as he ever mustered. "I think my son is capable of killing someone, including me."

Maria bit her bottom lip and rubbed her mouth. "Really?"

Raymond nodded.

"Then I'd get myself some big-time protection before he came home looking for a hunk of your hide."

"I always tell you the truth, Maria, and the facts are that I'm about half scared of Junior. Well, I haven't even stated the truth as it *actually is*. The boy and those friends of his give me the creeps." Bench cursed. "There's no question in my mind that they could do me in with the snap of a finger."

The extra layer of flesh above Maria's eyes narrowed, and she suddenly looked tough. "Raymond, baby, we have good times together, but when you tell me that son of yours is capable of killing, I don't fool around with that story none. I'd suggest that you get a gun and keep it where you can get at it in a hurry. That man's quite capable of cutting your throat."

Bench flinched and let her words roll around in his mind. He knew exactly what cutting someone's throat looked like, and the remembrance chilled him. A surge of fear crossed his mind, and he knew that Maria had told him the truth.

"Always been a little edgy about guns," he confessed. "Having one around could get dangerous."

"Not having one around could be *more* dangerous," Maria insisted.

"We both know that I tend to hit the sauce a little too much," Raymond confessed. "Way too much, is what I mean."

Maria shrugged and smiled wickedly. "Remember the last

time your old lady left town?" She laughed. "Sure, I know what you look like when you're half crocked."

"If I get a gun, I might reach over some night when I am half looped and shoot the wrong person."

Maria leaned over the table, her ample bosom resting on the wooden top. She pointed a finger in Raymond's face. "You'd better run that risk rather than have Junior slit your throat in the dark when *he's* totally loaded."

Bench felt anxiety hit him again. For a moment he remembered his son holding him up on one leg and slapping his face. The boy's mean eyes sent waves of terror through Raymond. He could feel himself falling helpless back in that chair, knowing that Junior could have done anything he chose at that moment. The man was strong and mighty enough to have broken his neck.

"Am I wrong?" Maria's eyes widened.

"No," Raymond growled under his breath. "You're absolutely right. I need to find a gun I can keep stashed somewhere out of sight in my bedroom."

21

DURING THE MORNING FOLLOWING HER conversation with Sam, Vera thought about the case. Sam's attitude had changed. No question about that fact. He definitely seemed to be open and talked about the investigation more easily with her. Vera sensed she was genuinely becoming part of a team.

As she worked around the house, Vera thought about the facts in the murder investigation. She wanted to find an aspect, some angle, a slant, which she could use to help Sam and truly make a difference. Hopefully something would open up, but nothing came to mind.

Vera gave her kitchen another long, thoughtful inspection. She liked being a housewife. No arguments there, but her world seemed to be shifting into a different orbit from where it had been in the past decade. Cara stood on the threshold to adolescence with her own cares and interests that didn't necessarily include a mother's oversight. Vera realized that every second of the day was no longer filled with important tasks and errands.

Time sometimes hung heavy on her hands, and she wanted her life to count for more. Vera could feel an inner urgency pounding away in her mind, demanding more of her existence. An unrealized potential lay hidden that now demanded expression. Horizons stood out there on the dawn of the morning, waiting for her attention. The beauty of the mountains no longer offered only a beautiful sight. She didn't want to miss climbing a single mountain.

For a long time Vera sat at her kitchen table, looking out toward Pikes Peak and the high mountains beyond Colorado Springs. She ran through the facts of the case again and again, thinking about and looking for unexpected twists that might reveal different dimensions of how the murder occurred. No matter how she thought or where she looked, Vera kept coming back to one conclusion.

"I need to get closer to the actual day-to-day operation," she said out loud. "If I could get my fingers more tightly around the facts, the data, the evidence . . ." Vera's mind wandered off again, pursuing several possible trails. Finally she stood up. "I know exactly what I'm going to do!" She hurried toward the bedroom and her clothes closet.

By 11:00 Sam had covered most of the details on several other cases that had crossed his desk. With the distractions out of the way, he could get back to the Allan Hammond/Al Henry case, where he really wanted to work. The phone rang.

"Got a couple of matters I need to talk over with you," Dick Simmons said.

Sloan leaned back in his chair and closed his eyes. Not another one of those needless conversations that did no more than devour his time! As he listened to Simmons, Sam rubbed his temple and shook his head. Five minutes later he hung up, still shaking his head.

Sam whirled around in his desk chair and reached for the file on the other side of his desk. Suddenly he felt someone standing in the door, watching him. He looked up. "Vera! What in the world are you doing down here at the precinct station house?"

"Thought I ought to come down for a little visit."

Sam blinked several times. "But you don't even like this place!"

Vera smiled. "Yeah, that's for sure. Smells like the courthouse over there." She pointed over her shoulder. "Can I come in?"

"Of course!" Sam leaped out of his chair, hurried around his desk, and reached for a chair standing next to the wall. "Here's a chair." He pushed it around to the front of his desk and sat back down.

Vera eased into the seat. "I wonder if this is what a criminal feels like, sitting over here looking across at you."

Sam laughed. "Good heavens! I wouldn't have any idea."

Vera scooted around in the chair. "It could feel a little threatening, sitting here looking across the desk at those cold eyes scrutinizing me as if I'd done something wrong." She raised an eyebrow.

"Heavens no!" Sam got up and scooted his chair from behind his desk to the front side. "Let me sit over there by you."

Vera smiled out of the corner of her mouth. "After all, I'm only your wife, who dropped by unexpectedly."

"No! No!" Sam waved his hand in the air. "I didn't mean anything personal. It's just that you've never dropped in on me down here. I'm completely surprised."

"Surprised?" Vera raised an eyebrow. "Who were you expecting this morning?"

"No one," Sam stammered. "Honestly, I was sitting here getting prepared to . . ."

Vera laughed. "Sam, you sound like I'm giving you the third degree." She giggled. "I simply came down here to find out what it feels like to be a genuine detective. You can relax."

Sam rubbed his chin and pulled at the tip of his nose. Seldom did anyone get the drop on him. Vera had completely outfoxed him. He'd have to admit she'd done a superb job of surprising him.

Vera winked. "Is that how a detective sneaks up on people?"

"You did a good job," Sam admitted. "Afraid you took me totally unawares."

"Excellent." Vera beamed. "I was sitting at home in the kitchen thinking about this case, and it occurred to me that I needed more insight into how the world of a detective worked. I couldn't think of a better place to find out than to come down here and see what happens in your office."

Sam shook his head. "Vera, you never cease to amaze me. The last thing in the world I would ever expect is to see you come walking into a place that, as you often said, you despised."

Vera looked around at the dull ivory color of the office walls that hadn't been painted in twenty years. "Sam, your desk looks used by who knows how many people before you, and the floor tile is vintage 1950 asphalt squares, which reminds me of every church bathroom floor I've ever seen. Let's face it. The place lacks class."

Sam chuckled. "We don't generally deal with classy characters down here. I guess that's the way the city likes us to look."

"Then the city council is a bunch of scumbags! Someone
who does the critical work you do should have one of the nicest
offices in town!"

"Oh, Vera." Sam laughed, then rubbed his chin as he
spoke. "Now. Why are you down here?"

"You didn't understand what I just said?" Vera raised both
eyebrows. "Or has your hearing gone bad, Sam?"

Sam stopped rubbing his chin and stared at her. The other
cops gave him the business for going to church. What would
they say if they thought his wife was down here checking out
what he did? Oh, man! He could be in real difficulty with
people like Dick Simmons.

Sam stood up. "Let me get you a cup of coffee." He walked
to the coffeepot in the back of the room, thinking as he walked.
"Plan to be here long?" He shut the office door.

"You're wanting me to leave this quickly?"

"No! No. Just thinking about how much time we've got."

Vera smiled but didn't say anything.

"Coffee's a little black." Sam handed her a cup. "I put in a
little sugar like you usually enjoy."

"Thank you, dear." Vera held the cup. "Actually I won't stay
long. I know you have much to do."

Sam felt himself relax. "Oh?" He tried to sound indifferent.

No point pushing anything negative. Might as well just go
with whatever Vera had in mind. Jack Sloan would have never
done that with his wife, Alice, but then again, Sam's father hadn't
proved to be much inspiration in how to get along with a wife.

"Do you have any new leads on where the corpse might
be?" Vera asked.

"Nothing more than I've told you. Probably won't until we find Jester and his gang."

"Hmm." Vera shook her head.

"The whole thing is truly an empty coffin," Sam said. "We've got no idea where that young man might be hidden."

"Sam," Vera's voice sounded much more tentative. "I would like to tell you something else." She stopped and looked down at the floor for several moments. The room turned silent except for the people walking up and down the hall. "I want you to know how important your conversation with Cara was. She talked to me yesterday and said your conversation with her was a real turning point in her life. Those were her exact words. 'Turning point'!"

Sam frowned. "I'm not sure I'm following you."

"Remember what you told her?"

"Told her?" Sam scratched his head. "Yes, of course."

"Darling, I've told you this before. You have no idea of the significance that you have on people's lives, but when the person is your daughter, the impact goes off the scale."

"I don't know what to say."

"Look. We know your job is demanding, but it's important you realize that your faith makes an important difference everywhere you go. Don't let the pressure of working on cases push that side of your life out of focus."

Sam took a deep breath. "I guess I needed the reminder today. Thank you."

Vera reached over and took his hand. "See! I can help you in ways that you don't even realize."

"Yes," Sam said soberly.

"Now, let's get down to business." Vera's smile disappeared and her eyes squinted. "I want to see the big map you keep down here."

"Big map?"

"Sure. Sam, we don't have one at home, and I need to take a sharp look at the possibilities of where that body might be found. I've been giving this considerable thought, and I want to look at a large-scale map of the area around Colorado Springs."

Sam's mouth dropped slightly. "Yes. Well . . . ah . . . sure." He pointed to the back of his office. "Over there's a government map of the mountainous country around here."

Vera stood up. "Excellent. I have a few ideas that I want to check out." She walked quickly to the map and began running her finger across several roads. "Just as I thought," she said more to herself than Sam.

Suddenly the office door opened. "Sam?" Dick Simmons called in. He stopped and stared.

"Just having a conversation with my wife."

"Oh!" Simmons started backing out. "Excuse me."

"Come in, Dick," Vera said. "I'll be leaving shortly."

"Don't want to interrupt anything."

"No." Vera sounded casual. "We're simply talking about our daughter."

"Great. Fine." Simmons laid a file on Sam's desk and glanced at Vera, who was reading the map. "Call me when you got a moment. See you around, Vera." He quickly closed the door behind him.

"Looks like I frightened your buddy Dick," Vera said.

"Simmons huffs and puffs around here like he's in charge of running the train's engine, but he puts out more smoke than anything else."

Vera turned around from the map. "I basically wanted to get a feel of what happens around here," she said. "Seeing your

office helps me think about the problems we're wrestling with."
Vera smiled.

Sam stared at her, realizing Vera was even more serious
than he'd dreamed possible. She truly meant business.

"Call me when you have time." Vera kissed Sam on the
cheek. "Be careful, dear." She pointed at the map. "I think that
I'm on to something." Vera waved and was gone.

For several minutes Sam sat behind his desk and thought
about their conversation. He was going to have to involve Vera
far more than he'd even thought possible. She wanted to help
and had more ability than he'd let himself recognize.

Sam got up and went over to the coffeepot and poured
another cup of steaming coffee. So what if the local cops
thought it was unusual or strange that his wife wanted to help
him solve cases? They laughed at him praying; they could
laugh at Vera being a resource. If it made her happy, then the
matter was okay with Sam. Of course, sooner or later he'd
need to clear the matter with the chief of police.

He walked back to his desk and set the coffee cup on the
end and picked up the phone.

"Simmons?" Sam said. "What can I do for you this morning?"

22

THE CALENDAR ON SAM SLOAN'S DESK AT the Nevada Street station reminded him that Thanksgiving Day was coming tomorrow. Time both appeared to race by and at the same moment stand still. Some of the day the Henry/Hammond case seemed to be resting next to a stone wall, then, at other moments, the entire investigation zoomed by. In fact, the murder case had unfolded at a high rate of speed, with crucial pieces simply falling into Sam's lap. Yet the problem of finding the young man's body and locating Jester remained unsolvable.

"Hey, Sam," a policeman called from the doorway. "That big ugly guy is back and wants to talk with you. I told the front-desk officer I'd relay the message."

"Where is he?"

"An officer took him down to interrogation."

"Thanks." Sam waved gently, sending the detective on down the hall.

Sloan sat at his desk, thinking about the situation. Ape possibly wanted to get on his way out of town. Did he need him? Maybe yes. Maybe not. Probably. Sam scratched his head and got up from his desk. All he wanted was a big clue to know where he might find that missing body.

When Sloan walked into the interrogation room, Ape sat in his usual chair, wearing the same T-shirt and overalls that he'd worn that first Friday night. The old clothes looked like they had gone through a washing machine sometime over the weekend. From the smile on his face, Ape appeared to be in a better frame of mind.

"How ya doin', brother?"

"Fine." Sam sat down across from Ape. "Still working the case."

"Good!" Ape smiled even more broadly. "Ex-so-llent."

"What brings you down here?"

Ape fidgeted in his chair. "Well, I've been thinkin' 'bout movin' on, and you told me to hang around until you gave me permission to leave town. So I thought I better check in."

Sam studied the man. George Barnes still had the overpowering awesome look that concealed a gentle heart. No questions about the fact that he had turned out to be one of the most cooperative witnesses Sam had seen in a long time.

"Kinda wanted to know what you'd turned up to date."

Sam leaned back in his chair. "Got two problems, Ape. Can't find the corpse. Can't find Jester. You developed any new memories on those two fronts?"

Ape shook his head. "I've been tryin' all weekend to jar my ole head, but nothin' new comes up. I think I drained everything out of my crankcase." He shrugged.

Sam pulled at his chin and rubbed the tip of his nose. "Ape, why don't you come with me and take a look at something."

"Yes, sir."

Sam stood up and beckoned for the man to follow him. They backtracked down the hall that led to Sloan's office. "I want you to look at a map that might help jar your memory a bit."

"Yeah?" Ape stayed right behind Sam.

Sloan opened his office door and pointed to the opposite wall. "I put up a map of the area that I want you to study." He pointed to his office wall. "Take a look."

Barnes ambled across the room and stared at a large multi-colored wall map.

"I want you to see if you can trace any possible route up into the high mountains and see what comes back to your mind."

Ape scratched his head. "Wel-l-l, there's that road down there by the Broadmoor Hotel that stretches out into the Victor Pass road that'll take ya over to Cripple Creek." He shook his head. "But I don't think they would've gone that way."

Sam said nothing but folded his arms over his chest and watched.

"Then we've got that big highway that stretches up through Woodland Park and runs over to Deckers." Ape ran his finger along Highway 67. "That road seems a better possibility." He scratched his head. "Of course, close to the Green Mountain Falls area, the highway turns off toward Divide and the Wilkerson Pass. Now that gets high up in there." He pointed to Cheesman Lake, which ran down through the whole area.

"You're guessing," Sam said. "The truth is that you don't recognize anything."

Ape shook his head. "I'm tryin', boss. Just don't see nothing that jars my memory none."

"Come back closer to Colorado Springs."

Ape stood closer to the map. "Just don't think they'd go out in the direction of the Air Force Academy. Too much security over there. Military police and all." His nose nearly touched the map. "That Ramparts Range Road has a nice name to it."

"Remind you of anything?"

"No, sir. I just like the sound of the place."

"Look, Ape." Sam fought to keep from sounding disgusted. "We're not playing a name-that-road game here. I want to know if any of these places kicks up a memory. Makes you recover something that's slipped away earlier."

"I'm tryin'!" Barnes peered at the map like a watchmaker putting a battery in a small wristwatch. "Just don't see nothin' easy though."

Sam pulled Ape's arm and pointed at the chair in front of his desk. "Sit down for a minute."

"Yes, sir."

Sam slipped behind his desk, then remembered what Vera had said when she dropped in for a visit. He got up again and pulled his chair around in front of the desk. "Doesn't knock anything loose in your head. Right, Ape?"

Barnes stared at the floor. "Honest t' God, Mr. Sam. I simply don't remember Jester ever tellin' me nothin' about where they put that poor boy except they left him tied to a tree, dead and all." Ape raised his eyebrows and looked menacing.

"Doesn't open up any memories of another name for Jester? Like his legal name?"

"Awful sorry, sir. Just don't get nothin'."

Sam gritted his teeth and rubbed his chin. "Nothing comes to mind?"

"Like I said, I do believe that I hit the bottom of the barrel."

The man sounded like he always did. Half there. George Barnes had told Sam the truth as best he grasped it at that moment. Sam rubbed his hands together. "Ape, I don't think that you've got anything left that you haven't told me."

Barnes shook his head. "I'm a-tellin' you the honest truth, Mr. Sam. If I could answer those questions, I sure would!"

"I do need to know how to get in touch with you if you leave town."

Ape pulled on his long beard. "Kinda hard since I ain't got no phone in my van, ya know."

"Umm-hmm."

"I guess I got no choice but to try and run you down. That's a long-distance call, you know."

Sloan raised one eyebrow. "Yeah."

"Probably don't have no choice but to spend my quarter."

Sam didn't say anything but kept looking at Ape.

The big man kept tugging at his bushy beard. "I think maybe I better think about this problem some more." Barnes stood up and put his rumpled black leather cap on his head. "Need to sit out in Acacia Park and think."

"Getting cold out there, Ape. Snow's all over the ground."

"Guess I ought to put a coat on." Ape kept frowning.

"I'd definitely get me a heavy coat if I was going to sit out there for long."

Ape nodded and turned toward the door. "I'll be back in touch before I does anything, Mr. Sam. Thanks for talking to me."

"Just let me know where I can find you quickly."

"Don't worry. I'll certainly do that." Ape wandered down the hall toward the front door.

Sam watched the man disappear, looking like a large ocean liner pulling out of port with smoke coming out of only one stack. Just wasn't enough fire in the engine room to get anything else going. Sam sat back down at his desk and picked up the file on the Henry/Hammond case to see if any other data had come in with a clue he might have missed. The phone rang.

"This is the lab," a woman said. "We've got an update for you."

"Yes?" Sam leaned forward on his desk.

"We don't have any DNA yet from this Hammond character, but we have done an ABO test on the bloodstains over there on the empty house. Guess what?"

"You tell me."

"The bloodstains turned out to be a type A positive. Guess who's got blood of that variety?"

Sloan hit the desk with the end of his palm. "Allan Hammond?"

"You got it, chief. We don't have all the work done but if you need a verification on those stains, all we need is DNA evidence from the man's body."

"Thank you!" Sam smiled. "You've at least put another nail in the coffin. Yell at me when you get anything more."

"Will do." The woman hung up.

Sam bent over the file to write the lab's findings on a sheet of paper. He suddenly had the strange feeling that someone was watching him. He looked up.

"Sorry to bother you again." Ape stood in the door with his leather hat in his hand.

Sam jumped. "What are you doing back here?" More than a small hint of irritation slipped through his voice.

"I thought of somethin'."

Sloan took a deep breath. "Okay, Barnes, what came up from the bottom?"

"Mind if I sits down?"

Sloan pointed at the chair in front of his desk. "Sit down."

"As I was walking out of the station house, I thought of somethin' I forgot to tell you earlier. About Jester . . . Jester is who I'm a-talkin' about."

"Jester?" Sam pushed the file to one side. "What about Jester?"

"Well, I didn't just leave him anywhere, you know. I dropped him off at a house. A particular house where he says to me that he's a-got family livin' there. Know what I mean?"

Sam held up a finger. "You're telling me that you left this man and his gang at the same place where they're probably still staying?"

"I expects."

"This just came back to you?"

Ape smiled. "As I was walking across the street this very minute."

"Can you furnish me an address? A direction?" Sam beckoned. "Anything?"

"I just followed Jester's directions, but if you had a map it'd help a bunch. A map of Lincoln."

Sam grabbed his phone and dialed an extension.

"Maria, this is Sam. How quick can you get in here with a city map of Lincoln, Nebraska?"

"I'll have to download a city map off the Internet," Maria said. "I can be in there as quick as I run it out."

"Excellent. Thank you, Maria." Sam hung up. "I'll have a map in here quickly, Ape. You're sure you can identify the place?"

"Sure. I came driving into town on Interstate 80. Coming across from North Platte and Kearney, don't you know. Remember we stopped at that rest park area only a few miles this side of Lincoln?"

"Certainly."

"Well, we come into that town and turned off on Highway 6, which is actually Zero Street." Ape stopped. "Not sure where next."

Sam's eyes narrowed. "I asked you about this matter of where you left these people earlier." His voice hardened. "Why didn't you tell me about where you let them out then?"

Ape shrugged and raised both eyebrows. "Hate t' say it, Mr. Sam. My drug usage kinda messed me up. Sometimes I remember. Sometimes I don't. All this direction sorta popped up in my head out of nowhere." He scratched his head. "Sorry."

Maria hurried into the room and spread a map before Sam. "I think this will give you some sense of the streets running through Lincoln." Maria stared at Ape out of the corner of her eye.

"Thank you, Maria," Sam said. "You've done very well." He nodded toward the door.

The secretary backed away, still staring at Ape.

Barnes reached across the desk and picked up the map. "Yes sirree, boss. I can sure read this thing . . . Don't got the exact address." He stuck his finger in the middle of town. "We went down Zero Street goin' east to the corner of Fifty-sixth Street." Ape stopped and looked closer. "But in that block right there is where I let 'em out, the whole batch of 'em. On that street right there."

"You're sure?"

Ape nodded enthusiastically. "You bet."

"If I send the Lincoln police out there to check the place out, you're sure they'll find something?" Sam looked straight into Ape's eyes.

"Can't promise nothin' today, but I can tell ya that's where I turned that pack of mules loose." Ape popped his palm with his fist. "But I'll bet ya they is still floatin' around that place. Yes sirree, Bob!"

23

THE CLOCK IN THE NEVADA STREET POLICE station read 3:45 when Sergeant Fred Pile called from Lincoln. Sam eagerly took the call.

"Did you get the information I faxed you this morning?" Sloan began.

"You aren't going to believe this one," Pile answered. "Turns out we know a great deal about your old buddy Jester."

"Really?"

"Police business started with his father, whose name is actually Raymond Bench, a town drunk and all-around jerk."

"Sounds like you've done a number of transactions with the old man."

Pile snorted. "You bet! I've run this guy around the block for years. Most of the time he's been nothing but a sot found asleep in a car parked in some inappropriate or illegal place.

Every town has a million of these guys. Bench and I had a nasty incident one night that got some people hurt. Bench hit me in the head with a pipe, and it took several stitches to sew the wound back up . . . In fact, the only reason I didn't pull him in for a lineup on this liquor store killing was that I figured it would have taken a fairly able person to have killed the liquor store owner."

Sam pushed the phone closer. "How is Raymond Bench tied to Jester?"

"That street your informant identified as the area where Jester and his gang were left is Raymond Bench's place. Didn't take much checking to identify Raymond as Jester's father. The murderer's legal name is Raymond Bench Junior . . . Probably that whole gang of people is all holed up in that house on the corner of Fifty-sixth Street."

Sam drummed his desk with his fingers. "Does this break-through look like it'll help your liquor store murder case?"

"You bet. José's Liquors is only a few blocks away from Raymond Bench's rented house. The perfect place for Jester to knock off."

"And you think Jester is still in the area?"

"We've seen some strange-looking people going in and out of the house, which causes us to believe the whole gang is staying there, but no one that recognizes Bench Junior has seen the man."

"Hmmm." Sam rubbed the side of his face. "What do you think Jester looks like?"

"We've got two very different pictures of him," Pile said. "One is his senior high school picture. Typical kid. Hair a little long and full. Brown hair. Black eyebrows. Usual Nebraska boy."

"How about picture two?"

"A real freak. We believe that today Raymond Junior has a beard and mustache. Lots and lots of hair. Hippie style. Weird dress and wears a black motorcycle jacket much of the time." Pile laughed again. "See how much we've turned up? Nebraska cops don't fool around none!"

"What's the next step as far as your people are concerned?"

Pile paused for a moment. "I'd suggest you get up here as quick as you can. Come prepared for action. I think our best bet is either to raid the place as soon as you arrive or hit it before dawn." Pile cleared his throat, sounding like a general. "With their history, who knows what they might do? Why, they could even knock off old Raymond Senior before we even got inside the house."

Sam glanced at his watch. "I'm going to have to step on it, or I'll end up in a private airplane and that costs a mint. I need to leave this minute to stop by the house and pack a suitcase before hurrying out to the airport and seeing what I can jump on. I'll call you from the terminal and let you know when I'll be in Lincoln."

"Okay," Pile said. "We'll have a police car out at the airport to pick you up. In the meantime, we'll start organizing *our* assault on the Bench house. Our policemen already have the entire block completely staked out."

"Keep your boys out of sight. I believe Jester is capable of running and letting the rest of the gang take the hit."

"Yeah, I read the cards the same way," Pile answered confidentially. "We'll play it cool."

After contacting his secretary by phone to set up the airplane reservation, Sam Sloan drove as fast as he safely could to the house, then to the airport. He discovered that the secretary had made reservations for him to board a flight flying out in thirty minutes. He hurried to the gate but stopped along the way to make a couple of phone calls. His easiest was letting Sergeant Pile in Lincoln know when he was arriving.

Sam listened as his home phone kept ringing. "Oh no!" he said to himself. "Sounds like Vera's still not there."

He kept waiting until the answering machine came on. Cara's childlike voice announced that the Sloans weren't in, but the caller could leave a message "on the house." Sam waited for the beep to record his message.

"Vera, I'm out here at the airport. We've had a big breakthrough in the Henry/Hammond case, and I must fly to Lincoln, Nebraska, tonight. I can't say much more over the telephone, but I'll call you as soon as I can." Sam took a deep breath. "Looks like there's no way I can be back in time for Thanksgiving dinner tomorrow. I'm truly sorry, dear, but I'll make it up to you and Cara as soon as I get back." He started to hang up, then added, "I love both of you." Sam placed the phone back on the hook just as he heard the boarding call.

"Flight 2641 to Lincoln is now ready for passengers. Please have your boarding pass available as you walk through the gate," the official behind the desk announced.

Sam picked up his briefcase and fell into the passenger line. He watched as the people in front of him handed the young woman their ticket slips.

I hope Vera understands. I'd much rather have been able to talk with her. Who knows what will happen when I get there? No telling! We may be shooting up the place by the time midnight rolls around. Surely she'll understand.

"Thank you, Mr. Sloan." The flight attendant obviously read the front of his ticket. "You may board now."

With the slow, careful gait expected of all passengers, Sam walked down the tunnel and onto the airplane. He found his way back to seat 10A and sat down. Within a few minutes, the small jet roared down the runway and up into the sky.

Sam stared out the window and watched Colorado Springs disappear beneath the clouds. Right, wrong, or indifferent, he was on his way to what might bring the entire case to a conclusion.

The airplane soared along the edge of the Rocky Mountains and over the foothills. Everywhere Sam looked, he saw the awesome beauty of the towering majesty of the mountains, lakes, and streams winding their way like small strips of ribbon through the meandering mountainside. Never had he felt more at one with the land that made Colorado a state of never-ending beauty. The airplane tipped slightly and started out over the long expansive prairie that would eventually take him to Lincoln.

"O Lord," Sam prayed under his breath, "blessed be Your holy name. Thank You for the wonder and awesomeness of all creation."

He kept looking out the window. Feeling more than seeing the earth buzz past.

Vera came back to mind, and he hoped she'd understand his being gone on Thanksgiving Day, just about the worst day of the year not to be with the family. He sure hoped that Cara would understand and be forgiving. After all, he'd been much more attentive lately. For several moments he thought about Vera and felt a nudge of apprehension. Surely she wouldn't have a problem with this flight. He swallowed hard.

Or would she?

24

VERA AND CARA PULLED UP IN THE driveway of their home. Evening had already fallen over Colorado Springs, and darkness covered the house and lawn. Vera turned off the car's headlights. "Cara, please help me take the groceries into the house. We've got quite a load to get for tomorrow."

"Sure, Mom." Cara opened the car door. "But you'll have to pick up the turkey. I think it might be a little heavy for me to carry by myself."

"Of course." Vera hopped out. "I'll open the trunk. I put the turkey in the back because it's so large."

Cara slipped out of the side door. "I'll get the grocery sacks out if you'll unlock the kitchen door."

Vera pulled a large box from the trunk and walked around to the back door where she set the box down. She unlocked the kitchen door and swung it open. "Go on in, Cara. I'm right behind you."

Cara put the grocery sacks on the kitchen counter and hurried back to the car. In a few minutes all the sacks were in the house, sprawled across the cabinet and on the kitchen table. "We sure have a lot of stuff for tomorrow."

Vera shut the back door. "We're going to have extra people, and that simply requires more food." She stopped and looked at her daughter. "You didn't tell anyone, did you, Cara?"

"What, Mom?"

"That I invited my parents and my sister's family."

Cara shook her head.

"You certainly didn't tell your father?"

"Mommy, you know I keep a secret."

Vera raised an eyebrow. "The whole thing is a big surprise for your father. I don't want him to know until the last minute that I brought my family from out of town. The celebration is special because your dad always enjoys a large gathering during the holidays, and he loves my parents. Since his father and mother died, he's become increasingly close to our family."

Cara started taking the groceries out of the sacks. "I like to surprise Daddy as much as you do. I can't wait to see the look on his face in the morning."

"He should be home by now." Vera looked at her wristwatch. "In fact, he should have been here when we arrived. I wonder if something happened."

"Probably one of those extra problems he keeps having at the police station," Cara said. "I'm sure he'll be home in a little bit."

For the next few minutes, Vera and Cara emptied the grocery sacks and filled the refrigerator. Vera finally looked at her watch again. "I don't understand why he hasn't called."

Cara glanced at the answering machine by the telephone. "Look, Mommy. The red light says we have a call waiting."

Vera frowned and walked over to the answering machine. "Let's see what's here." She pushed the button.

In seconds Sam's voice came on. Instantly Vera's mind drifted into a blank mode. Sam's words became a blur. She didn't need to hear anymore. She knew where the message would end.

"Looks like there's no way that I can be back in time for Thanksgiving dinner tomorrow," Sam's voice said.

Vera felt her rage starting to bubble up. She'd been here too many times before. Sam had not explained, talked to her, given any warning, nothing! He had simply disappeared into the sunset like the Lone Ranger riding off with his faithful sidekick Tonto! She and Cara were left standing in the dirt, covered with dust. Nothing but fools!

"Mother?" Cara's voice turned tentative. "Your neck is becoming red."

Vera turned her back on her daughter and started setting the milk cartons in the refrigerator. "Obviously I'm not happy about your father's sudden disappearance."

"Sounded like he didn't have any choice." Cara spoke no louder than a whisper. "He did try to call us."

"*Call us?*" Vera shrieked. "You think a message left on the recorder when we're gone is a serious attempt to talk with us about what he's doing?"

Cara's eyes widened.

"Let me tell you something, dear." Vera knew she sounded angry. "I feel like an abandoned dog left down at the pound to be shot." She stomped out of the room.

Cara bit her lip and watched her mother march into the bedroom. "Oh, boy! We've got trouble. Big trouble!"

The jet landed at the Lincoln airport and glided to the end of the runway. Within minutes, the airplane turned around and pulled up to the terminal. Sam Sloan stood up, poised with a briefcase in hand, ready to rush off the airplane. As soon as the passengers began filing out, Sam hurried into the terminal. Two policemen stood just beyond the gate, waiting for him.

"You're Sam Sloan?" The first officer shook his hand.

"Yes." Sam also shook the other man's hand.

"I'm Officer Malone, and my partner is Officer Johnson. We've got a car outside waiting for you. Sergeant Pile said to move you along, as we've got a great deal to do tonight."

Sam glanced at a telephone, then at his watch. "Well, okay. Let's get on with it."

The trio hurried down the hall and out of the terminal. Within a few moments, the police car's overhead emergency lights began flashing, and the Ford shot down the street.

"Where are we going?" Sloan asked.

"Sergeant Pile is down at the police station. He's trying to round up the officers who have the capacity to use some of those high-powered guns that we may need to hit these people."

"Anything else pending?" Sloan asked.

"One thing," the policeman added. "On the way to the police station, we're going to run by the courthouse. Sergeant Pile's already done the legwork, but we need you to swear out a search-and-arrest warrant for the operation tomorrow. Shouldn't take long."

"What type of warrant are we seeking?" Sam asked.

"We believe there's enough probable cause for a no-knock warrant."

"Thanks." Sloan settled back and watched the two police-men in the front seat. He felt good about what he'd heard.

After they got the warrant, the police car pulled up at the station and Sam hopped out, walking straight for the front door.

"Pile's there in the back," Officer Malone said. "Go on to the rear of the station."

Sam kept walking without turning around.

"Over there." The other policeman pointed to a door on Sam's left. "Go on in."

Sam opened the door and looked around the room filled with men. Some were in police uniform, while others wore jeans and casual clothing. A large athletic man stood at the blackboard, talking to the group. He didn't stop when Sloan came in.

"We need to make sure that all sides of the neighborhood are covered." The man's large neck hung over his shirt. His voice had the same intonation Sam had earlier heard on the phone. It had to be Pile. Sloan pulled out a chair and sat down. Only then did Pile's eyes show recognition.

"I believe Detective Sam Sloan from Colorado Springs has arrived," the sergeant said. "Am I correct?"

Sloan stood up, looking around the room, not registering any emotion. "Yes, I'm Sam Sloan."

"Welcome!" Fred Pile boomed. "Come on down here near the front of the room." He pointed to a chair in front of him.

Sam walked forward and sat down.

"We have a problem," Pile said to Sam. "Our surveillance people have determined that some of the gang aren't in the house yet. We're not sure where they are."

"I thought you had the entire gang under complete cover-age," Sam said.

Pile's face reddened slightly. "Looks like a couple of them slipped out the back door sometime during the day. We haven't yet determined where they went."

Sloan sat down and crossed his arms over his chest. "We're not going in until they come back. Right?"

Pile raised his eyebrows and shrugged. "Yeah, I suppose."

"What if they're not back by tomorrow morning?" Sam pushed.

"We haven't crossed that bridge yet," Pile mumbled.

Sam looked around the room. The attention of the officers had shifted. They were looking at him instead of Pile. A good moment.

"I'd suggest that we prepare to hit them at dawn, regardless," Sloan said slowly and smiled. "We might find those folks are still in there and our head counter missed them."

Pile stiffened. "I'm going to send you men out to get your weapons prepared for an assault, should we determine later in the evening that would be best. Get those rifles and protective vests out, and let's get ready. I'll stay here with Detective Sloan and Jack Downs for some ah . . . ah . . . executive decisions."

The policemen began filing out of the room. Malone and Johnson left with the group. As the last man went out, the door closed behind him.

"Now Sloan, you understand that I'm in charge here," Fred Pile said.

Sam smiled. "No problem."

Pile scratched his head. "I'm trying to understand the best and safest way to approach this assault." He frowned. "It's not easy to do this right."

"Certainly," Sloan said.

Pile sat down and pointed at the chair next to him for

Downs to sit down. "We've got the equivalent of a SWAT team assembled. You said that these people were a motorcycle gang. We aren't taking any chances."

Sam smiled. "Not much of a threat from these folks, but no point in exposing anyone to trouble. Sure. Sounds fine."

Pile's eyes narrowed. "Okay, Sloan. You got a few ideas?"

"Yeah," Sam answered. "I think I might have some things to add."

25

SAM GLANCED AT HIS WATCH AND REALIZED that it was past midnight. Even though Colorado Springs was in a mountain time zone and an hour earlier, he still didn't want to chance waking Vera up. Moreover, making a phone call would demand walking some distance to get out of the neighborhood, where he wouldn't be heard by anyone. He'd have to call home in the morning.

Sloan leaned back against an elm tree and looked through his binoculars. Today was Thanksgiving Day, so few people would pay any attention to who was coming and going on the block. The arrival of any stranger would be natural. He kept watching up and down the street, focusing on the target house.

Raymond Bench's dwelling looked small, and there hadn't been any movement inside for the last thirty minutes. All the windows remained dark. Bench's old dilapidated abode sat in the midst of two other seedy-looking rentals. The grass hadn't been cut in some time around all the houses. A couple of old cars parked in the driveways didn't offer much hope of ever starting up again. Pile kept saying that two people were still somewhere out in Lincoln floating around, but Sloan doubted it. The house looked locked up tighter than a drum.

Sam started walking back to the police car, thinking about other stakeouts he'd been on. The assignments felt the same, with an air of tension hanging over the officers before the assault. When he didn't know the other policemen or their level of competence, Sam found it hard not to be apprehensive about what the cops might do. Moreover, no one could guess when the subjects might try to make a break for it. Usually they had no idea they were surrounded by police and were taken easily, but sometimes there were problems.

In the spring of 1988, Sam had been part of a shoot-out south of the Springs in a town named Fountain. After hitting a savings and loan company on the edge of Colorado Springs, a couple of robbers had holed up in a condo on a back street, but had been spied by a neighbor who saw the holdup story on television. Apparently the two men got wind of the police coming and suddenly broke for their car, shooting at anything that moved. One of the Colorado Springs policemen stepped out to aim at the fleeing car and got hit in the back by one of his own men.

Sam could still see the thirty-two-year-old young cop lying dead on the street. One minute the man had been no more than five feet from Sam. Then *boom!* He was in the street. Gone. Sam cringed, seeing again the man's empty eyes staring straight ahead, the pavement pressing against his face, a pool of blood oozing out from beneath him. Sam shivered.

Sloan opened the police car door and got in the back. Pile turned around from the front seat. "I'd certainly expect those other two clowns to show up about now," he whispered.

Sloan said nothing.

"This town tends to shut down shortly after midnight. Even the bars close up then during the week. Nothing left to do. Nowhere to go."

Sam nodded but kept staring through the shrubs at the old white house.

"Guess we don't have much choice but to wait them out."

"Yeah," Pile said.

Moron! I'd bet they're all sound asleep while we're out here in this boondoggle doing nothing but waiting, Sloan thought.

In about ten minutes, Sergeant Pile said, "We've got more men watching this neighborhood than there are birds in the tree. Sloan, if you want to take a nap, we'll wake you up when anything happens."

"A nap?"

"Sure," Pike said. "I've got everything set up for the attack in the morning. Got an ambulance crew standing by with paramedics. Even alerted the fire department to be ready if something catches fire. If there's a child in there, we got the welfare people notified to take action."

"You've done well, Sergeant," Sloan said. "Doesn't look like there's much for me to worry about."

"Naw, Sam. Grab a few winks. You'll have plenty to do in the morning."

Sloan nodded and closed his eyes. He pulled the heavy coat more tightly around his neck to fend off any unexpected cold evening air. Within a few minutes he fell sound asleep.

Somewhere around 6:00, Sam woke up. Nothing had

happened through the night, and the first light of dawn was starting to break over the horizon. The street remained bathed in dim shadows. He unbuttoned the heavy coat and rubbed his eyes. Sam looked at the house again with his binoculars. No one inside seemed to be awake.

"Hey, Sloan," Sergeant Pile called from the front seat. "You awake?"

"Yeah," Sam said. "Ready to hit the house and get this over with? Cold out here."

Pile nodded. "The other two never came back."

"How much you want to bet me they're still in there?"

The sergeant didn't answer but looked with his binoculars. "No one's moved yet. Now would be a good time to hit the house."

"That's my feeling," Sam answered him. "Let's not waste any more time."

"We've got the street ready to be sealed off." Pile pulled out a .38 caliber Smith & Wesson Model 10 military and police revolver with a four-inch barrel. He checked to make sure it was loaded. "We've got plenty of people covering the alley if anyone tries to go out the back door. Seems like you and me ought to hit the front door first."

"Sure." Sam took out his snub-nosed Smith & Wesson pistol and cocked the gun. "I'm ready whenever you are."

Pile wiped the side of his face nervously. "You, me, and a couple of men will creep up to the front door. They'll bust it open. You and I will rush in."

"Okay," Sam said and opened the car door. "Let's go."

"We'll stay with the plans we made last night."

"Of course." Sam stood up. "The longer we wait, the more apt they are to wake up."

Pile nodded and spoke into his small telephone. "All right, boys, we're ready to hit the place." He glanced at his watch. "We strike in one minute." He got out of the police car and motioned to Sam. "Follow me."

Sam glanced around. The policemen picked up their weapons and started moving forward. Sloan looked up and down the street. Even the paperboy didn't appear in sight. Just another easygoing morning like any other Thanksgiving Day in America.

Sam started forward through the grass toward the old house. Dew covered his shoes. He stopped behind a car parked about twenty feet from Bench's house and checked where everybody seemed to be. Policemen kept inching toward the house on all fronts. To his surprise, he found Pile waiting behind him.

"You prepared to charge the front door?" Sam asked.

Pile nodded but didn't speak.

"Here we go!" Sam said and started running for the front of the house. The two policemen stayed directly behind him and Pile brought up the rear. "Hit the door!" Sam shouted.

The cops smashed the door with a small battering ram, and the front entrance flew open, crashing into the wall. Sam ran in with his gun pointed straight ahead at arm's length.

An old man with one leg lay sleeping slouched over a badly worn recliner chair. When the door smacked the wall, his eyes opened like the dead returning to life. The man's jaw dropped, and he abruptly sat up with a startled look on his face.

"Don't move!" Sam demanded with his gun on the old codger.

For a moment the white-haired man stared, frozen like a block of salt. Sam stepped past and took a quick look in the kitchen. He didn't see anyone.

Suddenly the old man grabbed an artificial leg lying beside his chair and started swinging it, catching the first policeman along the side of the head and dropping him on the floor. "I'll kill you, if it's the last thing I do!" He cursed and swung the leg in the opposite direction, hitting the second policeman still holding the battering ram. He slid to the edge of his chair with his good leg pouncing on the floor. "You ain't going to take me alive." The leg swung past again with a return sweep of the backhand, missing everyone.

The cop on the floor reached up and grabbed the man's artificial leg, stopping any more swinging. Pile rushed in and turned on the light switch.

"Bench!" Pile gasped. "Raymond Bench!"

The old man cursed. "I knew it was you, Pile, you rottin' worthless . . ."

The second policeman jumped on top of Bench, knocking him out of the chair. The two men rolled on the floor.

"Stay down!" the policeman yelled in Bench's face.

Sam had slipped next to the other door emptying out of the small living room, figuring it had to lead to a bedroom. He jerked the door open and leaped in with his gun moving back and forth across the room. A small man with loads of black fuzzy hair was half out of bed.

"Don't move or I'll shoot!" Sam yelled.

At that moment a naked woman popped up in the bed and grabbed for the sheets.

"Don't move!" Sam screamed again.

The woman let go of the sheets and fell back against the bedstead. The white around her black eyes turned into the size of quarters, and she held her hands straight up in the air.

The small man stood nude with his arms extended over his

head. "Don't shoot!" he begged. "I ain't armed." The only thing on his body was a wristwatch.

"One flinch and you're dead!" Sam yelled. He heard the back door smash open and cops yelling in the back rooms. "You even twitch and I'll fire."

The woman's mouth dropped, and she began shaking. Somewhere in the house Sam heard a child start crying. "Turn around," he growled at the man. "Put your hands against the wall." The man did as he was told.

"Okay, miss," Sam said to the woman. "You crawl out of bed slowly and put this robe on." He tossed a chenille bathrobe lying at the end of the bed. "Put it on, then keep your hands in the air."

"I ain't done nothing," the woman insisted.

"Don't talk!" Sam said firmly, waiting for her to get the robe on. "You both listen to me." Sam immediately recited the usual statement of their right to an attorney while feeling the pockets of the jeans on the floor, making sure no weapon was concealed anywhere. Sam threw the pants over the man's shoulder. "Put them on," he said.

The man slowly slipped his legs into the jeans. Sam tossed him a white T-shirt and he pulled it on.

"As I said, keep your hands on your heads and march into the living room."

"Yes, sir," the woman said, leading the way with her hands held up in the air.

Raymond Bench now lay on the living room floor with his hands cuffed behind his back. His long leg and bare foot stretched out on the floor. He wasn't talking, but reeked of whiskey. At that moment a small child came toddling into the living room crying. The little fellow immediately waddled over to the woman in the bathrobe, clutching her legs. He kept looking back and forth nervously, unable to grasp what was happening. The child kept whimpering.

"Go ahead and pick him up," Sam told the woman. "Just don't make any fast movements."

The police in the back of the house walked into the living room, driving three people in front of them. The large woman, wearing nothing but a man's long T-shirt, had her hands over her head, towering above the police in the room. An Asian woman and a young man followed her with their wrists cuffed together.

"Found the big woman sleeping on the back porch," the officer reported. "The other two were asleep in that small back room. We were on them before they even had a chance to move."

"Got 'em all?" Pile asked.

"Yes," the police reported.

"You expecting anybody else to be showing up here?" Sloan asked Pile.

Pile's eyes still had a wild look. He glanced around the group, counting the number. "Someone must have sneaked back in last night."

"Through our people out there?" Sam smiled. "You bet." He turned and looked at the young man he'd pulled out of the bedroom. "Who might you be?"

"Raymond Bench Junior," he said, rubbing his black beard and running his hands through the long strings of hair. The young man's black eyes looked frightened and on the edge of spinning completely out of control. Anger lurked in the corner of his glance.

Sam turned and walked up next to the young man, sticking his face only inches away from Junior's. "Raymond Bench Junior? Call you Jester, don't they?"

Raymond Junior looked away but didn't say anything.

"You want me to put this gun next to your head and ask the question again?" Sam said in a voice that meant business. "You'd be surprised at how quickly I could pull that trigger. Let's try it again. Do people call you Jester?"

With a slow sense of resolution, he shook his head. "Yeah, I'm the Jester."

Sam looked at Jester's arm again. "What's that you've got around your wrist?"

"My watch." Jester sounded sullen.

"Really?" Sam reached over and pulled the man's arm down, slipping the watch off of his arm. "Rather nice-looking watch for a guy like you, Jester." Sam flipped the Bulova watch over and looked at the back. "I'll be darned." He turned toward Sergeant Pile. "It's engraved. 'To Allan. Dad.'" Sloan looked Jester in the eye. "Your name is Allan?"

Jester looked away.

"I'd say you're wearing a fascinating piece of evidence. Looks like you took this off of your old buddy Al Henry. Huh?"

Jester stared out the window, refusing to speak.

"You know Al's full name was Allan?" Sloan spoke directly to Jester. "Looks like you took a little evidence of the murder with you."

The common-law wife looked at Jester intently. Her face had turned into a road map of fear. She obviously knew the ax had fallen.

Sam looked around the room. "You got any other people out there running around Lincoln this morning?"

Jester looked around the room and shook his head. "We're all here."

Sam smiled at Pile, who still stood in the living room with

a somewhat uneasy look on his face. "I'd suggest that we search the house and see what we can turn up. Sound good to you, Sergeant?"

Pile nodded mechanically. "Boys!" he shouted over his shoulder. "Come on in and search the place!" A team of five policemen hurried through the front door.

"Let's get them out into the police cars," Sam suggested. "Seem right to you, Pile?"

"Sure."

A couple of the policemen reached down and picked up Raymond Bench, standing him on his one good leg.

"When we came busting in, did you think we were trying to pull your leg a little?" Sam asked the old man.

Bench looked away angrily.

"Come on, Raymond," Sam persisted. "You were swinging that artificial leg like a baseball bat. We call that assault in police business."

"Sorry I didn't kill you," Bench hissed.

"You're a real mean dude." Sam smiled. "But I think your days at bat are over."

"Ain't saying nothin'." Raymond jutted his chin out and looked in the opposite direction from Sam.

"Whatever," Sam said. "Take him out to the car."

Police cars pulled up in front of the house about the time the cops started taking the seven people out the front doors. Old Raymond Bench said nothing. The gang members walked sullenly down the front walk and got in the cars. Jester stared at the sidewalk.

"Hey, Sloan!" one of the policemen called from the bedroom. "Come in here and take a look at what we found."

Sam walked into the front bedroom, filled with piles of

clothing. For the first time, he took a careful look around the room. The place had the feel of a pigsty.

"I think I've found something rather interesting over here in the corner." The policeman held up a blue jacket. "Look inside the collar." He held the coat out to Sloan.

Sam folded the jacket open. Across the top of the neck a name had been sewn into the lining. "Allan Hammond," Sam read the name out loud. "That's our boy. Looks like our raid was more than a success!"

"Hey, look at what's down here on the bottom," another policeman called from the closet. "Down here at the very back."

"What'd you find?" Sam asked.

The policeman walked out of the closet, holding a rumpled pair of pants and an old pair of shoes. "Sure looks like blood-stains to me."

Sam held up the pants. "Look a little large for Jester. Put this stuff in a bag and I'll keep it with me until this afternoon."

"Sure." The policeman picked up a plastic sack. "Looks like we sure won the war."

"Not yet," Pile said from the doorway. "You still don't have a body."

26

SLOAN STOOD ON THE FRONT PORCH AND watched the officers finish loading the gang into the police cars. A cold northern wind had picked up in the last thirty minutes, sending small swirls of snow down the street. The atmosphere felt like a storm might be rolling in.

Old man Bench ended up in a vehicle by himself, cussing and fuming like he might blow the whole parade apart. Sam glanced around the neighborhood. The raid had blown the usual Thanksgiving morning peace and quiet into a million pieces. Neighbors peered out of windows and stood in their yards, watching as if they were seeing the Fourth of July parade march by again. The residents looked more than a little surprised. They'd obviously remember this day for a long time.

Sergeant Fred Pile came walking up the driveway. "I think we've got this scene under complete control." The general sounded more like he'd turned into a private. "These people are ready to go to jail. Anything you see that's left? More searching to be done in the house?"

Sloan smiled. "Don't think so. You've accomplished a significant task."

Pile squinted and scratched his neck. "Naw, I haven't. I'll be honest with you, Sam. I have not done many of these assaults before, and I was half scared to death last night and this morning."

Sam studied the big man standing in front of him. The sergeant looked like a professional athlete, but during the raid he hadn't functioned like a tackle charging in to sack the quarterback.

"I tried to put the raid together right, but we truly needed you to make sure we hit the house correctly." Pile shrugged. "At least no one got shot."

"You did an excellent job," Sam responded. "Handled this raid from top to bottom like you'd done it a thousand times." He extended his hand and shook Pile's. "Listen. Anybody with common sense is frightened when the war begins. Your own men can shoot you accidentally."

Pile's face turned white. "I . . . I . . . I . . . didn't even think of that angle."

"Like I say, Fred, you did well."

"Thanks, Sam." Pile pointed to his police car. "Want to ride downtown with me?"

"Sure." Sloan slapped the sergeant on the back. "Let's put these strange characters under the bright lights and see what comes out of their mouths." Sam got into the police car, carrying the plastic sack with the pants and shoes.

"Okay!" Pile smiled and put his police cap back on. "Let's go."

Within fifteen minutes the police cars were back at the

ROBERT L. WISE   183

station. The cops booked Jester's gang as quickly as possible and set up the interrogation to begin soon.

"Sam, I know you're over here by yourself," Sergeant Pile said. "We're going to have Thanksgiving dinner this afternoon after we take care of these crooks. Why don't you come out to the house and dine with us?"

Sam smiled. "What a kind invitation! I'd love to. Thank you."

"We've always got more food than an army could consume. The missus will be delighted."

"Excellent." Sam looked around the station. "Could I make a quick phone call back to Colorado Springs?"

"Sure. Use the phone in that office over there." Pile pointed over his shoulder. "Charge it to us. We're glad to pay."

"I certainly appreciate the offer." Sam walked into the empty office and sat down behind the desk. In front of him stood an officer's pictures of his wife and children, who looked like good Nebraska people smiling back at Sam. "Good morning." Sam saluted the pictures. "Have a happy Thanksgiving Day." He picked up the phone and started dialing. When Vera answered he said, "Hey, it's me. I'm up here in Lincoln, Nebraska." No response came through the phone. "Hello," Sam said again.

"I can hear you," Vera said.

"Something's wrong?"

"No. Nothing." Vera cleared her throat. "Except that my parents and sister's family will be here shortly to enjoy Thanksgiving dinner with us, I have to prepare a huge dinner, and my husband is in another state."

"Your . . . your . . . *family's* coming?"

"You didn't understand what I just said?"

"Vera, of course, but no one told me we were expecting guests."

"You can jump on an airplane and get back by one?" Vera taunted.

"Dear, you know that's impossible."

"Then, Sam, I do have a big problem."

"You didn't get my message on your answering machine?"

"Sam, we found it last night. *Late* last night."

"Dear, let me explain what's happened. You see, this morning we raided the Jester's hideout and caught—"

"Sam," Vera cut him off, "I'm sure you've got a story that would simply curl my hair and make my eyes flutter for an hour. Unfortunately, I'm not interested in anything pertaining to your work. *Anything!*" Her voice abruptly rose in pitch and volume. "Do you understand me?"

"Vera, I didn't have any choice in the matter because—"

"Oh, I do understand. Sam Sloan never has any choice. He's simply swept along by the tides of fate to impossible ports that no one else's boat can reach. Not mine, at least. My, my, today you ended up in *Nebraska* of all places!"

"But, Vera, we caught this murderer and his entire gang. If I hadn't come up, they would have probably—"

"Gotten far away!" Vera cut him off again. "Yes, if you, Tonto, and the posse hadn't chased them into the canyon, no telling what would have occurred. Sam, *you listen to me well.* Our partnership in everything in this marriage is off. Forget me helping you solve criminal cases, pay your income taxes, take care of this house. You name it. *And don't call me back.*" Vera slammed the phone down.

The harsh click rang in Sam's ear like bells going off in his head. Sam could feel the strain pushing on the top of his emotional temperature gauge. He wanted to grab his wife and shake the living daylights out of her. For a full minute he stared at the phone and rubbed the side of his face. Finally Sam reached over and dialed again.

The phone rang for a long time.

"I told you not to call me back!" Vera shouted into the receiver.

Sam started to slam the receiver down but didn't. He took an extremely deep breath and remembered that exploding wouldn't get him anywhere. "Vera, I called yesterday but you weren't there. I had only a few minutes to board an airplane."

"You didn't call me *back* last night or first thing this morning!"

"I was in a stakeout with nearly the entire Lincoln Police Department. I couldn't call you without virtually destroying the entire operation."

"Sam, you're about to destroy the entire operation in this household!"

"Vera, I did everything I knew how to do."

"Sam, this is not the right time to talk to me." Vera's voice sounded strained. "I am trying to cook lunch for a small army, and the stove isn't working quite right. Do you understand?"

"Yes," Sam said hesitantly. "I'm sorry."

"Please, please do not call me again until *late* this afternoon. Good-bye." Vera hung up the phone.

Sam slowly put the receiver back in the cradle. *Life doesn't have to be like this. I go out and let the crooks shoot at me; I call home and the cook screams at me.* He slumped back in the chair.

Staring out the window, Sam thought about the battles he had seen between his parents. Jack and Alice Sloan fought like Trojan warriors. In the beginning, Sam gathered that his mother had been a rather quiet, reserved woman, but his father's drinking sprees changed her. By the time Sam was old enough to remember, Alice had switched from her soft approach to confrontation and become as aggressive as Jack. Sam hated those scenes and found them to be unforgettable. Now, one of those angry scenes slipped out of his memory.

"I don't care what your boss did to you," Alice had shouted across the kitchen at her husband. "You're not going to come home and do the same thing to us!" She leaned across the bare table and thrust a finger in Jack's face. "Understand?"

"Don't you scream at me!" Jack Sloan wobbled on unsteady legs. "I won't put up with any woman treating me like an inferior." He batted at her finger but missed and nearly fell over.

"And what will you do, Mr. Jack?" Alice stiffened. "Going to flatten me on the floor like you did those men down at the bar?" She reached down and pushed little Sam back against the kitchen wall, as if to make sure the boy didn't get hit.

Jack blinked slowly several times, weaving back and forth. "You don't think that I can?" His voice took on an air of superiority. "You want to see me try?"

Alice started backtracking across the kitchen toward the sink. "You mark this well, Jack Sloan. You hit me once, and it's the last time you'll ever have the chance. I'll take Sam and we're gone! Gone!" She shook her fist in the air. *"Got me?"*

Jack's head wobbled back and forth. His fist came up, moving around like as if wasn't sure where his target actually stood in the kitchen. "I don't like the tone I hear in your voice," he slurred, drawing back with a clenched fist. "You know what I think I'm going to do? Let me show you what I'm made of." Jack swung straight forward, and his entire body landed facedown on the floor. He didn't move. Out cold.

Alice had grabbed Sam's little hand. "Dear, you need to take a nap now." Her loud voice quickly began returning to a normal level. "Come in the other room and lie down, son."

She closed the door on Jack, who was stretched out like a slab of beef.

Now, Sam suddenly realized how much Vera and his mother sounded alike when they were both extremely angry. Each said harsh things they didn't really mean later. Cooling off was important for each of them to return to normal. He needed to remember that principle. Sure, Sam's father provoked the fights and his drinking always put the match to the firecracker. Mother had more justification than she needed to explode when those drunken bouts fired up, but time always tempered her. Vera generally did the same thing. Give her a little space and she became more moderate.

"Sloan?" Jack Downs stuck his head in the doorway. "You in here?"

"Yeah," Sam said slowly.

"Sorry to interrupt, but we're ready to start the questioning."

"I'll be there in a moment." Sam got up and walked to the door, again saluting the officer's happy family on the desk. "Have a happy Thanksgiving Day!" he repeated to himself.

27

SAM SLOAN STOOD IN LINCOLN'S POLICE station, staring at the asphalt tile that Vera always hated, pure 1950s. Rather typical old station house. Sam smiled and walked over to Sergeant Fred Pile, who was talking to Jack Downs and another officer.

"We usually interrogate the women first," Downs said with an authoritative air. "I assume that will be our procedure today."

Pile turned to Sloan. "What would be your suggestion, Sam?"

"I think I'd like to change things a bit, if you don't mind. I'm intrigued by the old man. Do you mind starting with Raymond Bench?"

Pile ran his tongue around inside his lower lip. "No, not at all. Actually the old man's the only one I know anything about. Got plenty of history with Granddad."

"You've got a facts sheet on the old guy?" Sloan asked.

"I can get one quickly."

"How does he feel about you?"

"Bench certainly wouldn't see me as his buddy. Of course, he hates me, but underneath I expect there's a considerable amount of fear," Pile concluded. "Raymond acts like one of those people who are afraid of all authority figures."

"Then we ought to start with Bench," Sam concluded. "See if we can rattle him."

Pile nodded. "Makes sense."

"We could do the good cop, bad cop routine on him," Sam suggested. "Since Bench doesn't know who I am, it would be natural for me to be the positive image. Fred, you'd make the expected bad guy."

Pile kept shaking his head. "Yeah, seems like as good a starting point as any. Why don't I go in and shake Raymond up with a screaming tough-man approach. Then you can come behind me like an old buddy stopping by to help Bench out of the sling."

Sam smiled. "You'd be surprised at what a nice cop I can be."

Jack Downs patted both Sam and Fred on the back. "Go get 'em, tigers!"

Pile turned to the other policeman. "Get the one-legged wonder boy and take him down to the interrogation room. Let's see what we can do." The policeman hurried off toward the jail cells. Jack Downs walked in the opposite direction.

"Won't take him a minute to get Bench in there," Pile told Sam. "I imagine he's getting close to sober by now."

"Yes," Sam said, "I'm sure the ride down to the station in the increasingly cold climate helped jar him awake, but I'm also sure the booze is still sloshing around inside of him."

"You do this tough cop, kind cop approach often?" Pile asked.

"Sure. More than occasionally."

Pile nodded. "Done it some, but this time the stakes are high. I truly hope this Jester character will confess to hitting the liquor store. Did you notice that he didn't say much?"

Sam nodded. "He's quiet and mean, but we believe that Jester is capable of fierce brutality. I don't think he'll break easy. Starting with the old man is probably our best routine."

"He's in the room," the policeman called from the end of the hall. "You men ready?"

"We're coming," Pile answered. "Keep your eye on Bench until we get there."

The policeman nodded and disappeared.

"I'll hit him first," Pile said. "If Bench is a tad bit on the inebriated side and we can slip into his fears, we might break him quickly."

Pile walked down the hall and turned the corner, with Sam following him. He nodded to the policeman and walked into the small room. Sam sat down in the corner. For a full minute, Fred Pile walked extremely slowly around Raymond Bench, saying nothing, but studying the old drunk as if he were a lion ready to pounce on the prey. "My goodness, Raymond. I haven't seen you in a while." Pile sounded almost as gentle as a Sunday school teacher. "A good while." Pile quickly rattled off Bench's legal rights. "You understand these interviews are both video- and audiotaped?"

Raymond Bench sat at the table holding his crutches. His hair appeared not to have been combed in days, and he still smelled like bad whiskey. Heavy bags hung underneath Raymond's bloodshot eyes. His hand shook slightly but his eyes stared straight ahead. Mean and hard.

Pile slapped the elderly man on the back. "Looks like you had a rough trip last night. Huh?"

Bench looked in the opposite direction.

"Having trouble hearing me, Raymond?" Sergeant Pile leaned next to his left ear and spoke softly. "Not loud enough?"

Bench turned the other way but didn't speak.

"*Not hearing me?*" Pile said in Bench's other ear.

The old man jumped as if he'd been hit with an electrical jolt and dropped his crutches on the floor with a loud thud. "Yes, yes! Of course I hear you." Bench's protest sounded blurry.

"Speak up, then!" Pile suddenly yelled in Bench's face, whirling Raymond around sideways. "We got lots of talking to do. You'd better be ready to start spilling your guts!"

Raymond squinted his eyes shut and gritted his teeth like he wouldn't talk in a thousand years. He crossed his arms over his chest, but Bench's whole body was still tense.

"Don't get tough with me!" Pile glared into Bench's eyes. "We're not playing with you anymore. We know the story. You read me? Time's run out on you, old man."

Bench glanced at Pile. For the first time, a look of fear gleamed from his eyes. His composure seemed to be slipping.

"We've been down this road before, but now the issue is much more serious than your drunkenness." Pile started speaking faster. "You don't think we broke into your house by accident this morning. We've had our eyes on you for a long time."

Bench's face twitched, and he got a firm hold on the table in front of him.

"You committed assault and battery this morning when we entered your house." Pile stopped circling the chair and sneered contemptuously at Bench. "By the way, we had a search warrant on the operation. The court already knows about you."

Bench took a deep breath.

"You realize that there's people all over this city who would think that I was doing the public a big favor by hauling you in here on Thanksgiving. Sorta cleans up our streets, doesn't it, Raymond?"

The old man rubbed the side of his face, but didn't say anything. He had definitely started to look frightened.

Pile stepped back and winked at Sam. Sloan moved over and sat down in front of Raymond.

"I'm Sam Sloan." He extended his hand across the table. "Glad to meet you, Raymond."

Bench slowly reached out and shook Sloan's hand. Sam squeezed strongly and smiled. Bench's hand went limp.

"I'm here to be your friend. Do you understand?"

Bench frowned and cowered.

"There are a few questions that I need to ask you." Sam kept smiling. "Ever been in José's Liquors?"

"No. Never." Bench shook his head emphatically. "Not once."

"We've got people that are witnesses to you being in there." Sam spoke softly and sounded concerned.

Bench blinked several times. "Oh." He shook his head. "Once I guess I did buy something in there."

"Oh, much more than once," Sam pursued.

Bench looked down at the table but didn't speak.

"The security camera got a picture of you," Pile suddenly yelled at Bench. "Don't you be lying any to us."

Sloan sat quietly, letting the effect of Pile's wild assertion settle. Bench had taken on a much more nervous disposition.

"Don't you dare toy with me!" Pile kept it up. "I want to get home and eat Thanksgiving dinner. You better talk now, or I'll throw the whole penal code at you."

Sam kept his calm composure. "Things don't look good, Raymond," he said quietly. "I'd like to be able to assist you in every way that I can, but you have to talk if I'm to be able to make any difference."

Bench swallowed hard. Light perspiration had already begun to form across his forehead. His head started to tremble, and he wiped his mouth with the back of his hand.

Sam pulled the plastic sack up on the table, taking out the bloodstained pants and shoes. Pile blinked several times, obviously not sure of what was coming next. "Ever see these before?" Sam asked.

Bench flinched and shook his head. "Never!" he said too dogmatically.

"Oh?" Sam kept smiling. "We found these in the back of your closet. Notice that one shoe is well worn but the other looks pretty good." He held up the better shoe. "Just like you'd expect from a one-legged man."

Raymond stared.

"Notice how bloody the bottom of the pants were when they were hidden," Sam continued. "I think that we know where the blood came from."

Pile's mouth dropped slightly, and he stared at Sloan.

Bench clenched his teeth.

"How much do you want to bet me that the bloodstains exactly match Johnny Gonzales's blood?" Sam bore down.

Raymond swallowed hard. "No! *No!*" he suddenly shouted. "I didn't murder the man, I tell you. *I didn't mean to kill the man.* It was an accident."

Pile stepped back from the chair as if he couldn't believe

what his ears clearly told him. Bench laid his head in his hands and started to sob. Sloan watched stoically.

"I tell you that I didn't mean to do it," Raymond cried. "The whole thing was nothing but an accident."

Pile looked over at Sam with a puzzled expression, as if he didn't understand what both men had obviously heard. Sam held up his hand for silence. Raymond looked at him with blurry red eyes.

"I'm new here, but I know you've been through a tough time, Raymond. I'll do my best to help you, but you've got to tell me the whole story."

Bench glanced up fearfully at Pile. "Don't let that gorilla hurt me."

"You've got to level with me," Sam said, pushing. "Just help me get the whole picture."

"I went in there to steal a little booze, that's all." Bench took a deep breath. "The man caught me at it, and I accidentally hit him with a bottle of wine."

"Certainly." Sam kept his voice low and filled with understanding. "You didn't mean to hurt him."

"I dropped the bottle of whiskey I thought was in my pocket." Raymond began talking faster. "Honest to God!" Bench cursed. "That worthless manager popped up out of nowhere at the end of the row and tried to catch me. I was only trying to get away from him."

"And you picked up a wine bottle?" Sam said.

"Exactly!" Bench's eyes started jerking back and forth in panic. "I don't know how I hit his throat. It was purely an accident."

"Of course." Sam moved closer. "Your son? Raymond Junior? The Jester." Sam's voice took on an even more appealing quality. "Jester waited outside in the car?"

Bench cursed violently. "No! Junior and that pack of idiots didn't even show up until later, don't you know. The liquor store job was purely my own doin'."

Sam slipped back across the table and looked up at Pile, now standing behind the old man. Pile's eyes were half shut, staring at the old drunk as if he didn't even know the man.

"Let me get this straight," Sam spoke gently, reaching over and turning up the volume on the tape recorder on the table. "You, Raymond Bench Senior, were stealing whiskey when the owner caught you in the act?"

Bench nodded. "Yes, sir."

"During your attempt at escape, you accidentally hit the man with a wine bottle and killed him?"

"It was an accident!" Bench whimpered. "Nothing more than a botched attempt to get out of the store."

Sam put his hand on the old man's arm. "Your son wasn't anywhere near the liquor store, and neither he nor his gang were involved in the robbery?"

"No, sir," Bench moaned. "Weren't anywhere near the area." He hung his head. "I done it by myself."

"And you'll sign a confession in this regard?"

Bench nodded slowly. "Yeah. You've caught me red-handed."

"Thank you, Raymond." Sam stood up. "Sergeant Pile will be back in a minute. We need to talk with several of our police officers. Write out what you've just told us. You can do that?"

"Yes, sir." Bench sniffed and took a deep breath.

Sam patted him on the back and walked out of the room, with Pile walking behind him.

The sergeant swore. "Can't believe my ears!"

28

THE MORNING SUNLIGHT HADN'T BROKEN into the police station's system of passageways. The hall remained dark with long shadows. Sam Sloan walked to the end of the corridor about thirty feet from the room where Raymond Bench now sat alone. Sergeant Pile's large athletic shoulders cast a long shadow on the white wall.

"I couldn't believe my ears!" Pile repeated, exasperated.

"Rather astonishing way to begin the interrogation process," Sloan answered. "The old man turns out to be your murderer, Fred."

Pile shook his head. "I still find it difficult to grasp. Apparently Bench thought we broke in solely to catch him."

Sam nodded. "Yes, appears Bench doesn't have any idea about Jester's crimes in Colorado Springs. We stumbled onto the truth."

"The killer of Johnny Gonzales was right under my nose all

the time!" Fred Pile kept shaking his head. "I simply didn't grab the one man I normally bring in on this type of crime."

"Happens that way, Fred. Who would have suspected a man with an artificial leg? By the way, what became of that leg?"

The sergeant shrugged. "Bench broke it when he hit our man. Looked like the mechanism was in bad shape. One of our officers brought it back to the station and put the leg back there in the evidence storage area."

Sam smiled slyly. "Sounds like we've put poor old Raymond out of joint for a good spell. At the least, we've solved your local murder case."

"Yeah, the newspapers will love this story, but we haven't done much on your case, Sam."

"I think we better try a different angle on Jester's gang. We need to hit the weak link in that chain as well. Once again we need to start by questioning the right person."

"Who'd you figure is our number one target?"

Sloan thought for a moment. "What have your people found out about the gang to this point?"

Sergeant Pile took a small notebook out of his coat pocket. "The big woman's name is Ginny Creager and they call her Big Gal," Pile said, reading slowly from his notebook. "We found her driver's license. My boys figure she's one tough customer. I don't think she'll talk very easily."

"Hmm." Sloan rubbed his chin. "What about the boy?"

"His name is Jack Alban. Seems to act tough, but I sense he's a coward. Nervous-looking guy."

"Got a soft center, huh? What about the Asian woman?"

Pile looked at his notebook again. "She says her name is Hoi Chin, but our computers aren't confirming the name anywhere yet. I think she's given us an alias."

"Another tough cookie?"

Pile shook his head. "Looks like Jack Alban may be our best bet if we're looking for someone to crack."

"Okay, Fred. Got another interrogation room?"

"Sure. Alban is already down there right now."

Sam kept rubbing his chin. "Let's go and see if I can put a little fear of God into our boy."

Pile beckoned. "Follow me." He started down the hall. "I'll watch and let you do the talking."

Sam followed the sergeant into an even smaller interrogation room at the other end of the hall from where Raymond Bench remained alone. Jack Alban sat on the other side of an undersized table. Several other chairs stood scattered around the room. Sloan quickly sat down in a chair across from the suspect and leaned across the table until he was eye to eye, four inches in front of Alban.

"Hello, Jack," Sloan said politely and extended his hand. "Nice to see you again." He shook hands.

Alban glanced nervously at both cops and leaned back as far as he could, but said nothing.

"I suppose you know that these interrogation rooms have video and audio recording equipment." Sam smiled. "Helps protect you." He laid an information sheet on the table. "I always begin by getting a few facts."

Alban stared at the sheet of paper.

Sam took a pen out of his pocket. "Just a few elementary facts that I write down." He immediately asked the questions in a friendly, casual voice. At the end of the page, Sloan read Alban's rights with an indifferent style, as if nothing important had been said. Sloan pushed the page aside. "I want to be your friend, Jack. Looks like you might need a buddy before this process is finished."

Alban stiffened, but he looked away.

"We have a significant amount of details to talk about with you, Jack. I'm sure you know why we raided the house this morning."

Alban looked around the room quickly, as if searching for help to pop out from one of the corners of the room. He glanced at Sergeant Pile, then looked away. "I don't know," he said under his breath.

"Don't know?" Sloan leaned even closer. "Come on now, Jack. Ever hear of Al Henry?"

Alban abruptly started blinking and looked away.

"Let me try the name again." Sloan's nose almost touched Alban's face. "Henry. Al Henry?"

"Don't know 'im," Alban mumbled.

"My goodness." Sam dropped back into his chair. "How strange. Your friends certainly didn't have any problem remembering poor Al Henry."

"My friends?"

"Big Gal. And the Asian woman you were picked up sleeping with this morning."

"What do you mean?" Al's face gnarled, and he started looking angry.

"I mean . . . that . . . they all knew about . . . all about . . . Al Henry. Knew a great deal about his death."

Jack didn't say anything, but looked at the floor.

"Alban, you're in a great deal of trouble," Sam said, continuing to talk in the same easy tone. "I don't think there's anybody left to cover for you, Jack. At least the women aren't of that turn of mind. They told us the whole story."

"Koo wouldn't squeal on me!"

"Koo?" Sam leaned back, letting the name float.

"Yeah, Koo Mae!" Jack pointed his finger rapidly at Sam. "She didn't say nothing."

"Koo Mae?" Sam looked up at Pile and nodded. "*Koo Mae.* You have confidence in her. I bet Big Gal rings with a different sound in your vocabulary."

Alban stiffened and didn't say anything.

"Big Gal has to look out for herself, doesn't she, Jack?" Sloan leaned back again, as if giving Alban all the space in the room. "Think about her dilemma. She doesn't want to end up doing a murder rap for Al Henry's death. Her problems tended to grease Big Gal's tongue."

"Listen." Alban leaned forward across the table. "She's the one who started everything by accusing Al Henry of stealing her junk. Big Gal is more responsible than anybody."

"Hmm." Sam raised his eyebrows. "You don't say."

Jack cursed at Sam. "Big Gal's got a big mouth, and you better take that fact seriously!"

"Lots of assertions come out of a big mouth." Sam sounded indifferent. "We're about to wrap this case up." He pushed back as if he might be ready to leave the room. "Big Gal signed off on a truckload of facts about her version of this story."

Alban rubbed his mouth nervously. "What'd she say?" He raised an eyebrow cynically. "What'd she say about me?"

"A significant amount. Jack, you'd better worry about telling us the straight truth. If your facts differ from hers, we'll certainly give you the benefit of the doubt and run everything you tell us down." Sam stood up. "Should you not have anything to say, then I guess we have no choice but to go with what Big Gal said." Sam shrugged. "If I were you, Jack, I'd certainly dig deep, because at this point the large woman has dug a coffin-sized hole for you."

Sam pointed toward the door and nodded to Pile. "We've got some other statements to take now. Doesn't look good for you Jack." He walked out, leaving Alban still staring at the floor.

Sam and Sergeant Pile walked around to the room next to where Alban sat and started watching him through a two-way mirror.

"What do you think?" Pile asked.

"He made enough mistakes to tell us that he's the man who will probably break first. I think we need to let him sit for a few minutes. Watch his eyes."

Pile peered into the mirror, watching Jack Alban stare nervously around the room.

Alban pulled a pack of cigarettes out of his pocket and lit up, a flurry of smoke quickly filling the air. The suspect kept drumming nervously on the small table with his fingertips and rubbing his forehead. He got up and paced around the room. Alban's glances darted back and forth nervously.

"'Jack Sprat could eat no fat,'" Sam quoted, "'and his wife could eat no lean.' We'll let our little man simmer over the fire for a few minutes, then go back in and see if he'd like to chew on a little lean for a change."

29

THANKSGIVING DAY FESTIVITIES AT THE Sloans' house predictably began with a table filled with magnificent food arranged like the composition of an artist's masterwork. The smoke from steaming mashed potatoes mingled over the table with the aroma of French-style green beans. A huge turkey sat in the middle of the table, basting in the glory of the midday sunlight. Greens, browns, reds, and yellows merged with the seasonal decorations on the table, reflecting the wide range of the colors of fall. The abundant style gave the appearance of affluence and opulence, a long way from the world of the first Pilgrims. Once everyone gathered around and had been seated, the eldest said the traditional prayer of gratitude, and devouring the feast began with earnestness. In thirty minutes, the pile of food settled in size and scope, while the happy family members chatted and joked as they continued eating.

Vera picked up the large plate covered with the remains of the Thanksgiving turkey. "Let's send the meat around the table again," she said. "We've got to finish off this bird before we stop."

"Yes, but we've got to save some for Sam," Henri Leestma said. "Have to protect my son-in-law, don't you know."

"Come on!" Vera glared at her father. "Sam can take care of himself!" She glanced around the table. The decoration of fall flowers in the center of the food lent an additional touch of beauty to the dinner, but didn't make up for Sam's absence. "He's more than capable."

"Ooh." Maria Leestma raised an eyebrow. "You still sound a little on the peeved side. Got a big spat going on?" She took the tray of turkey and passed it on.

"Daddy tried to call us before he left town," Cara said, without looking up from her plate, "but we missed him."

Vera glanced around the table. Everyone seemed to be smiling except Cara, who kept looking at her plate in an obvious attempt to avoid her mother's eyes. The spirit of Thanksgiving appeared to be alive and well with everyone but her and Cara.

"Oh, the tiff isn't that big a deal," Vera hedged. "Sam left town without giving me what I felt was proper notice. He only left a message on the answering machine."

Henri raised an eyebrow. "You weren't here?" He didn't wait for Vera to answer. "What else could your husband have done?"

Vera smiled. "Dad, you're *always* on Sam's side."

"I have to be . . . lest the women in this family overwhelm the poor man." Henri winked at his wife. "We men must hang together."

"Okay, okay! I shouldn't have gotten quite so angry," Vera admitted. "Sometimes these misunderstandings simply get out of hand before anyone knows what's occurring. I guess I essentially blew up a little quickly."

Cara looked up and smiled.

"That's what *all* of you think, isn't it, Cara?" Vera looked around the table.

"Daddy *did* call," Cara said. "He tried."

Vera shook her head. "I can tell when I'm outvoted. This whole family is clearly on Sam's side."

"Let's say that the good detective has our sympathy," Vera's sister Rachel Miller added. "Not getting into issues that we don't know anything about, we do miss our *friend* Sam."

"I hear you!" Vera held up her hands and answered good-naturedly. "I promise to be nice when he calls later this afternoon. You people win!" She started a plate of green beans back around the table.

Henri nodded. "Good. Tell my hardworking son-in-law that we drove up from our winter home in Phoenix especially to see him, but we know that his work is very important. No problem here."

"Daddy's going to catch a bad man," Cara insisted. "Maybe he's already got the killer in jail. My daddy always gets his man."

"That's certainly worthwhile," Rachel added. "Helps everybody."

"I'll get us some more rolls hot from the oven." Vera stood up with the empty bread plate in her hand. "Be right back." She walked into the kitchen.

Vera looked around her once lovely hand-polished kitchen. Stacks of dirty cooking utensils stood in the sink. Pans still sat on the oven surface. The room looked a mess, but she still liked cooking and didn't mind cleaning up the cabinet tops. She valued preparing food for her family. Nevertheless, something inside Vera had changed, although she couldn't put her finger on exactly what was happening.

Exactly why was Sam's leaving so offensive? Vera sat down at the kitchen table for a moment. The longer she thought, the more a new realization became clear. *The truth was that I wanted to go with him, to be right out there on the cutting edge! Obviously, Sam hadn't done anything wrong in flying to Lincoln! I felt cut out of the excitement of the chase and that's what angered me so significantly. I wasn't a partner in the pursuit.*

Vera got up and opened the oven door, pulling out the tray of golden brown rolls. "They're hot!" she called out. "Save room for what I'm bringing in."

"Room?" Henri yelled back. "We're reaching the saturation level!"

Vera dumped the rolls into the basket and covered them with a cloth napkin. She stopped and looked out the kitchen window as she so often did. The beauty of Pikes Peak towering over the town lent a majestic glory to Colorado Springs. The sight moved her in a new way, even though she had seen it so many times before.

From whence comes my strength? My hope comes from the Lord, who created that mountain. Oh Lord, give me the capacity and insight that I must have to walk down this new path that is opening up before me. Please forgive me for getting so angry when things don't go the way I want them to.

She opened her eyes and picked up the bread rolls. "Oh yes! Thank You so much for all that You've given me," Vera whispered. Vera walked back into the dining room and set them on the table. "Here's the rolls. Leave a couple for Sam."

Henri grinned at her.

Sam looked at his watch. "We didn't get much out of Big Gal or Koo Mae, but we've let Alban stew in that room by himself for the last forty-five minutes. Fred, you ready to go back in and see if we can finish cracking him? Jack looks very close to the edge. We can get Jester last."

Pile nodded and stared into the see-through mirror again. "We've got nothing to lose, and I'm starting to get hungry. Thanksgiving dinner is waiting at my house." He glanced into the mirror again. "Look at him. Alban appears more than a little apprehensive."

Fred opened the door to the interrogation room, and Sam walked in quickly. Jack Alban jumped, looking as though he'd suddenly been hit with a jolt of electricity.

"I see that you're still here, Jack," Sam began casually. "We've been clarifying the story of Al Henry's death with your friends."

Alban's eyes glanced back and forth between the two men, but he didn't speak. His mouth twisted downward, and beads of sweat started forming on his forehead.

"I've had a little time to check on your police record, also." Jack leaned back in the chair and smiled. "You've been a naughty boy for quite a while. Looks like you've done a little bit of everything from burglary to car theft."

"Nobody ever convicted me of stealing cars," Jack groused.

"You're lucky that you slipped by that charge in Denver, although you did spend time in a juvenile facility." Sam suddenly leaned forward into Alban's face. "You won't get by with killing Al Henry. We've got you nailed!"

Alban stiffened. His jaw tightened and his eyes widened. The man's breathing became heavier.

"We've been working on your friend Jester." Sam returned

to his previous easy, steady voice. "He didn't turn out to be nearly as tough as we had expected. Big Gal's testimony basically scattered his defense." Sam smiled and paused. "Jester talked! Looks like everyone's pinning the killing on your backsides, Jack old boy."

Alban stared at the table, but didn't speak.

Sam looked at his watch, then at Pile. "Fred, I don't see any point in wasting time worrying about what Jack has to say." He stood up indifferently. "Let's save our energy and simply charge him with first-degree murder. We've got enough testimony from the rest of the gang to hang him." Sam turned around and took a step toward the door.

"Wait!" Jack held up his hands. "Wait." He spoke more quietly. "I want to know what you say that my friends said."

Sam shook his head. "No dice, Jack. We didn't have the complete story an hour ago. We do now." He took another step toward the door. "I don't really need anything more."

"No!" Jack shook his head. "Let's talk."

Sam turned around slowly. "Sorry, Jack, this isn't an *us* proposition. Pile and I aren't here to talk. You're the guy who has the opportunity to speak. If you don't have anything to tell us, we have no alternative but to take what we've heard at face value."

"Okay, okay." Jack exhaled deeply. "I only did what Jester commanded me to do. He's the boss, you know how that works. If I didn't follow his orders, he might have killed me."

"Killed you?" Sam sounded sincerely concerned.

"Look." Jack nervously pushed his hair back. "Jester can get angry. Fly into a rage. When he does, you don't want to be on the receiving end because that's where people get killed."

"I don't understand." Sam frowned. "You need to be more exact."

"Jester has a strange tick. Some little problem will set him off like a firecracker." Jack shook his head. "Pain means nothing to him. Jester simply explodes and beats people to a pulp." He gritted his teeth. "The sight of blood does something strange to him. Makes the man crazy."

"That's how you killed Al Henry?" Sam asked.

"I didn't kill him," Jack insisted. "Jester did."

Sam looked at Pile. "You're going to have to be more specific."

"The whole problem started with Big Gal claimin' that Henry stole from her." Jack spoke slowly and deliberately. "She got Jester hacked off because he has this communist theory that we have to follow." Jack shook his head and smirked. "You know, the gang owns everything and you take only what you need. Stealin' violated the whole thing."

"Jester's father knew nothing about this killing?" Sam asked, to check Raymond's story.

Alban shook his head. "Nothin'. The old man just had a house we stayed at in Lincoln."

Sam stood up and rubbed his palms together. "I have the picture that you and Jester beat Al Henry twice." He started walking around the table in a slow steady pace. "Twice? That's correct?"

Alban nodded. "Yeah, once down on Fifth Street and then at the place we was stayin' at."

"Why the second time?" Sloan asked from Jack's back, still walking around the man.

Jack twisted, trying to see Sloan. "'Cause of Big Gal's huge mouth! She kept accusing someone of stealin' her stuff. The woman's nothing but trouble."

Sloan changed his pace and started back around Jack the way he'd first come. "Tell me what happened," he demanded in hard uncompromising tones.

Jack kept looking back and forth behind him to see where Sloan was standing. "She thought John-boy, you know John-boy Walton, done it. You know John-boy, the male prostitute that hangs around down there on the streets?"

Sam switched directions behind Alban again. "Done what?"

Jack turned back the other way, still trying to see Sloan. "Stole her stuff. Leather jacket. Motorcycle club badges. Junk." Alban twisted around the other way to find where Sloan had gone. "We beat Walton good, and he's the one who told us that Al Henry did the number on the gang's property."

"You're not lying to me?" Sloan said. "Making up a little story?"

"No! No!" Alban gestured aimlessly. "I'm tellin' you jist like it happened."

Sloan asked gently, "And you hid his body up in the mountains?"

"Yeah." Alban coughed. "Yes. Sure."

"Where?" Sloan yelled in his ear. "I want to know the exact place!"

"I was so scared that I didn't even look at what part of town we drove through."

"You don't remember anything? A street sign? A monument?"

Jack wrung his hands. "I couldn't even tell what day of the week it was."

"Nothing!" Sam pushed.

Alban rubbed his forehead and swallowed hard. "I . . . I . . . don't know." He shrugged. "I simply sat in the backseat. Koo Mae drove the car." Jack rubbed his mouth nervously. "The area was maybe twenty, thirty minutes out of town at the most."

"I want to know *exactly* how Al Henry died," Sam growled directly into Alban's ear.

Jack sobbed like a broken man. His face twisted in a painful stare. "We beat Henry," he said slowly. "Beat him unconscious in the basement of that old house we stayed in. Koo Mae came by with a car she borrowed from some guy down at the 7-Eleven store up the street. We drove Henry up into the mountains." He stopped and rubbed his mouth harder. Alban's eyes looked disconnected and out of focus.

"Keep going," Sam insisted, speaking softly in his ear.

"We tied the man to a tree," Alban said slowly. "Al kept bleeding and looked terrible. Tied him up." He bit his lip. Jack took a deep breath. "Jester had a knife . . . a long blade . . . he started cuttin' on Al." The color in Alban's face changed, becoming whiter. He looked drained. "The more Al bled, the crazier Jester became. Started stabbin' Al." Alban stopped and started weeping. "It was awful, terrible. I couldn't stand it, but there wasn't nothing for me to do but watch. Al started screaming, 'Don't kill me. Please stop.' But Jester went totally nuts. Started stabbing Henry everywhere. Cut open his coat. Cut on his chest. His arms. His face." Alban sobbed harder.

"Take your time," Sam said. "Make sure you have the facts right."

"Jester kept cuttin' on 'im. Stabbing him. Pokin' Al. Finally the knife tip broke off in Al's head." Alban again took a deep breath. "Don't know how many times that Jester stabbed Al, but he wouldn't stop. Finally Jester stabbed the broken knife into Al's heart and twisted it." Alban looked up at Sloan with tear-filled eyes. "That's when Henry died . . . I'm so sorry."

Sam patted Alban on the shoulder. "You never had the knife?"

"No, sir. Jester did the cuttin' and butcherin'. Blood made him go nuts." Alban rubbed his eyes. "No, sir, I only watched."

"Thank you." Sloan gently squeezed Jack's shoulder. "Your account of the killing helps us significantly." He nodded to Pile, and both men walked out of the room.

30

FRED PILE'S HOME PROVED TO BE A modest residence on Adams Street off the Cornhusker Highway and not far from Nebraska Wesleyan University. Dorothy Pile seemed to be genuinely enthusiastic about Fred's bringing Sloan home for Thanksgiving dinner. The rest of the family had come down from Omaha and Wahoo, making a houseful. The various and sundry members of the Pile clan turned the noon dinner into a belly-busting experience. People laughed, joked, and told stories. Once the massive feed had been devoured, the men drifted out on the front porch for cigars and conversation, while the women cleared away the dirty dishes. Sloan and Pile stood away from the others where no one could hear them.

"I saw you talking to your wife on the phone," Fred said. "I trust everything is okay back in Colorado Springs." The sergeant looked at his watch. "You're an hour behind us on mountain standard time."

Sam nodded. "Our phone call went better than I expected. Wives aren't generally too thrilled when their husbands disappear on holidays. Mine certainly wasn't."

Pile grinned. "You can bet that my wife wouldn't be happy if I didn't show up in my chair by dinnertime." He puffed on his cigar. "I'd say that we handled this whole raid rather well this morning. Grabbed 'em, slammed 'em in jail, and even had a confession before lunchtime." Pile blew smoke up toward the sky and sounded like the general again.

Sam smiled. "Sure. We got everything but the most important data that I came for. Nobody caved in to tell us where the tree is that they tied Al Henry to. Alban didn't know, and the two women's jaws stayed shut tighter than frightened clams. I don't expect Jester will give us any more information."

The sergeant scratched his head. "Yeah, those women are tough characters. Koo Mae never would admit that her name wasn't Hoi." He shook his head. "I personally talked with the Alice character, and she didn't do much more than sit there with a strange grin on her face. Claimed she didn't know anything."

Sam looked at his watch. "If I could get back down to the station and try to talk to Jester, I think I might catch the night flight back to Colorado Springs. Is that possible?"

"Sure." Pile puffed on his cigar. "We should be able to get these criminals extradited tomorrow if they waive extradition hearings. No reason for them not to go back."

Sam nodded. "We'd be delighted to have Jester and his friends back in the Springs by sundown tomorrow."

Fred laughed confidently. "We'd be happy to get all of them out of the state of Nebraska!" He patted his full stomach.

"How much time do you think you'll need for deposing Jester?"

Sam shook his head. "Hard to say. I need to give the interview some thought."

Pile checked his watch again. "Let's aim to ride back to the station house in, oh, say, fifteen minutes."

⊢━•━⊣

Sitting in the police car sailing through the peaceful streets of Lincoln, Sam thought about the man he was preparing to interrogate. What could have created a wild, frenzied killer who would murder at the sight of blood? Something undefined but horrible and horrendous in the childhood of Raymond Bench Junior or, at best, along the way. At the least, he had been physically abused as a child. Maybe even sexually assaulted. His head had to be filled with fearful images of psychotic proportions. If Sam's impressions were correct, was there any hope for such a man? Sam didn't know, but talking with Jester would take every ounce of skill he had. The young man probably couldn't be pushed anywhere.

Sam said little, thinking about the vast amount he'd discovered in the past week. From the moment Ape wandered into the police station on Friday night, Sam's life had been a rollercoaster ride. He wanted the free falls to stop and police work to even out.

Pile's police car pulled up at the station house which was relatively empty since most of the staff was on Thanksgiving leave. Only a skeleton crew would be maintaining the cells, and Jester was probably sitting isolated in a remote cell, wondering what had happened to the rest of his gang. Enough time had passed since the early morning raid that he might be in a more accessible state of mind. Sam slammed the car door behind him and walked into the police station.

Ten minutes later a police officer brought Jester into the interrogation room. Sam and Fred sat on the other side of the two-way mirror, watching the young man for several minutes. Jester's thick dark brown hair puffed out around his head and hung down his back. He wore an orange jail jumpsuit, looking like everybody back in the cells. The beard and mustache had more of a goatee look, but covered the bottom of his face. He sat at the table with a sullen, hard look of indifference.

Sam stared at the young man's fingernails, clearly chewed to the quick. Hidden forces drove something frightening in the man's emotions. Maybe a joint or two of marijuana helped ease the pressure sometimes, but obviously the need wasn't diminished. No matter how brutal Jester had been, his basic inner drive had to come from his own pain.

"Help me, Lord," Sam prayed under his breath. "I'm about to enter a den of turmoil and confusion with a violent undertow. I need all the help You can lend me." Sam shook his head. "Amen," he said out loud.

"What?" Pile turned away from the window. "What'd you say?"

"Just thinking out loud. I feel I ought to go in by myself. Why don't you stay here and watch what happens. Maybe a Lone Ranger approach will loosen our boy up a bit."

"Sure." Pile didn't sound as if he liked being left behind. "I'll watch from this side." He crossed his arms over his chest. "Think he's a psycho?"

"Don't know." Sam shook his head. "Sociopath? Yes. Real character disorder in this guy."

"Yeah?" Pile nodded. "Hmm."

Sam smiled. "Here we go." He picked up Jester's file and

walked out of the observation room, quickly entering the inter-rogation area.

Jester looked up without changing his expression. He stared at Sam with a blank emotionless gawk.

"Good afternoon," Sam began and extended his hand.

Jester stuck both of his hands under his armpits and clutched his chest tightly. He looked away without saying a word.

"I'm Sam Sloan." The detective kept smiling. "I don't think I've had the honor of meeting you before this morning."

Jester kept staring at the wall.

"I'd like to be of help to you if possible." Sam sat down at the table and pulled out the information sheet. "Mind if we fill this out?"

Jester shook his head. "I ain't telling you nothin'."

Sam kept smiling. "Let me read you your rights." He quickly covered the Miranda statement. "Of course, our con-versations are being videotaped for your protection." Sam pushed the sheet aside. "I thought maybe we could talk some."

Jester looked straight ahead with a stony gaze, not saying anything.

"The records indicate that your legal name is Raymond Bench Junior but you go by Jester," Sam began. "Which name would you prefer that I use?"

The man shrugged. "Jester, I guess."

"Thank you." Sam smiled politely. "Do you feel like talking some?"

"You've got to be kidding." Jester flipped his shoulders indif-ferently. "What else I got to do but talk to someone like you?"

Sam opened the file he had carried in and looked at the record for a moment. "I'm sure that you are aware of why you were arrested this morning."

Jester stared straight ahead.

"And I'm sure you've been concerned about the Al Henry murder in Colorado Springs for some time."

Jester didn't even breathe.

"I have the complete story in rather definite detail. I think we know fairly well what happened."

Jester took a deep breath, sighed, and shrugged.

"Care for a cigarette?" Sam asked. "Feel free to smoke."

Jester seemed to relax slightly. He pulled cigarettes out of his pocket.

"I've got the fire for you." Sam reached across the table and flipped a lighter.

Jester puffed until the cigarette lit, then leaned back in his chair, still not saying anything.

"Your friends were confronted with the facts in the case and took the opportunity to talk." Sam leaned forward and smiled. "We found the backpack and materials you threw in the portable toilet near the Lincoln city limits."

Jester stopped smoking and stared at Sam. His body tensed, and for a couple of moments fear registered in his eyes. "Ya don't say," he finally muttered.

"I am not threatening you, Jester." Sam spoke slowly and kept a smile on his face. "I want you to know that the evidence is overwhelming and puts you in a bad light. Do you understand the implications of what I am saying?"

Jester's mouth twitched. He nodded slightly.

"As I said, I am not in any way trying to frighten you, but what we have accumulated to date puts you in an extremely guilty position. I am sure that you will be charged with murder."

Jester's easy demeanor shifted, and he kept puffing on the cigarette without speaking.

"I am also sure that you've had many difficult and painful experiences in your life, Jester. I am not interested in adding to the heap that you carry on your back. If I can be of help, I'm here."

Jester eyed Sam suspiciously.

"What you need most is a friend. I'd like to try to help you."

"You've *got* to be nuts!"

"Let me say it again." Sam kept his voice on an even, non-threatening keel. "I'll do anything I possibly can to assist you." He sounded more like a therapist.

Jester looked away and stared at the wall, as if trying to avoid Sam.

For several minutes Sam sat across from Jester saying nothing. The silence became ominous and heavy but Sam didn't move. Eventually Jester lit up another cigarette and smoked it to the end.

Sam finally broke the ice. "You like motorcycles, right?"

Jester nodded. "Sure."

"Ever ride one of those big Harley Hawgs?"

"Couple of times."

"Lately?"

Jester looked disdainfully at Sam, then his face lit up slightly. "Not recently. Ain't been around anyone who had one."

"Lots of money in those machines," Sam said casually. "Big money."

"Yeah, as much as buying a car."

"I used to ride one," Sam said. "Really liked that powerful thrust you get when they're fired up on the open highway."

Jester pursed his lips and looked out the corner of his eye. "You had one of them big ones like a Road King?"

"Yeah, I drove it on the police force in Colorado Springs."

"Traffic man, huh?"

"For a short period of time, but I really liked driving the bike out on the long haul over the flat plains."

Jester nodded with more enthusiasm. "Get one of those bikes running out there up around eighty, ninety miles an hour and it feels like you're flyin'."

Sam laughed. "That's getting close to nearly leaving the ground and sailing off into the sunset. Know what you mean."

"Had a bike, a Fat Boy, a couple of years ago, but one of my people wrecked it. Ran my Fat Boy off a cliff north of the Springs."

"Totaled it?"

Jester sneered. "Left it down at the bottom of a canyon all twisted up like a ruined hunk of junk."

"Happens that way every now and then."

"Especially when you let idiots ride." Jester lit up another cigarette.

Sam abruptly changed directions. "What will you do if the state charges you with murder?"

Jester turned nervously in his chair. "I don't know," he mumbled. "Never been down this road before."

"Rather long and scary path to walk."

"Yeah." Jester twisted around some more.

"Like I said in the beginning, Jester, I'll do everything that I can to help you."

Jester rubbed at his nose nervously, pushing it back and forth above his lip. He didn't say anything.

"What can I get you right now?"

Jester eyed Sam suspiciously. "What do you care what happens with me? I'm the bad guy, ain't I?"

"I wouldn't call you bad, Jester. Troubled? Yes. If I can be of help, I want to try."

Jester looked hard at Sam. "I'm running out of cigarettes."

"What brand do you smoke?"

"Camels."

"I'll send some back to you."

Jester again eyed Sam cautiously. "I'll wait and see." He looked away.

"The Lincoln police will probably return you to Colorado tomorrow," Sam continued. "I would anticipate that you'd be back in a Colorado Springs jail by nightfall. Got any response?"

"Not much that I can do about that action." Jester slumped back in his chair. "At least I get a free trip out of the deal."

"I'll be there and still ready to help."

"*Humph!*" Jester exhaled caustically.

Sam leaned forward. "Would you want to tell me where you and Jack tied up that body?"

Jester jerked and swallowed hard but didn't speak.

"I think that information would be of significant help to your case." Sam smiled broadly. "You'll need all the help you can get."

Jester's demeanor instantly changed and he cussed at Sam. "Been helpin' myself for years. Just me takin' care of me!" His eyes blazed with fire. "Don't need no help from you or nobody else. Get me?" He jabbed toward Sam with his index finger, then fell back into the chair with his arms over his chest like steel bands.

Ooh! Sam thought. *Went too far and hit the wrong button.* "I'll be available if you need any assistance," he said. "Let me know."

Jester stared straight ahead, avoiding any eye contact.

"Okay." Sam smiled and stood up. "Camels? Right?"

Jester looked at the wall and said nothing.

31

MOUNTAIN STANDARD TIME GAVE SAM
an hour back on his return flight to Colorado Springs. The jet
glided over the flat plains of Nebraska and northern Kansas.
Flying on the cold, cloudless night, Sam could see dots of light
signaling the farm communities that he zoomed over. From his
window, the world looked deceptively peaceful, quiet, and
orderly. For the moment everything seemed in its proper place.

Sergeant Fred Pile had driven him to the airport and given
every assurance that Jester and his gang would arrive by Friday
afternoon at the latest. Pile sounded as if he'd even drive
them down in a pickup truck to get the crooks out of town.
Somewhat to Sam's surprise, Pile had turned out to be a decent
guy with but a few hidden quirks, a man who could be counted
on if the future demanded it.

Sam's thoughts drifted to Vera. What a difference between

how she sounded early in the morning and later that afternoon! Perhaps the war clouds had drifted to the south.

Vera didn't explode often, but when she did the blast went a long way straight up in the sky, which tended to set Sam off. When the two of them collided, the sight wasn't nice. But Sam felt that he had done better emotionally with everyone on this murder case, not blowing up but keeping his cool. In fact, he'd not even let Fred Pile have it when the sergeant acted like an overbearing slob. It wasn't easy, but Sam had definitely stayed on the clean side of any arguments or fights. To his surprise, Pile had come around in an accepting way, without even realizing that Sam would have liked to have poked him in the face a couple of times.

The airplane speakers came on, and the pilot announced that they would be at the Colorado Springs terminal in fifteen minutes. Sam checked his watch. He should be home by 9:30.

⊱⋙✦⋘⊰

Twenty-third Street proved to be a welcome sight. Sam even liked the flurries of snow. It felt as though he had been gone for half a century. Last night's snooze in the police car had helped some, but he was still ready for a good night's sleep in his own bed. The wear and tear of these out-of-town jaunts got old quickly.

Their home wouldn't be far ahead. Sam slowed down and started thinking about what Vera had said on the phone: "I want to be there with you where the action is."

Sam had to think about that assertion for a while. What had started out as an impossibility had turned into a challenge, and now Vera sounded as if she was ready to lie in the grass with an assault weapon in her hands. Even the hint of such an extreme boggled his mind. No question about it. Vera remained in a state of full alert!

Sam hit the button to open the garage door and pulled in, snow swirling in behind him. He hit the button a second time, and the door closed. Sam hurried into the house.

Vera waited for him in the living room, with the television dispatching the latest news. She gave him a big kiss.

"Welcome home, dear. Unfortunately, Cara's already gone to sleep, or she'd be here to get her hug."

"Vera, I'm sorry about how this trip worked out, particularly when your parents were—"

Vera put her finger on his lips. "It's all been said. You did the best you could. Mom and Dad are staying at the motel and will be glad to see you in the morning." She pulled him toward the couch. "Sit down and tell me where we are in this case."

Sam sat down on the couch and rubbed his chin thoughtfully. "As I told you, we caught the entire gang, and they'll be shipped back here tomorrow. That's no small accomplishment."

Vera squeezed his hand. "I'd say so! Must have been quite an attack on their hideout."

"Turned out that five adults and a child were staying with Jester's father." Sam laughed. "When the interrogation began, the old man thought we'd already pegged him as the killer of the liquor store manager! He confessed. Can you believe it? Jester's father killed the clerk."

"Excellent!" Vera snuggled closer to Sam. "What do you make of this whole scene?"

Sam took a deep breath and sighed. "On the airplane I thought about these people, a strange combination of strength and weakness, arrogance and fear. The gang believes that they look cool when they're actually a bizarre collection of individuals with severe emotional and legal problems."

"Sure."

"Big Gal looks like a fierce Amazon who'd be glad to stomp any man who wrongly crossed her trail. Rough, tough woman. Koo Mae's so obstinate that she won't even give us her correct name. And Jester's common-law wife, Alice, sits around holding their child, with a silly grin on her face."

"Jester?" Vera asked. "Tell me about that guy."

"He's a killer," Sam said slowly, "but I see something common in all of them. They're people who played with evil until the hooks of depravity were firmly set in their souls. Each of those gang members got pulled across the line so many times that eventually they belonged to the wrong side. Jester's gang is behind bars because they thought it was possible to do the devil's business and still walk away unscathed." Sam shook his head. "Well, it's certainly not!"

"Yes, you are so right. What a sad story."

"Sad *indeed*!"

"But did you discover where the gang left the body of that poor boy they killed?"

"I hate to tell you about that part of the story." Sam rubbed his chin. "We didn't discover one thing. No one either knew or confessed."

"You're kidding!"

"Wish I was." Sam abruptly yawned.

Vera straightened up and crossed her arms over her chest. "You've got the killers, but not the victim?"

"The coffin is still empty. The problem worries me. Eventually these criminals will get an attorney. If the lawyer is clever enough, we'll have a hard time in court, since we're claiming a victim whose name we're not even sure about. Everyone says his name is Henry; we say it's Hammond. Who knows for certain?"

Vera nodded slowly. "A big problem."

"Big!"

"We've got to find out where that body is." Vera ran her hands through her hair. "That's the next objective."

Sam yawned again. "Sorry. The lack of sleep last night is catching up with me. I'm starting to fade."

Vera nodded but didn't seem to hear him. "I've been thinking about this exact problem for days. It's why I wanted to see the map in your office. I don't think there's actually as many options as we think for where that boy's body is."

Sam frowned. "We're talking the whole state of Colorado . . . speaking metaphorically."

"Not really," Vera insisted. "Criminals often don't have a long attention span. They're impulsive. Want to get the action over and done with quickly."

"Yes," Sam spoke slowly, "that's true."

"I don't think that they would have driven more than twenty minutes to get rid of the young man."

"Yes . . ."

"And we're surmising that they would have gone as high as possible before they dumped him. Draw a radius around this area with roads taking you up as high as nine-thousand feet in twenty minutes. We're not talking about that many places."

Sam kept rubbing his mouth. "Hmm."

"On the map at your office, I identified the possibilities. Bear Creek Regional Park and North Cheyenne Canyon Park are close possibilities. Gold Camp Road runs through both areas. I'm sure they wouldn't have taken Old Cripple Creek Road through the Seven Falls area because of the possibility of being seen by a tourist. Of course, that rules out the Pike National Forest in the south."

"How about farther north?"

Vera nodded. "The Blair Bridge Open Space goes by Glen Eyrie, but the Navigators have their headquarters there, and they'd have to go by an inspection area to enter that land. Ute Valley Park is north, but I don't feel like the area is high enough."

"How about taking Highway 24 and going north of Manitou Springs?"

"The Rampart Range Road runs up into the Pike National Forest to the north, but it has to wind around near some tourist sights. The area's not a strong possibility, but could be."

"That makes sense."

"Once you start north of Manitou Springs, you've got to drive a ways to get out of the tourist area. After all, that entire area is filled with special sights and lots of tourists. I'm sure they wouldn't dump a body on the road going up Pikes Peak."

Sam leaned back against the couch with his hands behind his head. "You're postulating that there are only about two or three strong possible areas."

"I think so." Vera smiled confidently.

"Of course, that's still quite a good expanse of land."

"Far less than the entire state of Colorado!" Vera raised an eyebrow.

Sam laughed. "You got me. Let's sleep on the idea."

"Are you taking me seriously?" Vera sounded determined.

"Dear, if there's anything that I've learned in the last couple of weeks, it is that I need to take you *quite* seriously." Sam stood up. "Believe you me! I'll never underestimate you again." He leaned down and kissed her. "I've just got to go to bed." Sam shuffled toward the bedroom. "I can hardly stay awake."

"I'll be there in a minute," Vera called after him but didn't get up off the couch. She listened and heard Sam running water in the bathroom.

I don't think that dead body is nearly as far away as Sam does, Vera thought. *I bet they left that unfortunate young man someplace around here. Jester's gang is a bunch of drug users. Thickheaded. Not reasoning well. Hit-and-run types. It simply stands to reason that they wouldn't waste much time cruising around in the mountains at night.*

Vera got up and straightened the pillows on the couch.

Vera could still hear Sam rustling around in the bathroom. Their house looked fine after such a big day of holiday events. She'd enjoyed having her parents but still wished Sam had been there for their surprise appearance. She started to turn down the lights but stopped.

I've got to find some way to get beyond what we've talked about tonight. I need to figure out where they left the Hammond boy. Some twist to getting at this information that no one would expect.

32

FRIDAY TURNED OUT TO BE AN EXTENSION of Thursday's Thanksgiving Day. Particularly because of his time in Lincoln the previous day, Sam didn't work. He and Henri Leestma spent the morning hitting the shopping malls, while Vera enjoyed the day with her mother and sister Rachel. Cara tagged along behind, but by the end of the day was out playing with a friend. Whatever had been missed on Thanksgiving returned on Friday.

As night fell, Dick Simmons called from the Nevada Street station and left word that Jester's gang had been returned and were safely locked up. Raymond Bench stayed in Lincoln, accepting the hospitality of the Nebraska police system. Agents of the welfare department had been called in to care for Jester's children. The legal system was working quite fine.

Vera listened, making her own mental notes as events

unfolded. She was calculating what might next be needed to help Sam finish solving the case.

"Everyone's in jail?" Vera asked later that night as she brushed her hair before coming to bed.

"Simmons seems to be content with the situation downtown." Sam turned the covers back and punched up the pillow. "He feels that the gang's secure."

"I wonder if they talked with each other," Vera said. "You know, while they were being flown back here."

"I don't think so." Sam picked up the alarm and set it for the morning. "My impression is that each of the suspects has been kept isolated from the other. At best, they couldn't have exchanged more than a hello."

"So they don't actually know what each person told the police on Thursday?"

Sam shook his head. "No, they only know what we've let them think."

Vera watched herself in the mirror, thinking about what Sam had just said. The gang had to be worried about the nature of the exact story the police had extracted. No matter how tough they acted, inner doors had to be swinging off the hinges and their fears surging around like Halloween ghosts.

"Don't you think the gang ought to be afraid?" she called into the bedroom.

"Afraid?" Sam scoffed. "If they've got good sense, they'd be terrified. Underneath the bluster and the baloney, they know we've got them dead to rights." He stopped and thought for a moment. "Of course, the exception is Jester. I imagine he'll become more resistant as he realizes we've got his number."

"And what will that precipitate?"

"I imagine that Jester will turn into a stone wall."

Vera kept brushing her hair. "Interesting. Why did you come to that conclusion?"

"My hunch is that the man has been severely damaged. Probably got worked over brutally as a child. Jester protects himself with extreme resistance to authority."

"How about the rest? The women?"

"I'm not sure." Sam slid into bed and pulled the covers up around his neck. "Ginny Creager is also an extremely resistant woman. Large. Tough. Seems to like pain. Probably masochistic. Not very bright."

"And the Asian woman?"

"Much the same, except she's more intelligent. I don't think she likes the rough stuff like Ginny does."

Vera put the brush down. "What about that other woman? Jester's girlfriend?"

Sam thought for a moment. "I don't know what makes Alice tick. She doesn't say much, but leaves me with the impression that she might be the brightest of the entire bunch. She sits around with that strange smile on her face like she's not sure what's going on, but I think she knows every inch of what's happening." Sam rubbed his chin. "Don't know what her actual name is, but the woman calls herself Alice Bench. At least, that's the way we booked her for the time being."

Vera turned around. "She had a little boy, right?"

"Yeah. Poor little fellow cried most of the time."

"How did she deal with that problem?"

"Bothered her a great deal. Left me with the impression that Alice truly cared about that baby."

Vera turned back around and started putting skin cleanser on her face. "Interesting. Very interesting."

In the middle of the night, Vera awakened and glanced at the clock. Three o'clock was far too early to wake up, but her mind was working like a machine. Thoughts and ideas kept bubbling up from unseen corners of her past, mixing and intermingling with her conversation with Sam before they had drifted off to sleep.

Vera remembered growing up on a Dutch dairy farm in Shelton, Iowa. She had spent time with the cows and lambs. Her father's barn appeared, always long, dark, immense, even a little on the scary side. Out across the pastures, the meadows felt fresh, warm, and alive.

In the winter, when the barn felt like an ice factory, the meadows were covered with snow and cows walked through the cold. The softness of the fur of the lambs and cows always warmed and encouraged her. Most of the time the cows acted afraid, but she still spent many an hour wrestling with the little lambs and the goats. Playing with the livestock remained one of her warmest memories from the past.

She'd been there in the barn when the calving came in the spring and always remained awestruck, watching the little ones being born. The experience left her reeling with emotion. She was always ready to jump into a stall and get right in the middle of a delivery. Her father, Henri, always called that instinct "being an earth mother."

Vera was such an earth mother. Cara's grip on Vera's mind and emotions ran deep and firm, not unlike a cow with a newborn calf. That same fierce concern and protection for her daughter could push Vera slightly toward the edge. The fact that she sometimes got a little strange about Cara didn't make any difference. Earth mothers carried an inordinate concern to care for, to protect, to guard the little ones. The maternal drive stuck in her craw like a hook in a catfish.

Vera's remembrances touched something in her thinking, adding an unexpected tug to her reflections. Maybe here was a hint that she needed to pay attention to.

=====

The alarm rang for several moments before Vera realized it was time to get up. She slowly turned and reached out for Sam's hand.

"Got to roll out," Sam mumbled. "Your folks are going back to Arizona early this morning."

"Yeah." Vera sighed. "They're coming over here for breakfast. It would never do if they found me still in bed."

Sam suddenly kissed Vera and held her tight. "Let's just not get up and scandalize them when they finally show up."

"You bet!" Vera laughed. "We'd hear about being lazy forever."

"Oh, *pain!* I know you're right."

Vera threw the covers back. "Sam, I'm so tired. I woke up in the middle of the night."

Sam sat up and put his feet on the floor. "Probably thinking about what you'd fix them for breakfast."

For a few moments Vera didn't say anything but thought about what had been running through her head in those wee hours of the morning. She remembered again what had touched her and brought new insight.

"Guess I better take a shower." Sam stood up and reached for his bathrobe. "The hot water usually gets my engine started."

"What are you going to be doing today?" Vera asked.

"Of course, getting your folks on the road will take most of the morning, I expect." Sam shifted slowly across the room. "Got some errands to run, but I want to watch the big football game on television this afternoon."

"Hmm." Vera rolled over and looked out the window. "Yes, you'll have a full day." She heard the shower turn on. "And I think I know what I'm going to do."

33

THE THANKSGIVING SATURDAY AFTERNOON battle between the University of Colorado and Iowa State had been on the television for only half of the first quarter when Vera quietly slipped out the side door. Sam was settled so deeply into the game that he didn't notice the sound of Vera driving away. Sam Sloan had for years demonstrated an insatiable love for football that seemed to be the only thing that surpassed his preoccupation with "who-killed-who" down at the precinct. He wouldn't come up for air again until the fourth quarter had been officially declared finished.

Vera sped down Twenty-third Street until she reached the corner of Colorado Avenue, then went south toward Nevada. Traffic seemed lighter in the slush created by the snowfall, but multitudes of holiday shoppers filled the streets as they rushed from store to store on the busiest shopping day of the year. She didn't stop.

Vera finally pulled up in front of the county jail and turned off the car. She'd never been inside and felt reluctant to enter. She got out of the car slowly, but kept walking innocuously toward the front door. Vera quickly observed that in the usual pace of judicial business, any slack from the Thanksgiving holidays had disappeared.

For a moment she watched people coming and going, paying no attention whatever to her standing alone, trying to figure out what to do next. A couple of women sat behind a thick glass reception window, transacting the business of allowing visitors to enter and leave the visiting area. She watched them checking credentials, but didn't know either of the clerks. Vera did recognize a couple of attorneys entering the cell area and noticed that they had to pass through a metal detector, checking them out to make sure they didn't carry concealed weapons. The visitation process looked simple enough. Tell them your name, show your identification, and move on down to the gun detector gate.

Vera pulled out her driver's license and pushed it under the thick glass. "I'm here to see Alice Bench," she said clearly.

The receptionist looked at the license and frowned. "You're part of the family?"

"Do you know Detective Sam Sloan?" Vera asked.

The jailer nodded. "Sure."

"I'm his wife. I'm here to question the incarcerated woman."

The woman looked at Vera's driver's license again more closely. "Vera Sloan?" She read it out loud. "Well . . . Okay. Enter through the big doors and do what they tell you." She pointed over her shoulder with her thumb. "Go on back."

Vera smiled politely and hurried through the metal detector lest anyone stop her. The prison personnel treated her with professional kindness, and within five minutes, she was in a small room that only two people could occupy, waiting for Alice Bench to appear. Ten minutes later a young officer opened the door, and a thin woman walked in, dressed in the usual women's blue work suit. She sat down and smiled thinly but didn't speak.

"Alice?" Vera began. "Alice Bench?"

The woman nodded but kept her mouth shut. The smile stayed.

"My name is Vera Sloan, and you've met my husband, Sam, one of the detectives in Lincoln that arrested Jester? Remember?"

The woman frowned and turned her head slightly, looking at Vera out of the corner of her eye.

"I work with Sam and would like to speak with you."

The woman only nodded.

"I'm not here for any reason but to try and alleviate the suffering that is still going on because of Al Henry's death."

Alice Bench stopped smiling and took a deep breath. "What do you mean?"

"I've been part of a team working on this case from the beginning." Vera stretched the truth a tad. "I know how the young man's death occurred."

Alice kept staring at Vera, but the smile was gone.

"I've seen the data and know what the police have gathered as evidence in this case." Vera worked to sound sincere and nonthreatening. She watched Alice's eyes carefully. "The police have a solid confession from Jack Alban. Probably nothing else is needed to convict Jester."

Alice took a deep breath and flinched.

"You've not been involved in this sort of crime in the past, have you, Mrs. Bench?"

Alice shook her head. "I have not," she said factually. "You'll not find a police record on me."

"But we'd have to look under another name besides Bench, wouldn't we, Alice?"

Alice sagged slightly. "Look, Mrs. Sloan. Why are you here talking with me?"

"You have a small child, Vera. I believe that anyone who observed you in the last several days knows that you love little Georgie."

Alice's composure crumbled. "Where is he?" Her voice trembled. "What have they done with my baby?"

"The welfare department has Georgie in a good home."

"Are you sure?" Alice's voice trembled.

"If you would like, I will personally check on him."

"Would you please?" Alice's eyes took on a frightened twitch. "I'm concerned that he'll be afraid without me there to care for him. He's so small."

"I'm a mother, Alice. I know the care and concern you feel."

"Look, Mrs. Sloan—"

"Please," Vera interrupted her, "call me Vera."

"Vera, the little boy has never been away from me. Sure, sometimes we didn't take as good a care of him as we should have, but Jester and me are all that he's got." Tears began swelling up in Alice's eyes. "I don't want Georgie hurt because of something stupid that Jester did. Do you understand me? My baby shouldn't have to pay the price for my husband's sins."

"Yes, Alice, I understand, and that's why I'm here today."

Alice dabbed at the corners of her eyes. "Georgie means the world to me. I'd do anything to make sure that he's okay."

"I think I can help you." Vera scooted her chair closer to the table between them. "We know how Al Henry died and have ample testimony concerning Jester's role in killing him. You understand me?"

Alice nodded and looked frightened.

"You're a mother and know how painful it is when you can't help your child. What if Georgie was lost and no one could find him? How would you feel under those circumstances?"

"I'd be terrified, hysterical." Alice put her hands to her face. "Awful."

"Then you know how Al Henry's mother feels at this moment. Can you imagine the terror that fills this poor woman's heart, believing the boy's body is lost out in the forest?"

Alice nodded her head and sobbed. "I understand," she groaned. "I know."

"I need you to help me locate where Jester and Jack Alban left this poor boy. Can you do that?"

"I wasn't with them. Honest to God. I didn't have anything to do with that murder."

"I understand," Vera continued to talk softly and compassionately. "But you must have heard them talk about the place where they left the boy tied to a tree."

Alice continued to nod her head. "Yes . . . Yes, I did."

"We need you to help Al Henry's mother find the peace of mind that you want for yourself, Alice. Can you simply tell me where they took Al?"

Alice wiped her eyes and sighed deeply. "What will you do to Jester?" she asked.

"I have nothing to do with your husband, Alice. The testimony about Jester has already been gathered. My only concern is to help find Al Henry's body."

Alice slouched back in her chair and shook her head. "Koo Mae borrowed a car. Got it from the manager of the 7-Eleven Store on Bijou and Spruce. She couldn't keep the car long, so they had to take Al Henry to the mountains quickly." Alice started weeping. "They had beat Al into a terrible condition." She spoke slowly and painfully. "The boy looked like a bloody mess. Most of the time he was unconscious." Alice chewed on her knuckle and shivered. "The murder was so completely unnecessary. A stupid beating over stealing nothing but trash."

Vera didn't move, as if a subtle shift of her weight might break the spell of Alice's talk.

"I didn't know where they went at the time, but later I heard Koo Mae tell Big Gal that they went up Gold Camp Road into the mountains."

"Up North Cheyenne Creek Canyon?"

"Yeah." Alice nodded.

Vera struggled to suppress her emotion, as she felt she was about to explode. "North Cheyenne Creek Canyon! Good heavens, I nearly had it!"

"What?" Alice's eyes widened.

"We were solidly onto their trail!" Vera's voice became low and intense. "Please continue."

Alice started crying harder. "Koo said that she went through two tunnels winding around the mountains, then came to a place to park their car before entering a third tunnel. They dragged Al up above the road." Alice pulled out a tissue and dabbed at her eyes. "He never came back."

"Think carefully, Alice. How far did they take Al Henry up into the forest?"

"I don't know," Alice stammered and shook her head. "Knowing the shape Al was in, I'd guess they couldn't have dragged him more than fifteen or twenty minutes. After all, Al was a good-sized boy."

Vera glanced at her watch. "Mrs. Bench, I will find out about Georgie and bring you a report. I want you to know that today you've helped relieve the pain of another mother somewhere who loved her son as you love yours. Earth mothers understand these matters."

"Earth mothers?"

"Just a favorite term of mine." Vera smiled and stood up. "Thank you again, Alice. I'll be back in touch." She reached over and hugged Alice before hurrying out the door and gesturing for the officer to return Alice to her cell.

34

VERA DROVE HOME WITH GREAT URGENCY; every blood vessel in her body pulsated with new life and energy. An emotional charge of purpose and conviction made it difficult not to push the pedal to the metal.

When she turned into the driveway, the unmoved position of Sam's car made it clear that he probably hadn't even gotten out of his chair watching that blasted football game. She slammed the back door much harder than usual and tossed her keys on the cabinet.

"That you, dear?" Sam called from the living room chair without getting up.

"Who else would it be?"

No answer.

Vera poured a cup of coffee and walked into the gladiator's

den as the battle was going full tilt in the fourth quarter. "Interesting game?"

"Umm-hmm," Sam groaned more than said. "Hmm."

Vera sat down but Sam kept his eyes glued on the television and didn't speak. She sat there drumming her fingers on the chair, waiting for him to talk.

"Important moment?" Vera finally asked and set the coffee cup on the end table.

"Yeah." Sam leaned forward as if being magnetically pulled into the television. "Yes!"

Vera looked at him, saying nothing, as if she were an observer in a mental institution watching a catatonic slip in and out of a trance. No one spoke for a minute and a half.

"Yes!" Sam suddenly clapped and plunged his fist straight up into the air. "They made it! Got the third-down yardage! I know Colorado can score now."

Vera twitched her lips and drummed harder on the chair. The scene shifted toward the totally ridiculous. "Who's winning?"

"Colorado by two touchdowns."

"What difference is a third score going to make?"

"Helps the national ratings."

"Sam, I have something I'd like to ask you if it wouldn't be too great an interruption." Vera's voice carried a slight sarcastic twist.

Sam blinked several times and looked at her more completely than he had since she had come home. "Oh, sure." He smiled and leaned back in the chair. "What's on your mind?"

The sound of his question didn't set particularly well. What sounded like a condescending tone in his voice suggested that he was allowing Vera to come into the room during a football game. Big deal. He needed a little something to get his feet back on planet Earth.

"Sam, why don't you deputize me?"

"What?" Sam's mouth dropped. "What did you say?"

"I was thinking that it would be easier if I were a deputy."

Sam stared blankly. "I've missed something here."

"Well, if I'm going to find Al Henry's body, it seems to me that I ought to have some authority, since I'll be roaming around in the mountains."

"Al Henry's body?" Sam's voice rose. "What in the world are you talking about?"

"I'm going to be up there looking for it this week, and I thought that I ought to have some special authority . . . unless of course, you planned to go with me."

"Up there *looking* for it? Why in the world would you be wandering around in the vastness of the mountains haphazardly looking for a body?"

"Because I know where it is." Vera smiled innocently.

"You know *what?*"

"I said that I know where the body is."

Sam's mouth dropped again, and he slid to the edge of his chair. "How in the world would you have the slightest idea where Al Henry's body is?"

"Alice Bench told me." Vera sounded as straightforward and factual as if she were asking Sam if he wanted a cup of coffee.

Sam swallowed hard and he coughed. "You're telling me that Alice, Alice the common-law wife of Jester, told you where the body is tied to a tree?"

"Yes."

"When did this revelation occur?"

Alice looked at her watch. "About forty-five minutes ago while you were glued to the TV set."

Sam's mouth dropped again. "She called you up on the jail phone?"

"No, I went down to the jail and talked with her. Mothers have more in common than you might think, Sam."

Sam rubbed his chin and pulled nervously at the tip of his nose. "You're not kidding me?"

"Al Henry's body is up North Cheyenne Creek Canyon on Gold Camp Road above the entrance to the third tunnel. I'd guess about fifteen to twenty minutes' walking time from the tunnel's entrance."

Sam stared at her as if his mental faculties weren't working quite right. He pulled at his bottom lip. "You're serious, aren't you?"

"Absolutely. I'm ready to go look right now."

"Alice told *you*?" Sam's voice had a far-off quality.

"That's exactly what I just said. And if I'm the one who got the information, I certainly expect to be there when the body is found!"

Sam sat back in his chair without saying a word.

"I'd suggest that we call Dick Simmons and have him gather up several officers to help us." Vera continued talking as if she were now in charge. "The body may not be so easy to find. After all, a twenty-minute walking distance could cover a significant amount of territory."

Sam took a deep breath. "Yes, of course." He looked completely undone.

"I've been thinking about the weather that we've had the last several days. Quite possibly there's a great amount of snow up there at that height."

"Yes, of course."

"And I imagine it will be rather cold. Down around freezing."

"Yes, of course." Sam stood up. "I'll go and call Dick." He walked into the kitchen like a robot moving mechanically. "Right now."

Vera nodded. She didn't often pull Sam's chain so hard that he went into overload, but his preoccupation with football was nonsense.

+‑═━═‑+

Thirty minutes later Sam came back into the bedroom where Vera was putting their laundry into the dresser drawers. "I've made a number of phone calls," Sam said slowly. "For one thing the weather people are predicting a snow tonight and tomorrow for the mountains. I don't think that we've got much possibility of a significant search until the snow clears. Probably Monday morning is our best bet."

"You're kidding?"

"Sorry, but Simmons agrees. Eight o'clock Monday morning is the earliest we can start, if the snow has stopped by then. We'll need to wear snow protection suits and heavy boots at best. The temperature can get brutal at those heights this time of the year."

Sam sat down on the bed. "Vera, I obviously don't doubt a word that you've said but I need to make sure that . . ."

"That Alice told me where the body is?" Vera raised an eyebrow. "You think I'd come home and tease you about such significant information?"

"No, no!" Sam waved his hand as if to fend off the question. "I'm simply checking before we run a squad of men up there on that mountain."

"And I wasn't kidding when I said that I intend to be part of the search." Vera kept the same tone of seriousness in her voice. "We are both understanding each other quite well."

"Yes." Sam bit his lip. "I caught that part as well."

"So!" Vera abruptly smiled. "We're going on the search come Monday morning?"

Sam stood up, nodded, and started walking out of the room. "Yes. Monday morning."

Vera smiled. Her Sam-Wham speech hadn't been half bad.

35

SNOW BEGAN FALLING ON SATURDAY NIGHT and continued through Sunday morning. Much of what fell in Colorado Springs turned out to be light and sporadic, but the downfall in the high mountains proved to be significant. By Sunday night it was clear that Pikes Peak had turned completely white. No one questioned that the old Gold Camp Road would be covered. The glorious blue of the Colorado sky broke through on Monday morning, and the sunshine sparkled across the snow, covering the white like a million diamonds.

As Vera pulled on her waterproof ski pants, she glanced out the bedroom window. A jaunt across the mountainside wouldn't be easy this morning. She would need her heavy gloves and sunglasses. The exercise should be arduous.

"My woolen gloves in there?" Sam called from the living room.

"Look in your coat pocket!" Vera yelled back.

She slipped her feet into her snow boots and tightened the leather belt at the top. Today wasn't the time for any leaks, accidental slipups, oversights, whatevers. Vera knew that she had to perform well. The entire police force would have an eye on her.

"Ready to go?" Sam called again from the living room.

"Yes!" Vera stuffed a stocking cap in her coat and walked out of the bedroom.

At the Nevada Street police station, the Sloans left their car behind and loaded up in two police cars filled with officers. Dick Simmons drove with Vera in the front seat. Sam sat in the back with another officer. No one said much as they wound their way south to Gold Camp Road. The crew seemed to be a determined and silent group that knew what they were doing. Then again, maybe a woman outsider was the silencer.

Vera knew most of the officers in a casual way. They always treated her respectfully because, after all, she was Sam's wife, but things had changed on this Monday morning. She was the one who had the information that none of them had thus far secured. Vera felt that silence seemed to be the only way they could deal with the edge her conversation with Alice had given her.

In about fifteen minutes, they started down Gold Camp Road with the other police car behind them.

"You'll have to give me some advance warning," Dick said. "I expect we'll be going through some areas with heavy snow. It may not be easy to slow down quickly."

"We're in a four-wheel drive?" Vera asked.

"Yes." Dick kept watching the highway. "We shouldn't be stopped unless we run into a snowbank."

"Might happen," Sam added.

"You bet." Dick put both hands on the wheel. "Can't ever tell about the mountains at this time of the year."

"We must pass through two tunnels cutting across the mountains before we slow down," Vera said. "We're looking for the third tunnel."

No one answered, and the car settled into silence again, winding through the canyon as the grade of the road continued to increase. Vera leaned back and watched the beauty of the pine trees and snow-covered slopes go by. Covered with a dusting of white beauty, the scene looked like a winter wonderland.

"There's our first tunnel." Dick pointed ahead. "We're getting up to a good altitude."

"Excellent!" Sam leaned up against the front seat. "Vera, we're one-third of the way to our goal."

"Anyone ever been up here before?" the policeman in the back asked.

"No one's worked this area," Dick said. "Our action happens down in the valley."

The police car crawled through the tunnel and continued down the road at the same speed they had been going, but the crunch of the snow increased.

"I'm going to have to slow down," Simmons told his passengers. "We're the first car up here today. Looks like we're the trailblazers."

"How difficult is it?" Sam asked.

"Not a problem yet," Dick said, "but if we pick up a couple more inches, we might have difficult moments."

By the time the car reached the second tunnel, Simmons

was driving even slower and more judiciously. "How much farther?" he asked Vera.

"We must start watching for a third tunnel," Vera said. "We will want to stop on this side and not go through that last tunnel."

Dick slowed down a notch. "Okay, let's all keep our heads up." Again silence descended over the car.

"Look!" Vera pointed straight ahead. "There's our last tunnel!"

Simmons slowed the car. The tunnel's entrance stood surrounded by a rock wall to prevent dirt slides, and on the right side there seemed to be a small parking area.

"That's it!" Vera kept pointing. "Yes! That's the place where Koo Mae parked the car!"

Simmons pulled over to the side. The crunch of breaking snow sounded heavy and brought their car to a quick stop. He looked in the rearview mirror and waited for the last car to pull in behind them before he turned off the switch. Then the officers and Vera piled out.

"Gentlemen," Sam called the group together around him. "My wife, Vera, got the information on where this man's body is from Jester's wife. What instructions do you have for us, Vera?"

Vera took a deep breath as the freezing wind cut through her like a knife. "I understand they dragged Al Henry up this hill for something like fifteen to twenty minutes. I believe that we should walk approximately to that area and start searching."

Sam squinted at the sunlight flashing off the snow. "It's not going to be easy, boys. You each have a whistle. If you find anything that requires assistance or that we should see, simply blow hard and we'll come in your direction. Blow loud."

"Do we know that the story about this location is authentic?" one of the officers asked. Silence fell over the group.

"No," Sam said, "we don't. It could turn out to be a wild-goose chase."

Vera caught the glances exchanged among several of the officers. For the first time, she realized her credibility was totally on the line. The realization of what might happen if Alice had misled her hit Vera with an iron thud. Should this trip turn out to be an exercise in futility, she'd be done as Sam's silent partner. For the first time, Vera shivered.

"Let's go." Sam pointed up the mountainside. "Spread out up and down the slope and see what you can find."

"The snow's fairly deep," Simmons groaned.

"Come on, Dick!" Sam slapped him on the back. "Let's enjoy our little romp through the drifts this morning."

Simmons shook his head and started off behind Dick. Vera watched the men spreading out down the road and suddenly felt very alone. Sam had truly gone out on a limb for her. She needed to remember that he, too, could lose face if this search went badly. Clutching the whistle firmly in her hand, Vera started up the hill.

On all sides the drifts of snow quickly revealed the obvious: Al Henry could be so deep under a snowbank that they would miss him and never realize they'd simply walked past his body. Not only could Alice's story mislead, but the frozen terrain might prove to be a deceptive factor.

Vera marched for what seemed like thirty minutes before she realized that she hadn't checked her watch down at the road. She looked again at her wristwatch. Everything was now a guess. Off in the distance she could hear the officers punching and plowing through the snow, but no one had found a thing. She kept walking.

After forty-five minutes, Vera sat down on a large rock to

catch her breath. A creeping sense of discouragement had begun to work its way into her carefully laid plans. Never had she been part of anything more difficult than this search.

For the first time, Vera took a long careful look around the terrain. In some places the snow looked thin and barely covered the ground; it also stood six to eight inches deep over the rest of the ground. Probably the blowing wind made the big difference. Many of the piles and drifts appeared to be at least three feet high. Al Henry might easily be hidden in such a drift around a tree.

Resolutely, Vera stood up and started back the way she'd come until she returned to the road. A glance at her watch told her that an hour and a half had passed. No one had blown a whistle.

"Okay!" Vera talked to herself. "Got to keep moving so I don't get cold." She turned and faced up the hill again. "They would have dragged Al Henry some of the way," she mumbled, walking slowly up the mountainside. "Twenty minutes might prove to be much shorter than I thought." Vera slowed down and began timing herself much more methodically. "I think I overshot the area." She kept talking quietly to herself.

Vera watched the ground, looking for what might make a natural trail through the trees. Her steps became slow and sure, avoiding trees lying on the ground and seeking the easiest path through the brush. She paid attention to everything in front of her. In twenty minutes, Vera came to an open area.

If she'd been Jester, this area would seem to be a natural place to stop, but the snow covered everything in sight. Nothing protruded that looked strange or unnatural. Vera closed her eyes for a moment, then opened them slowly, trying to envision what the area must look like without the snow. Two three-foot piles had drifted up on both sides around the large pines that probably extended fifty feet into the sky.

Vera walked around the first tree, kicking at the snow, but nothing came up except a spray of white powder. She backed away toward the other tree, wondering if she ought to get a large stick and start poking into the snow. As she scooted backward, her foot hit something hard under the snow that didn't feel like a branch.

Vera used her toe to push away the snow and find out what was hidden beneath eight inches of snow. In a matter of seconds, she saw cloth, denim jeans. Vera dropped to her knees and pulled her gloves off as she feverishly felt around the cloth until she knew for sure that underneath was a frozen leg!

36

VERA BLEW WILDLY ON HER WHISTLE
until Dick Simmons burst through the trees behind her. "Okay!
Okay!" Dick waved the whistle away. "We can hear you over
the entire mountain."

Vera stopped and took a deep breath. "I think . . . I think
. . . I've found something." She pointed at the cloth on the
ground. "A body."

Simmons dropped down to one knee and stared at the blue
denim protruding from the snow. "My goodness, you've been a
busy girl, Vera. If this ain't our boy, then you get the prize for dis-
covering an unexpected body out here in the middle of nowhere."

Vera put her hand to her mouth. "You truly think it's him?"

Simmons began pushing snow aside, and the clear shape of
an entire leg emerged. "Looks like the real McCoy to me. I can
identify toes anywhere."

Sam Sloan hustled into the clearing, with an officer hurrying behind him. "Found something?"

"Looks like your little lady hit the jackpot, Sam." Dick kept piling the snow to one side. "Welcome to the frozen-leg club."

Other officers broke into the clearing. "What's happening?" someone called out. "Somebody got somethin'? Found the guy?"

"We hit the pot of gold at the end of the wrong rainbow," Simmons called back. "If there's a body attached to this leg, we're in business. Any of you boys care to give me a hand cleaning off this former specimen of humanity?"

Immediately, officers began pushing the snow aside around the tree, and soon the entire shape of a man's body broke into view. Vera stared, more horrified by what she saw than whatever it was that she had expected.

The man's shirt had been slashed to shreds and was splashed with dried blood that had now turned into dark brown stains. Over his arms and across the man's face, horrible slashes and cuts had ripped his skin open. The body looked like he'd been dropped into a meat grinder.

Vera suddenly felt quite nauseated.

"Well, Dick." Simmons turned to Sloan. "If this isn't Henry or Hammond or whatever the guy's name is, it's got to be his twin brother. Look at this guy. They cut him to pieces."

Sam pushed closer and started making a quick count of the wounds he could see. "Two, five, ten, twenty." His lips kept moving as he counted.

"Must have used a small knife," Dick concluded. "They slashed at him more than tried to plunge the blade into his body. Sure whacked up his face."

Vera ground her teeth, terrified that she would vomit. Everything in her wanted to come up, but she couldn't embarrass herself and Sam. She turned away and tried to get cold fresh air into her lungs, to still her churning stomach.

"I bet they stuck this guy thirty, forty times," Simmons concluded.

"Every bit of that," Sam answered. "The man is positively frozen like a rock."

"Look at that face!" Simmons shook his head. "Any of you boys ever see one worse than this?"

"Vera?" Sam said. "How'd you find him?"

Vera heard her husband's voice but wasn't sure she could answer. She took another deep breath.

"Vera, you all right?" Sam asked.

Vera was instantly aware that every one of the men was looking at her. If she blew this moment, she'd forever be a pariah to her gender. "Yes, I'm catching my breath." She turned around slowly.

Before her lay the ravaged figure of a young man frozen solid, with ropes holding him against the trunk of the large pine. His eyes had frozen shut, although one had obviously been stabbed. His jaw hung over at a strange angle. Maybe this was business as usual for the local cops, but it was a living nightmare for her.

Sam brushed the snow off the young boy's foot. "The shoe is gone," he muttered, more to himself than anyone else. "Can't study what he was wearing. Guess it doesn't really matter now."

"What are you talking about, Sloan?" Dick asked.

"Nothing. Just talking to myself."

"Look!" a police officer said, pointing at the head. "There's a piece of the knife broken off in this man's skull."

Dick Simmons bent over. "By golly, there certainly is. Looks like the knife broke."

"What do you do when you find a body like this?" Vera asked.

The men shrugged. "We call the coroner to come and get him," Simmons said.

Vera nodded. "He was a human being. One of us. A young boy. I think that we ought to pause and ask God to bless his memory, regardless of whatever his life might have been."

Sam and Dick looked at each other blankly. No one spoke.

"Doesn't that seem proper?" Vera asked, feeling tears welling up in her eyes. "He was someone's son." Vera's own words cut through her like the knife that had slashed Allan Hammond.

"Let's stop for a moment of silent prayer," Sam abruptly said and stood up.

The men took off their hats and looked at the ground. Eventually, Sam said, "Amen." A few murmurs of "amen" followed.

"Okay," Sam said, "let's cut him loose and prepare to collect any evidence. Dick can call the coroner on his mobile phone."

Vera started back to the car without looking over her shoulder. What had been an overpowering victory had turned into a towering defeat. She'd never seen a body before, except at funerals, where they'd been fixed up to look as if they might take a breath at any minute. Instead, she had found someone's son, sliced and cut to shreds with less sensitivity than butchers used in killing animals. Whatever joy she'd felt the day before in being Sam's helper had turned sour, very sour. Police work wasn't solving a mathematical problem, but picking up the pieces after the butcher went home.

Vera hurried through the trees, not wanting any of the men to see the tears running down her cheeks. She slipped and slid around the big pines, trying to stay ahead of Sam lest he be walking behind her.

How could such a horrible death have occurred? I never knew that the dimensions of evil could look so horrible! I don't want to see anything like that poor man's frozen face ever again.

The branches of the trees pulled at her thick coat, but nothing stopped Vera from feeling cold and raw inside. How could any parent endure viewing their child in such a torn condition?

A branch grabbed at her leg. Vera slipped and went spinning down the steep slope until she slid to a stop next to a large tree at the bottom. Her arm hurt and her knee ached. She didn't want to get up and go on. All the bravado and daring had been drained out of her. Vera lowered her head into her hands and started crying.

"Vera!" Sam came sliding down beside her. "Vera, are you okay?"

"I slipped and fell." Vera tried to suck up her tears. "I guess I didn't see the log in the snow."

Sam put his arm around her. "It's okay, dear. I know the boy's a terrible sight." He hugged her. "I understand. The men act indifferent because it bothers all of them." He squeezed her tightly. "I was proud of what you did and said up there."

"Oh, Sam! I had no idea the sight could be this terrible!" She cried freely.

"You never get used to these things, Vera. Bodies are the hardest part of the job." He stood and took her arm. "Let me help you down. Come on. Lean on me."

Vera struggled to her feet and walked along with Sam's arm around her waist. "Sam, I simply wasn't prepared for this."

Sam hugged her again. "Don't worry. You did well today, Vera. You found our man."

37

AT 5:30 MONDAY EVENING, SAM DROVE into the driveway at an unusually early hour for him. The car engine stopped and the front door slammed. Vera had been sitting in the living room for an hour while Cara worked in the bedroom, finishing her school homework.

"Hey, I'm home," Sam called from the kitchen. "Anybody here?"

Vera took a deep breath. "I'm in the living room."

Sam walked in and sat down. "You've had quite a day, dear. I guess you know that you're the talk of the entire police force."

Vera frowned. "Is it that bad?"

"Bad? Come on, you've got to be kidding." Sam laughed out loud. "Listen, everybody in the place is talking about the fact that my wife both sniffed out the location *and* found the body. You put the victim back in the coffin."

"And are they all getting a good laugh out of my running back to the car?"

"Vera, no one's said a thing about what you felt up there on that mountain. The fact is, nobody wants to talk about the ordeal. Simmons always acts tough and sounds nonchalant, but underneath he feels just like you do."

"You're putting me on."

"I'm telling you the straight truth. Everybody in the department is buzzing about your breaking the case wide open." Vera shook her head. "I've been sitting here for an hour and a half trying to make sense out of what I've seen today. To be truthful, I feel confused."

Sam sank back into the soft chair. "You've lost me. I thought solving cases made your headlights shine."

Vera looked at the rug for several moments, then out the window. "I don't know how to describe my struggle, but something inside of me is far out of place."

She rubbed her forehead. "Cara is growing up!" she said abruptly. "Do you realize that this little girl is standing on the threshold of adolescence? She's going to be gone before we even know it, Sam. Do you understand what this means?"

Sam didn't speak.

"I've always thought of myself as a mom, but in a short time I'm out of a job. The shift bothers me."

Sam nodded knowingly.

"And my husband is so in love with his job that he only shows up when it's convenient."

"Now, Vera!"

"You know exactly what I mean. Until I got tough with you, Sam, you slid around here like a bumper car. You came and went from this house more like a yo-yo than a husband."

"I'm trying to do better."

"You are," Vera agreed. "Yes, you are, and I thought that if I became part of solving these crimes, I could find a special place that would be closer to you."

"Good heavens, dear! What more could any human being want than what you've done this past week?"

Vera ran her hands through her hair and sighed. "This morning blew everything to pieces."

Sam rubbed his chin and nodded. "The sight of that body was terrible. Yes, I know. Probably the worst I've ever seen."

"Sam, I've seen bodies on television and in the movies, always assuming that the gore and bloody makeup looked like real life." Vera took a deep breath. "Nothing compares or is in the same league with how horrible real life can be."

Silence settled over the room. The house almost seemed to be empty, with the couple looking at each other like statues.

"I can't speak for anyone but myself," Sam finally said. "Every profession has its adjustments, and some of them never come easy. Sure, brutality and injury always bother me, but I guess detectives and undertakers develop a certain sense of humor, a caustic distance, a casualness about the horrible. If we didn't find some way to stand back from the tragic, we'd be consumed by the dread we feel. Examining a corpse is tough work, Vera."

Vera rubbed her cheeks. "I couldn't ever do it." She shook her head. "I love people and can't stand to see them destroyed."

"I love people too. That's why I keep doing my job."

Vera often looked for those Sam-Wham statements of energy and vitality that exploded from this remarkable man, but what he'd just said was one of those Sam-Whammers she'd have to think about for a minute.

"I don't understand," Vera finally said.

"Vera, let me explain how I operate." Sam stood up and started gesturing with his hands as the preacher did on Sunday morning. "I know that it may sound strange, but what I'm about to tell you I learned from reading Martin Luther."

Vera laughed. "Luther. The Protestant Reformation theologian? You're kidding!"

"Martin Luther taught the world that there's two kinds of government on this planet. One is the right hand of God and the other is His left hand. Got me?"

"No."

"The church and the good folks are God's right hand, running the world with goodness and truth. If people only believed what they heard on Sunday, there'd be no problems."

"So?"

"Some of them never go to church on Sunday or any day of the week. Ever! Jester and his cronies are exhibit A!" Sam started marching back and forth as he spoke. "God has to have a left-hand government, or the good folks would be eaten alive by the bad guys. People like me and Dick Simmons are that left-handed government. We clean up the messes."

He stopped and whirled around, pointing his finger directly at Vera. "If we didn't stop the Jesters in this world, everyone's playing cards would be called. We have to look at those mutilated bodies, or do you know who'd finally pay the real price?"

Vera shook her head.

"Our daughter, Cara!"

Sam stopped and hitched up his pants. "I guess I'm getting a little far out. I'm not preaching at you, dear, but getting back in touch with what makes me tick when the alarm goes off in the morning. I'm no preacher, but I believe that when I hit the front door of the station house, I'm doing God's will as much as anybody in America."

Vera didn't say anything, but kept staring at the rug.

"I think I need to go back to the bedroom and change my clothes. I've still got on these blue jeans from this morning's chase through the woods." Sam left the living room and disappeared down the hall.

He is right, she thought. *Somebody has to do the dirty work, but I guess I didn't expect it to be so dirty. Martin Luther? When in heaven's name did he read that theologian?* She shifted her weight around uncomfortably in the chair.

Vera got up and walked into the kitchen to start getting supper ready. She reached up for a pan, but when a hand grabbed her arm, Vera jumped like a rattlesnake had bitten her.

"Dear," Sam said, "let's eat out."

"Sam! I didn't hear you come in!"

"I don't have my shoes on yet. Tonight you're my guest as thanks for all that you did today."

Vera stopped and looked deeply into Sam's eyes. She saw nothing but genuine kindness. Vera suddenly hugged Sam fiercely. "I love you!"

+≈⋯≈+

An hour and a half later, Sam, Vera, and Cara returned home and settled in for the evening. Sam and Cara played a game for a while, then Cara drifted off to her bedroom, getting ready for bed. Vera read a book and kept to herself. Sam didn't talk and settled into one of his more contemplative moods. The offerings of the ten o'clock news weren't much, and the time to go to bed drifted in.

"Sam, I have a favor to ask."

"Sure."

"I promised Alice that I'd bring her a report on how the little boy was doing. Remember? The child she and Jester had. Georgie? Anyway, could I get a report on him?"

Sam thought for a moment. "Sure. I can work out something. I'll do it in the morning."

"I'd certainly appreciate it. If possible, I'd love to see the child and bring back a firsthand report. You got any more going on this case?"

Sam nodded. "We're trying to find John-boy Walton to collaborate the testimony we have on him saying Al Henry stole objects belonging to Big Gal or the gang."

"You're going to be successful?"

"Sure. Big Daddy Wilbanks owns that hot dog stand. I think we can scare a little information out of the old man and maybe find out where old John-boy is hiding."

Vera sat down on the couch. "I want you to know that you helped me out tonight. I didn't know what to do with all the pieces that fell at my feet this morning. I certainly am not ready to put them back together yet."

38

FOR A LONG TIME AFTER SAM HAD DRIVEN to the office and Cara had left for school, Vera thought about what occurred the day before. Monday's discovery collapsed something she had been building deep inside. Now she found herself faced with the dilemma of trying to resurrect whatever had been built all over again from the foundation. The pieces of the broken structure revealed aspects of her past that Vera didn't often visit. Like it or not, she had to think on those things today.

By midmorning Vera wandered out onto the porch and sat in the bright sunlight, letting the warmth cut through the cold morning. The snow had melted from the steps, and the porch top had dried. Vera sat on the cement and stretched her legs out on the walk. Halloween seemed like only yesterday, yet Christmas waited round the corner. Time certainly moved too fast on Twenty-third Street.

Rising out of the snow were old memories of life in Shelton, Iowa. The Leestma farm lay bathed in white for most of the winter and looked much like her own front yard. Ponds froze over and children skated.

Farm life had been good. Not that the work couldn't be hard and long—the summer harvesttimes certainly proved to be rough—but overall the work had a clean-cut purity to it. The Leestma farm had been a wonderful place for a child to grow up. Vera had watched her mother and father work together like a skilled precision team, making the farm run like a Swiss clock.

And what had it meant to grow up in that place in the country? Her mother offered only one answer. From time immemorial, the Leestma women had been wives and mothers. Was there anything more a woman could want? Not in her mother's opinion. Motherhood stood at the top of the ladder. That option had to be Vera's choice. Discussion closed. Question finished.

But any fool knew the times had changed. Not that motherhood had diminished, but life on the farm existed far away and in the past. Vera lived in a city filled with harsh realities that didn't exist in Shelton, Iowa, thirty years ago. Her choices happened in a world filled with mountains and airplane flights coming and going every hour from an airport only minutes away. Her alternatives were framed by the circumstances of the present, and she had to think of them in the harsh terms of the moment. The task wasn't easy.

Working as Sam's silent and unseen partner had popped into her head from out of nowhere, yet it was the most natural consequence of her childhood Vera could have imagined. Though it must have scared the liver out of Sam, the idea was nothing more than an imitation of her parents. The harsh, bitter side of the criminal justice system hadn't even entered her mind. The possibilities of pain had remained an abstraction.

No longer.

Now the question was whether she had what it took to go with the quest or whether she was at the end of the journey. If she meant business, other terrible sights awaited her. Could she adjust? That was the question. Sam might speak of undertakers casually, but did she want to rummage around in that world with them?

A couple of collies ran down the street, and Vera could see the postman delivering mail two blocks away. The street reflected the simplicity with which she had lived most of her life. Routine. Predictable. The expected unfolding at the usual pace, one day following the next.

Sam's world had always been the opposite. From the moment he walked into the police station, no telling what would be coming next. He stumbled over more mayhem and chaos in a day than Vera experienced in a year.

For the first time, Vera realized how much she'd let tragedy become an exciting adventure without ever stopping to consider what the struggle must cost Sam. She kept his work in the simple terms of solving crimes like algebra problems. Start at X in the morning, end with Z by nightfall, and come home with a paycheck.

If she really intended to be his partner, then she'd have to be prepared to chase the devil. Sam always talked about walking in the criminal's or the victim's shoes, symbolically trying to fathom the depth of the mind or finding the last heartbeat of a slain victim. Now the job had become clear. Though he didn't say the words, Sam had always been walking through forbidden territory marked with *No Trespassing* signs for the general public.

Tough stuff.

Vera had heard of doctors beginning their careers by being squeamish at the sight of blood. Occasionally someone would remark about how the best doctors often began as frightened orderlies. Still, the sight of the mutilated frozen body of Al Henry remained a horrifying memory. She couldn't escape the fact that people walked down the street every day with the capacity to perform such a horrible deed. Did she truly want to face the results of what these characters did?

Vera's answer was firm. No, she didn't want the job.

The wind picked up and shook the empty branches of the birch tree hovering over the front lawn. A pine tree next door rattled in the breeze when the gust swept down the street. Quiet returned and the mailman walked by, not stopping at the Sloans'. In the quiet, a new thought emerged.

Should she pursue this battle with evil whether she wanted to or not? The answer was equally certain. Yes, she should be willing to face the war.

One of the certainties that the childhood Sunday school classes had left with Vera Leestma was the hard-nosed Christian fact that you did what you were supposed to do, not what was comfortable. Every good farmer knew that simple truth. *Ought* always took precedence over *want*.

Vera took a deep breath and closed her eyes. She envisioned her father moving from stall to stall, caring for the family cows. She blinked. Her mother stood there pouring the milk into large jars, preparing for their sale of the town's people. *Ought* prevailed. She could think of a hundred examples. *Ought* always prevailed.

Vera stood up and went back into the house. She had no idea how long she had been out there on the porch, but the time had done an important work in her. A sudden burst of happiness hadn't swept over her, nor had she felt any mystical sense of resolution. Instead, a basic, clear sense of urgency prevailed. Nothing of value came without work, struggle, and often pain. Her choice would be shaped by the basic value that had always molded her life. The foundations remained strong enough that rebuilding wasn't necessary.

She picked up a dust cloth, made a few swipes across the bookcase, and tossed the rag back into the pantry.

At five minutes after two o'clock, the phone rang.

No one calls at this time of day, Vera thought. *What now?* She picked up the phone.

"Hey, it's Sam."

"Sam? My gosh, what's happened?"

"Happened?" Sam paused as if searching his memory. "Nothing. Nothing at all."

"Then why in the world are you calling at this time of day?"

Sloan laughed. "Tell me, is there a law against talking to my wife in the middle of the afternoon?"

"Well, no. No. Not at all. You simply never call me."

"I was just sitting here going over some of the pictures from yesterday, and I wanted to make sure you were okay."

"Oh, Sam! Don't worry about me. Yesterday morning caught me a bit by surprise. You know. Crept up on my unexpected side. That's all. Hey, I'm back in the saddle."

"Really?" Sloan's voice sounded mystified and surprised.

"Sure. Look, I wouldn't want to find a frozen body every day of the week, but I'll be up to it the next time one comes around."

"I am talking to Vera Sloan?"

"Sam, we all have our moments. Just one of those things. I'm fine today and ready to go."

"Well, more than I expected. Vera, want to go by and see Alice's baby tomorrow?"

"Of course!"

"Okay. I'll set it up and you can bring the woman a first-hand report."

"Sam, I truly appreciate your effort."

"My effort?" Sam's voice rose. "Vera, I am amazed at how you've recovered from that sight yesterday. And I might say, quite proud!"

"Thank you, dear. I'll see you this evening."

Vera hung up the phone, not feeling nearly as exuberant as she had sounded. Her shakiness lay hidden not far around the corner. She'd best keep those awful sights that caused her to quake and tremble out of sight for a while longer. At least she had made progress.

39

BY WEDNESDAY MORNING, DECEMBER HAD begun in earnest, and even the jail took on a more festive air. Sam led Vera down the hall, instructing as they went. She said little but listened carefully. Christmas trees and snowmen hung taped on doors now and were supposed to signal cheer.

"Remember that your being here is highly irregular," Sam said. "Jester won't have any idea about what's going on, but be aware that we don't do things like this most of the time. I got permission from the chief based on your finding Allan Hammond's body."

"I understand," Vera said, trying to sound professional. "I'll keep my mouth shut and just be an observer."

"I don't expect any problems with Jester, but you never know."

"Certainly."

"If he should go for you, I'll whack him on the head."

Vera laughed. "Now, that would be the event of the day. Your knocking the little man on the head with your gun."

Sam laughed. "Never had it happen before, but then again most of the past couple of weeks never occurred before either." He stopped and pointed at the door. "Jester's already sitting in there. You ready to start?"

Vera only nodded.

Sam opened the door and they both walked in. Jester sat in a plain wooden chair. He was wearing one of the jail's usual orange work suits that immediately identified him as a prisoner.

"Good morning, Jester," Sam began. "We're here to clarify a couple of facts with you. Like to talk a minute?" He didn't say anything that identified Vera, who slid into a side chair, saying nothing.

Jester stared at Sam, ignoring Vera. His dark eyes seemed harder and angrier than the last time Sam talked with him. After thirty seconds of silence, he looked away.

"You do know that you have the right to representation by an attorney." Sam reached over and switched on a tape recorder. "You've been given this right previously, but I want you to be aware of your choice in the matter."

"Can't afford one of them bottom feeders." Jester spit out the words.

"We can obtain a lawyer from legal defense funds," Sam countered.

"Forget it." Jester cursed. "My boat's sunk anyway."

"Ooh," Sam took on his professional therapist tone. "By the way, did you get those cigarettes I sent over?"

"Yeah. Thanks," Jester said reluctantly.

"Good." Sam kept smiling.

"You're shootin' with me straight that Alban gave you a

confession?" Jester wrung his hands together, his knuckles turning white.

"We got your wife, Koo Mae, and Big Gal to add to the testimony list. Everybody's protecting their own backsides, Jester." Sam smiled.

"Alice talked?" Jester pushed the mop of bulky hair that had dropped down over his eyes back around his ear.

Sam shrugged. "That's what we came to talk about, friend. Alice told us where the body was, and we found Al Henry on Monday. Of course, his actual name is Allan Hammond."

"I don't believe that Alice talked," Jester hissed. "You're setting me up."

"Does Alice love Georgie?" Sam asked again calmly. "Think she'd want to go on being the baby's mother?" Sam shrugged. "Consider the issue carefully. How much time in the jug would she trade to go on being with her child?"

Jester's mouth opened as if he were going to say something, then closed slowly. He sank back in his chair and glanced over at Vera. Cold disdain seeped out of his eyes.

"Alice talked with the person you're looking at." Sam pointed at Vera. "She found the body up above tunnel three on Gold Camp Road."

Jester jerked and his jaw tightened.

"Cold weather froze the body," Sam continued. "We have Al Henry down at the morgue in exactly the same condition you left him—tied to that tree with a piece of the knife still lodged in his head." Sam reached into his pocket and laid a piece of bloodstained rope on the table. "I cut this off of the rope you used to lash him to the tree. Recognize the cord?"

Jester stared at the rope lying on the table but didn't speak.

Sitting on one side of the room, Vera could study the action and reaction between Sam and Jester. She was keenly aware that Sam's casualness was a strategically practiced act. His seemingly casual conversation was filled with carefully measured words and phrases to maneuver Jester to the place where he wanted the man to be.

The *ooh* sound in Sam's voice had been used effectively on her as well. She realized that his intense listening posture caused the speaker naturally to say more than he intended.

Mostly Vera watched Jester's face. The beard and mustache must have required hours of careful work to look so bad. Then again, maybe he simply slept on the mess and got the same effect. His shaggy hair hung down Charles Manson style, and the man looked capable of murder.

Jester's hands were equally interesting. On one hand a dragon had been tattooed, its body winding across the top of his knuckles and down the side of his hand. Jester kept cracking his fingers and popping his joints from the sheer pressure of squeezing his hands so tightly. Vera could tell when Sam hit pay dirt because Jester's knuckles turned whiter.

"Does Alice love Georgie?" Sam asked again. "Think she'd want to go on being the baby's mother?"

Vera noticed that Jester's eyes narrowed slightly. Not much, but enough. He got Sam's message. In fact, Vera had the distinct feeling that the battle ended at that moment. Oh, Jester wouldn't quit easily and it might take several more interviews, but with those words Sam had brought the entire issue to a head. Jester knew that Alice cared more for the baby than she did for him.

They weren't actually married, but the baby truly belonged

to Alice. Somewhere along the line Alice must have pushed Jester to marry her and he had backed off. Therein was the issue. His decline had sealed the man's fate.

Jester finally reached over and picked up the piece of rope. For a few moments, he toyed with it, running it through his fingers. "So, Copper, what's the point of the conversation? You've got me. You've got the body. You think you've got the testimony. What's left?"

"A confession could save you many problems," Sam said. "It might change the way in which you are charged."

Jester's face didn't register any response, positive or negative. The man simply stared straight ahead.

Sam didn't speak.

Vera watched Jester's eyes but couldn't read any intent. In fact, the longer she looked, the more Vera realized that nothing seemed to be going on inside Jester's head. He had simply slipped into a vast wasteland that appeared to be emotionally empty, as though a piece were missing. A big piece.

The criminal began staring at the ceiling and finally looked down again. "That's all you got?" Jester asked Sloan.

"All?" Sam smiled. "We've got you dead in the saddle, partner. I was trying to give you a reprieve."

Jester laughed. "You're funny, Sloan, but I like you." He laughed again. "Come back and see me again when you've got another deal for me."

"I don't think we're communicating," Sam suddenly screamed into Jester's face. "Let me reframe it for you. I offered you an opportunity. If you don't want it, we'll fry you like a piece of bacon."

Vera's mouth dropped. Never in her life had she seen such an abrupt change of action. Sam had gone from the therapist to

Dirty Harry in three seconds. Jester looked totally shocked. His emotional state of distant cool had turned into total disorder.

Sam leaned into the man's face. "This is a take-it-or-leave-it situation." Sam abruptly stood up. "Got me?"

Jester sat in the chair with his mouth open, looking shocked.

"See you around, kid." Sam sounded hard and unforgiving. He pointed toward the door and beckoned for Vera to follow him. "If I were you, I'd give the whole thing a considerable amount of thought."

Sam walked out with Vera following him, then he slammed the door behind them. They walked down the hall to another room, and Sam shut the door quietly behind them.

"Good heavens!" Vera gasped. "That was like a tornado blew through!"

"That's how the technique works." Sam shrugged. "Jester's a sociopath, at best. Maybe a tad on the psychopathic side. I think that pain and suffering cut through the fog his brain stews in. Hopefully I shook him enough that he'll go back to the cell and slip toward rationality. We'll see."

"What if he doesn't?"

Sam scratched his head. "I'm betting on the possibility that this guy was abused as a child. The problem is that I simply don't have any idea how bad the abusive treatment was. It's possible that he may slide over into a black depression."

Vera shivered. "Sounds terrible, but I guess we'll see. Where to now, Sam?"

"I'd say that it's time to go over and take a look at that child you wanted to visit."

40

BY LATE WEDNESDAY AFTERNOON, VERA was ready to talk with Alice. Sam set up the interrogation, and Alice ended up in the same room where they had talked with Jester earlier in the morning. In sharp contrast, Alice sat fairly composed, looking like a chastened schoolgirl. Vera walked in by herself.

Alice brightened and smiled. "Hello," she said first.

"Good afternoon, Alice." Vera returned the smile and sat down. "They've been treating you well?"

"Oh yes. No complaints."

"Good." Vera kept smiling. "You've seen your friends in the gang?"

Alice shook her head. "No. I understand that they're in different parts of the building."

"I guess you know that we found the body."

Alice looked slightly surprised. "No, I hadn't heard that rumor. You really did?"

"It turned out that I was actually the person who stumbled over the poor boy covered with snow."

Alice's strange little smile reappeared. "Snow? My goodness. I don't think that anybody thought about that possibility."

"I want you to know that you did the right thing by telling me where the boy was. We were able to move the body back down to the morgue before there was any damage from animals. I'm sure Al's mother will be a very grateful person."

Alice kept the smile in place but didn't show any other emotion. She continued to look straight ahead, nodding slightly.

"I personally checked on your baby, Alice."

The woman's eyes brightened, and her smile widened. "Good! I appreciate your effort."

"I watched Georgie playing in the foster home where he's kept and found him to be happy and very well-cared for."

"That's so good to hear." Alice's demeanor shifted into a genuine expression of delight. "He looked in fine shape to you?"

"I can honestly tell you that the foster mother is an excellent Christian woman who cares for children because she loves them."

Tears filled the corners of Alice's eyes. "I'm so relieved. When the police came, everything happened so fast I didn't even have time to know what to do next. One minute the baby was with me, then I was handcuffed and put in the police car. I didn't even know where he'd gone."

"Let me reassure you that they took good care of Georgie in Nebraska, and the welfare people in Colorado have only his best interests at heart."

Alice dabbed at her eyes with a tissue. "I didn't like Jester's older son being with his father. Raymond Bench made me uncomfortable."

Vera nodded. "I understand."

"Now I need to tell you that I don't really know that older child of Jester's." The artificial smile crossed Alice's face again. "To be right honest with you, I never even seen the little boy yet."

"But Georgie is important to you, Alice?"

"Oh, very much so."

Vera leaned over the table. "Alice, I want you to listen to me. You know Jester is in big, big trouble. Right?"

Alice nodded, and the smile faded.

"You may have a chance to avoid jail time if you're straightforward and honest," Vera continued. "Your help in finding the body speaks well for you."

Alice kept nodding.

"I want to encourage you to walk a straight line with the law enforcement people, Alice. You have a chance to help yourself."

"Yes." Alice sounded meek and beaten.

"And I suspect you've got some bad feelings toward Jester because you and he never got married." Vera stopped and looked straight into Alice's eyes.

Alice swallowed hard and looked away, saying nothing.

"The fact that you've stayed single may turn out to be an asset. You're not tied to what happens with this man. You have a chance at starting over again. Think about the difference that can make for Georgie."

"I'm not sure I understand."

"At best, Jester will probably spend the rest of his life in jail,

Alice. If you can walk away from this incident, you and your child won't be tied to this terrible murder. You've got the possibility to become a productive person."

Alice rubbed the side of her face. "I come from a poor background. Never had much."

Vera shrugged.

"Fact is that I met Jester in a bar one night and that's how everything got started." She rubbed her neck nervously. "I didn't even graduate from high school. The baby was the first real joy I ever had in my life."

"Then you've got to guard that opportunity," Vera encouraged her. "I want you to know that I'll do everything I can to help you graduate from high school or whatever it is that you want to do."

Alice's eyes widened. "You mean it?"

"I most certainly do, but you've got to hold up your end of the bargain. You can't let Jester talk you into changing your story. You've got to stand tall and strong for the truth."

"Strong and true?" Alice took a deep breath. "Those are powerful big words."

"Yes, but they can reshape your life into becoming what you most want it to be."

"And the baby's just fine?"

Vera smiled. "Believe me, Alice. You don't have to worry about him tonight."

Alice extended her hand across the table. "Thank you, Mrs. Sloan. God bless you for what you've done."

Vera shook her hand. "I'm serious, Alice. You take care of yourself, and I'll be there to help you. Is that our agreement?"

Alice kept shaking her hand. "I'll certainly try to do my best."

"And if you call me, I'll be there to help in any way that I can."

"Thank you, Mrs. Sloan. Thank you." Alice's smile looked real and genuine.

Vera left the room and walked back to her husband's office, where Sam sat bent over his desk, scribbling away on the papers in front of him. Vera walked in and sat down, almost unnoticed.

"Ah, dear!" Sam jumped slightly. "Just finishing up the files on what happened today. Fred Pile called from Lincoln."

"Pile?"

"Yeah. You know. The officer in charge of the investigation there."

"Oh, yes. Yes."

"Pile thinks that Raymond Bench will be quickly convicted of killing the liquor store operator. Looks like the nasty old man is out of the way."

"Alice won't be sorry to hear that."

Sam closed the file and leaned back in his chair. "They had John-boy Walton downstairs for about an hour. He hasn't wanted to say much, but enough has leaked out that the stories the people in Jester's gang have told us are verified. In some ways, old John-boy has some responsibility for Allan Hammond's death. The whole thing is a sordid mess."

"I've certainly learned a ton of things from this crime," Vera said. "I've made a decision, Sam. I'm going back to college and finish my degree in criminology. I think that's one of the most helpful things I can do."

Sam straightened. "You're serious?"

"Yes. I lacked about a year and half on a B.A. degree when we got married. I can work out classes that fit with Cara's school schedule. I believe I'd grow significantly."

"I can tell you that you've certainly picked up a host of supporters down here this week, dear. If you need any references, there's plenty of cops that'll send a letter on your behalf." Sam finished shuffling the papers on his desk and pushed them into a neat stack. "That's what I'll have to take care of tomorrow." He grinned. "Or the next day."

"Or the day after that," Vera added. "Let's go home, Sam."

41

THE MONTH OF DECEMBER SHOT PAST, filled with the usual parties and gift exchanges. On the day after Christmas, a heavy snow shut down Colorado Springs, closing the airport for several hours and limiting travel on the interstate. However, by the end of the week, business became more routine around the police station, and the snow stopped. Vera enrolled at the University of Colorado at Colorado Springs, planning to start classes when the winter semester began in a couple of weeks. By January 1, the Christmas decorations started coming down and the new year began. Snow stayed piled up a foot deep over most of the town.

On the Tuesday after New Year's, Sam went back to work at the Nevada Street station. The new year always created a sense that things would be different, which, of course, they weren't. Sam put his overcoat on the rack behind his office door and prepared for the arduous job of completing the files piled up on his desk. Not his favorite job in life.

"Hey, Sloan," Dick Simmons called from the doorway, "you had a great New Year's Eve?"

"Yeah, we flew to Las Vegas and partied the entire night."

"You're lying. You probably didn't even leave your house."

"You're saying that I wasn't out at the shindig at the Broadmoor Hotel?"

"Definitely."

Sloan laughed. "Here I am, sane and sober. What more could you ask for?"

Simmons waved Sam away. "I never get a straight answer out of you."

"You never ask a straight question."

"Baah!" Simmons walked on down the hall.

Sam sat down and was reaching for a file when the phone rang. "It's the front desk. I've got an old friend of yours up here. This hulk says he's your buddy."

"Is his name Ape?"

"That's exactly what the clown said."

"Send him back."

"You're serious?"

"Sure. The guy's harmless."

"Yeah, if he don't step on you." The phone went dead.

Five minutes later, George Barnes's enormous frame filled the doorway. He stood politely with his beat-up leather hat in hand. "Yes, sir, Mr. Sam," Ape said, kicking off the conversation. "I'm here to talk."

"Well, it's my old buddy." Sam stood up. "Come in, Ape, and sit down."

"Thank ya." Ape shuffled across the floor. He wore an old

leather bomber jacket, clearly too small, over the same dirty overalls that looked like they hadn't been washed since Halloween. "Good to see ya, boss."

"Getting a little cold out there for you, isn't it Ape?" Sam sat down.

Barnes shivered. "Yes sirree. Mighty cold."

"You still sleeping in your van?"

Ape rolled his eyes, looking more embarrassed than anything else. "Well, boss. Saves me a heap of money, but sure is cold to wake up out there these mornin's."

Sam frowned. "How do you keep from freezing?"

Ape stuffed his worn black leather cap in his pocket. "You know I got that barbecue oven in the back. That's what the chimney's for. Helps some, but when it gets too cold, I jist switch on the van for a while and let the heater warm things up for a bit. Then I turns the car off."

"Hmm." Sam smiled. "Interesting."

"Just come by to say good-bye. 'Spects you don't need me no more."

"You're leaving town?"

The big man leaned forward in his chair and nodded. "Last night convinced me that I needs to be a-gettin' to a warmer climate. Been a-thinkin' I'd go back to California."

"Wouldn't freeze out there in Pasadena."

"That's how I sees it, boss."

Sam leaned over his desk and looked pointedly at Ape. "You wouldn't be playing Roy Rogers and disappearing into the sunset so that you won't have to testify against Jester and his gang, now would you, Ape?"

"Oh, no, sir!" Barnes shook his head, causing his shaggy beard to fly in all directions. "I wouldn't kid with you, boss."

Sam smiled slyly. "I bet you wouldn't!"

"Now, I'm a-bein' honest with ya."

"Well, the good news is that I doubt if anything that you might say will be needed, Ape. I think we've got Jester wrapped up in steel chains, ready to be shipped to some nice rest stop like the state pen."

Ape's face lit up. "Really think so?"

"Looks like Alice will walk, but Jack will spend time in there with Jester."

Ape nodded up and down. "He should, sir. Yes sirree, that bad boy deserves a lifetime in the big house." Barnes pulled on his beard. "How about them women? What happens with them?"

"I imagine that Big Gal will get off." Sam shrugged. "After all, she didn't do anything to Al. Koo Mae? I don't know."

"Yes, sir." Ape pursed his lips and kept nodding. "I'm mighty glad I came in here and spilled the beans on those guys. Wouldn't ever got it off my conscience."

"You did the right thing, George, and I appreciate it." Sam extended his hand across the desk. "I truly thank you."

A reddish tint swept across Ape's face, and his cheeks turned crimson. "Shucks. Just doing my part." He shrugged self-consciously. "Thinking about driving to Arizona today. Just see how far I can get, but I want to be where the weather don't freeze none tonight. Then's I can cruise on into L.A. tomorrow. Somethin' like that, at least."

Sam studied Ape's face. The big man's eyes looked tired and his features worn. Barnes's lifestyle might not cost much in money, but he paid daily out of his own hide.

"Jist don't want to spend another night 'round here, as cold as it's been and all."

"Tell you what, Ape. You call me collect every couple of weeks and I think you can go wherever you want. I simply need to be able to get in touch with you should the unexpected occur. Okay?"

Ape beamed. "Can't tell ya how much I appreciate the opportunity, boss. I'll call you every Monday morning."

Sam walked around his desk and sat down on the top. "Ape, where you going in life? You hop around like a summer grasshopper, but where is it taking you?"

The big man drew a deep breath as if to answer, but didn't say anything. Finally he mumbled, "I don't know. Guess I never did have any idea of what I was up to. Best I kin do seems to be just floating around."

Sloan reached over and patted Ape on the back. "I don't think so, George. I read something the other day that I think might apply to your life." Sam picked up a small Bible off the corner of his desk, thumbing through the pages. "They tell me that I'm not supposed to share these thoughts here in the police offices, but this will be just between us."

"Sure thing, Mr. Sam."

"In the Bible, the apostle Paul wrote these lines to the Philippian church. 'Forgetting what lies behind and reaching forward to what lies ahead, I press on toward the goal for the prize of the upward call of God in Christ Jesus.' Know what that means, George?"

Ape shook his head.

"I think these words are saying that we have to forcefully put the past behind us. Push ugly experiences out of our minds. Know what I mean?"

"Absolutely, Mr. Sam. Plenty on this murder case like that."

"And the way we do that is by setting our face toward what God has called us to be and to do."

Ape scratched his head. "Don't know much about religion and all. Didn't grow up in that sorta world, boss."

"But have you ever tried to talk with God?" Sam smiled. "That's how the Jesus Christ part helps. Because Jesus was a person, talking to God is like talking to Him. I simply tell the most important friend in my life what I have on my mind, then I try to listen to what He might tell me. I find that the prize of the upward call of God comes out of the cultivation of that relationship. Ape, maybe what you need in your life is to discover who God is."

Tears welled up in Ape's eyes. "No one ever talked to me like that, boss. I promise to take everything you told me right seriously."

"Good." Sam reached out and shook Ape's massive beefy hand. "God bless you, George. Take care of yourself."

"I'll pay attention to what you told me." Barnes kept waving as he walked away. "Yes sirree! I shore will."

Sam watched the strange man disappear out of the building. From his window he could see Ape climbing into that bizarre van with the black stovepipe sticking out the back window. The putt mobile fired up, and Ape disappeared into the traffic.

42

WHEN SAM RECEIVED A PHONE CALL FROM Bill Hammond, only two days had passed since Jester's trial ended on February 20. The murder victim's older brother called from California to talk about flying in to view the site where Al had been murdered. Sam agreed to take Hammond up Gold Camp Road on Friday.

Jester had received a life prison term, and Jack Alban would be next on the chopping block, with possibly an equally harsh term. Koo Mae might receive some sort of probation, but Big Gal and Alice would undoubtedly walk. Once the body was recovered, the gang's house of cards had simply tumbled.

The phone rang in Sloan's office.

"Hello. Sloan here."

"Sam, this is Gibbons over here at the county jail, Ward D-2, where the really bad guys stay. Got a special message for you."

"What's happening? Someone escape?"

Gibbons laughed. "That's fairly close. At least they're dead."

"Humph!" Sloan snorted. "Who died?"

"Actually, the man committed suicide. Your old friend Jester. Remember the killer? Raymond Bench Jr. hanged himself with his own bedsheet."

Sam bolted forward in the chair. "What did you say?"

Gibbons coughed uncomfortably, as if Sloan weren't responding as he had expected. "Actually, the suicide occurred last night right after our last bed check around midnight. The inmate in the cell next to Bench heard Jester gagging and called the guard. Of course, we got a jail paramedic to give cardiopulmonary resuscitation, but the man was in terrible shape. The medics rushed Jester over to Eisenhower Hospital, but he was dead on arrival."

Sam ran his hand nervously through his hair. "No question but that Jester's dead?"

"Come on," the jailer protested. "The hanging happened early this morning. Of course, he's dead! I imagine that by now they've started the autopsy down at the coroner's office."

"I see," Sam spoke slowly.

"Just wanted you to know that we've got one less beggar taking up jail space."

"Thank you." Sam hung up the telephone. For several minutes Sloan thought about Jester and his gang. Now the case had been closed on Jester by his own hand.

Jack glanced at his watch and realized that his wife and Bill Hammond ought to be there shortly. The trip up old Gold Camp Road shouldn't take long, then Sloan's work on the case should be finished.

Only moments later, Vera walked in through his office door. "Our man here yet?"

Sam shook his head. "Any minute and he should come rolling in." His voice dropped, becoming more serious. "You can certainly back out on doing this project, Vera. Going back up there where you had that terrible experience isn't in your contract."

"If nothing else, I need to go back," Vera insisted. "I need to climb that mountain one more time."

Sam rubbed the back of his neck and gritted his teeth. "Vera . . . there's something else I need to tell you. A few moments ago I received a telephone call that you should know about."

"Sure." Vera shrugged.

"Gibbons over at the jail called me to say that last night Jester hanged himself. He's dead."

Vera's mouth dropped. "You're kidding!"

"Afraid not. Looks like our killer has killed himself."

Vera dropped down in the chair in front of Sam's desk. "I'm completely flabbergasted. He's dead?"

"Hanged himself."

"Oh, my. What a shocker!" Vera caught her breath. "I guess his conviction pushed him over the edge."

"I saw that as an option, but I didn't think that he'd kill himself. Well, at the least, we have one less problem to worry about."

"I guess so."

Sam stood up. "Come on. Let's go down and see if Bill Hammond has shown up in the reception area."

The couple walked back to the Nevada Street entrance of the police station. To their surprise Bill Hammond was already sitting in the lobby.

"Mr. Hammond!" Sloan extended his hand. "Good to see you." Hammond looked to be about the same height as his brother Al, and his features bore a striking resemblance, but his hair had a short-combed appearance. Hammond wore a business suit and looked like a professional man.

"I appreciate your taking time to help me today." Henry spoke to Vera as much as to Sam. "Our family is trying to get closure on this entire episode, and it hasn't been easy. I thought that visiting the site of Allan's death might be a step forward."

Sam turned to Vera and explained, "Bill is one of three boys. He's the eldest, and Allan was the youngest. Larry is the middle boy."

"My brother lives in California," Bill explained, "but wasn't able to come with me. His job didn't allow an absence."

Vera shook his hand. "I'm glad to meet you, Bill. We hope that we can help."

Sam pointed to the front door. "Please follow me, and I'll drive us up the old Gold Camp Road."

"Thank you, Mr. Sloan." Hammond fell in behind the couple. For the first couple of miles, no one spoke. Finally Sam looked over his shoulder. "Rather paradoxical that you came in today, Bill. I just received notice from the city jail that Jester hanged himself last night."

"What!" Bill jerked forward. "You're serious?"

Sam watched the road but kept talking over his shoulder. "I guess the prospect of life in prison proved too much for our bad boy. He's been depressed for weeks and must have seen a life sentence as worse than a death penalty. He wasn't performing an attention-getting stunt. Jester did it right."

Bill Henry sighed. "Maybe it's better this way."

Vera kept looking out the window but didn't say anything.

"I brought Vera with us," Sam said, "because she found Allan's body. She can also help us identify the spot more quickly."

The car wound around the turns in the canyon until it came to the third tunnel, where Sloan pulled over. "Looks like we've still got plenty of snow up here, but there's less than what we found a couple of months ago." He shut off the engine. "Vera, please lead the way for us."

Vera smiled and started the hike. Bill Hammond said little. They slowly walked over logs and fallen debris up the steep slope. White snow had piled up deeply in some places, but proved shallow in others. Snow that had fallen before the first of the year still covered some of the ground.

"I'm surprised that I remember the path as well as I do," Vera said. "I think we should almost be there."

"I imagine that the discovery area is now covered with snow," Sam said. "At least it's not nearly as cold today as it was in December."

Vera pushed through the underbrush. "We're here, gentle-men." She looked around the open area. "There's the tree over there." She pointed to her left.

Bill Hammond stopped and took his hat off. The cold northern wind swept through the trees, and the sound of rustling leaves filled the forest. Stillness settled over the clearing.

"Al was tied to that large pine tree," Sam explained. "As best we can tell, Al was badly beaten back in Colorado Springs, driven up here, and then dragged up the hill to this spot."

"They beat him some more?" Hammond asked.

"Yes," Sam said.

"And cut him up."

"I'm sorry," Sam said.

"Allan wasn't a bad boy," Bill explained. "He just had a habit of being rebellious. Because Allan was the youngest, he tended to get away with behaviors that should have been punished. I think that's where the problems began."

"Mr. Hammond," Vera spoke softly, "I don't find any mention

of your and Al's father. Where was he during this troubled time?"

Bill shook his head. "My mother and father struggled with each other and had problems long before they married. They probably shouldn't ever have married, for that matter. At best, they didn't provide much of a home life for any of us. By the time I became a teenager, Dad had been gone from our home for a number of years." Hammond started walking back and forth in the snow, his face pained. "I guess Allan took their separation harder than any of us understood."

Vera nodded understandingly. "Younger kids can do that."

"Dad started coming around now and then. He'd take us out for a walk, a ride, anything that kept us entertained for a short while. He did that more with Allan than the rest of us. Even gave him a nice watch."

"There was competition among you?" Vera asked.

"No. No, that wasn't our problem." Bill took a deep breath. "The difficulty lay elsewhere."

"Yes?" Vera said.

"Two years ago, Dad picked up Allan for one of those typical afternoon jaunts." Hammond turned his hat nervously in his hands. "As they were returning, my father got sideswiped by a truck on the freeway. The result turned into a massive car pileup, killing Dad and severely injuring Allan."

"Good heavens!" Sam exclaimed. "No one gave us that piece of the story."

"Allan blamed himself for Dad's death." Hammond pulled out a handkerchief. "Shortly after he got out of the hospital, he became deeply depressed. Allan seemed to struggle with feelings of self-worth. He didn't have many friends and worried that no one liked him. After the car wreck, his self-esteem sank even lower. I think Allan only wanted people to love him and care about him. Unfortunately, he made that difficult for us. Eventually he started running away. On the last trip, Allan never came back."

"And that's how he got to Colorado Springs." Sam patted Hammond on the back. "I'm sorry, Bill."

"We were simply average people," Hammond explained. "Not that different from people all over the Los Angeles area. I guess Allan wandered off to the place where the water proved to be too deep for him."

"Tragedy isn't easily explained," Vera answered. "There's never a good reason why bad things happen to people who don't deserve them. Allan simply got caught up with the wrong people in Colorado Springs."

Bill shook his head. "I'll tell you this, at least Allan's disappearance and death have turned my life around spiritually. I started going to church and have found a new relationship with God that has sustained me through this black night."

"We're Christians," Vera said. "In fact, ever since you called Sam about coming up here, we've been praying that this time would prove to be a positive experience for you."

"Thank you," Bill spoke softly.

"I don't want to push an analogy too far, Bill." Sam walked closer to the big pine where a few pieces of rope still hung from one of the branches. "But we believe that Jesus Christ died on a tree, and we know Allan died at the foot of one. Maybe in that last struggle, God granted him the peace that he needed to leave this world. Obviously, the hand of God has been upon this investigation, bringing it to a quick conclusion."

Bill Hammond nodded but didn't say anything. He wiped his eyes.

"Would you like for me to say a prayer?" Sam asked.

"Please," Bill mumbled.

"Maybe something that I learned at church would help." Sam closed his eyes and folded his hands. "Father in heaven, we affirm that You are our shepherd. We shall not want. You make us to lie down in green pastures and lead us beside quiet waters. Please, today restore our souls and guide us in the paths of righteousness for Your name's sake. Even though we have to walk through the valley of the shadow of death, we will not fear evil because You are with us. Your rod and Your staff comfort us. You prepare a table for us in the presence of our enemies. You have anointed our heads with oil. And I believe goodness and loving kindness will follow us in the days that are ahead, allowing us to dwell in the house of the Lord forever. Amen."

The wind picked up again, rubbing the pine branches against each other. Snow powder got caught up in the draft and whirled down the hill. For five minutes no one spoke, hearing only the sound of the northern gale.

Bill Hammond finally turned away. "I'm ready to leave now."

The threesome hurried down the hill toward the car. When they reached Sloan's parked vehicle, Bill Hammond turned to Sam. "Thank you, Mr. Sloan. Thank you for that prayer."

Sam put his hand on Hammond's shoulder. "A couple of days after the police first heard of Allan's death, Vera and I went to church on Sunday morning." Sam grinned sheepishly. "To be honest, I thought more on this case than I did about the sermon, but the preacher left an important idea in my head. He was explaining the awesomeness of God's power and trying to persuade the congregation to trust God more than they had before." He patted Bill Hammond's shoulder. "As I've watched this case come to a conclusion, I believe that we all can, Bill."

"Thank you," Bill said again.

43

THE JOURNEY BACK TO THE STATION
house didn't take as long as driving up Gold Camp Road. Soon
the Sloans pulled up in front of the police station and turned
the car off.

Sam turned to Bill Hammond in the backseat. "I hope we
can send you back to California with a bit more peace of mind
than you came with."

Hammond patted Sloan on the back. "Standing up there in
those tall pines put some of my questions to rest. I guess I can
now envision what happened, and insight helps."

"You'll stay in our prayers, Bill," Vera added.

"Thank you." Hammond squeezed her hand, then opened
the car door. "Let's keep in touch."

As Bill Hammond drove away, Sloan turned to his wife.
"Dear, you did that task well. I appreciate your coming with us."

"I was glad to, Sam. Got a minute to talk?"

"Sure. Let's walk up to my office."

Vera fell in alongside her husband. "I know that the police department isn't going to like my knowing about what is happening in your cases, Sam. Confidentiality has always been a big thing."

"You're certainly correct about that one," Sam said. "I hate to say it, but spending much time down here at the police station could become a problem."

"I've been giving considerable thought to what I could do next. I'm sure that finishing my college degree is important."

"It puts you in an excellent position to be hired by any police department," Sam added. "At least that offers you an angle to pursue."

Vera put her arm in his. "You know, I could become a private investigator. A confidential agent? What do you think of that idea?"

Sam squinted and shook his head. "I've reached the place where I simply try to roll with the punches. Who knows what your next idea will be?"

"Come on, Sam. You're putting me off. Tell me your real thoughts."

"You need a great deal of training, Vera. Tracking criminals has become technical and sophisticated. The days of Wild Bill Hickok riding in and being appointed the town sheriff are long gone. Computers, testing, and investigating are a science."

"Sure. Doesn't bother me a hair. I enjoy learning."

"But I'm talking about an enormous amount of data to be absorbed."

"Fine with me."

Sam led Vera down the hall toward his office door. "I think

you'd better get that degree in criminology done before you lay out any more plans."

"You're not doing anything but avoiding my question."

Sam shrugged and laughed. "Yeah, you hit that nail on the head. I'm not even sure what to say anymore, but I believe that you can do whatever you put your mind to." He walked into his office and stopped abruptly. "Cara! What are you doing here?"

"Hi, Daddy, Mommy. I came to visit."

Sam hugged his daughter. "What in the world are you doing down here at the police station?"

"School's out, so I came for a visit."

Vera put her hand on Cara's shoulder. "I thought you were going home after school?"

"I was, but a friend of mine was coming downtown so I caught a ride." Cara smiled.

"But why'd you come all the way over here?" Sam asked.

"Dad, it used to be that you were always gone on police business," Cara explained. "Now Mommy's doing the same thing. You're both gone all the time."

Vera and Sam stared at each other dumbfounded.

"So-o-o"—Cara grinned as she spoke—"I thought if I came down here you might take me down the street and buy some ice cream."

Vera laughed. "Now the picture is coming into clearer focus. Very clever, young lady. You're simply trying to push us to buy you a good time."

"I made a 100 on my math test today," Cara threw in.

"What can I say?" Sam laughed. "I've got the two most scheming women in the world in my life. My only hope is to keep you from collaborating. I guess I don't have any alternative but to get you an ice-cream cone, Cara."

"What if we hadn't been here?" Vera scolded.

"But you *were* here!" Cara countered. "See how well everything has worked out?"

Sam took his daughter's hand. "We can't make a habit out of this, young lady. You understand?"

"Sure, Daddy."

"But I do think you'd enjoy a double dip from the ice cream shop up the street."

"I sure would." Vera grinned at her mother.

Vera and Sam started down the hall, with Cara skipping in front of them.

"I meant to tell you that Ape came by again, and this time he is definitely leaving for California," Sam told Vera. "Looks like things are fairly well wrapped up on this case."

"Time to start a new one." Vera smiled mischievously at Sam. "Huh?"

"I'll have to admit that you made a whale of a difference in how this case was solved."

"Couldn't have done it without me." Vera raised an eyebrow and squeezed his hand. "Isn't that true?"

"Yeah. I guess so."

Vera hugged Sam and laughed. "Just takes a little humility, doesn't it, dear?"

"Oh, my!" Sam reached out to take Cara's hand. "Where in the world is all of this going?"

"We may *all* be surprised before it's over," Vera said.

About the Author

ROBERT L. WISE, PH.D., IS THE AUTHOR
or coauthor of twenty-five books, including the bestsellers *The
Third Millennium*, *The Fourth Millennium*, and *Beyond the
Millennium*, *The Secret Code*, *The Tail of the Dragon*, and *Be Not
Afraid*. He is a bishop in the Communion of Evangelical
Episcopal Churches and is the founding pastor of Church of
the Redeemer in Oklahoma City. He has planted churches in
Canada, England, Hungary, Romania, and the United States.
Dr. Wise and his wife, Margueritte, live in Oklahoma City,
Oklahoma.

Don't Miss These Titles by Robert L. Wise

BE NOT AFRAID

A stack of forgotten letters, a diary, and an old photograph are pieces of a troubled past hidden for five decades and ready to explode. When Mary Oliver's daughter finds them collecting dust in the garage, the mementos awaken her curiosity. Who was Lieutenant Robert Walker? Why had her mother's letters come back unopened? Her persistent questions force Mary to reopen a chapter in her life that started in 1944 but came to an abrupt finish when Lieutenant Walker disappeared during World War II. In looking back at her past, Mary wonders if she missed a vital truth.

Be Not Afraid is a story of war, sacrifice, and love. Ultimately, though, it speaks of a journey we all can take to search the hidden corners of our hearts and uncover the secret of courage.

ISBN 0-7852-6977-0 * Trade Paperback * 384 pages

THE TAIL OF THE DRAGON
Robert L. Wise and William Louis Wilson, Jr.

Dr. Greg Parker, head of the National Security Agency's Geological Research Department in Washington, D.C., discovers that the CIA is using technology to manipulate earthquakes. His highly respected journalist daughter, Sharon, finds that these events fit a pattern amazingly parallel to predictions found in Scripture. In this fast-paced techno-thriller, father and daughter quickly learn that they must overcome their estranged relationship and learn to trust God if they are to expose the U.S. government's sinister plans. They race against time to stop the destruction of their country at the hands of CIA operative Alex Majors and his coconspirators—a battle that could place their own lives in jeopardy.

ISBN 0-7852-6983-5 * Trade Paperback * 286 pages

THE SECRET CODE
Paul Meier and Robert Wise

For eight years, Judy, computer whiz Ben Meridor, and Judy's strangely gifted brother, Jimmy, have been unraveling the code embedded in the Torah. Considered subversives by Israeli intelligence because of their warnings of an imminent terrorist attack, they covertly reenter the country. And now, what began as an engaging mathematical puzzle becomes a race against the clock to save Messianic Jews from the impending fulfillment of end-time prophecies.

Paul Meier and Robert Wise create a gripping thriller based on the actual historical predictions and prophetic dates encoded in Scripture and only recently revealed through computer technology.

ISBN 0-7852-7090-6 * Trade Paperback * 310 pages

THE MEGAMILLENNIUM SERIES
Paul Meier and Robert Wise

Based on years of biblical research, the popular Millennium Series *(The Third Millennium, The Fourth Millennium,* and *Beyond the Millennium)* is now captured in one compelling, must-have volume. Expertly written with top-notch suspense and absorbing plots, these novels speculate on future events as well as God's role in the coming age. This is fiction like you've never experienced!

ISBN 0-7852-6971-1 * Hardcover * 934 pages